Warwickshire
County Council

DISCARDED
014366373 6

Mother Loves Me

Abby Davies studied English Literature at the University of Sheffield, then went on to teach English. She lives in Wiltshire with her husband and daughter. *Mother Loves Me* is her first novel.

@Abby13Richards

Mother Loves Me

ABBY DAVIES

HarperCollins*Publishers*

HarperCollins*Publishers* Ltd
1 London Bridge Street,
London SE1 9GF

www.harpercollins.co.uk

First published by HarperCollins*Publishers* 2020
1

A catalogue record for this book is available from the British Library

ISBN: 978-0-00-838951-2 (PB b-format)

Set in Sabon LT Std 10.5pt/13.5 pt
by Palimpsest Book Production Limited, Falkirk, Stirlingshire

Printed and bound in the UK by CPI Group (UK) Ltd, Croydon CR0 4YY

This book is produced from independently certified FSC™ paper
to ensure responsible forest management.

For more information visit: www.harpercollins.co.uk/green

To Mum and Dad

Little Simplicity

Dear little Simplicity's
Five years old,
She thinks that the moon
Is made of gold.
She fancies the stars
That shine so bright
Are put out in the morning
And lit at night.
She thinks that her Dollies
Are really alive.
But then, you know,
She is only five.
And we're good friends,
She and I,
And I know she'll be wiser,
By and by.

Ernest Nister

Chapter 1

Mother had painted my face every morning for as long as I could remember and today was no exception. But today was different in one way. It was Friday, 23 April 1976. My thirteenth birthday. Today I was another year older.

This fact clung to me like the plague, oozing and pulsating inside my mind. Beside this terrible fact hovered my big question. A question that made my tummy screw itself up into a hard knot.

If Mother sensed my mood, she did not show it. We sat at the dining room table and Mother placed her make-up bag on her lap. Humming softly, she unzipped the shiny red purse. I wrinkled my nose. The dead roses in the centre of the orange table smelled like urine. They had been dead at least a week, but Mother seemed not to notice.

The first part of me that Mother painted was my forehead. With her tongue pinched between her small, yellow teeth, she smoothed white powder over my skin, working up and along my hairline, down and around my eyebrows then down the bridge of my nose and around my nostrils. She applied powder to each cheek and my upper lip, finishing with my chin and jaw. Eyebrows were next. With a black pencil she coloured in the fair hairs above my eyes. When the pencil was due for sharpening, the lead scratched, but Mother grew angry if I complained or fidgeted, so I counted the freckles on her face to distract myself. I was up to twenty when she moved on to my eyes.

'So big and blue,' she murmured, as she often did when she reached this part.

Her warm breath touched my nose and I smelled coffee and buttered toast. I looked at her small, brown eyes, tried to focus on them, focus on anything except the fact that I was another year older. I thought about how unalike our eyes were. I didn't have freckles, but I did have blonde hair like Mother, whose hair bobbed around her chin. Mine reached my knees. It was ratty at the ends because Mother never cut it. She said she would trim the ends when it reached my ankles. She loved my long yellow hair. Always complained that hers would not grow past her shoulders. Sometimes as she walked by she ran her fingers down my hair, admiring its glossy feel.

My question trembled on my tongue, but I pushed the words away. Mother didn't like me to talk when she painted me and I had to get the timing absolutely right. For months I had been building up to asking this question. For months I had tested the words on my reflection, watched my eyes widen with anticipation and fear and something else I couldn't name.

Mother patted and smoothed blue powder onto my eyelids, careful to be gentle, then blew the excess away and picked up the mascara wand. When I was little I'd feared this part, but I was used to it now. I kept my eyes open and looked down at the fuzzy tip of my nose, making myself go cross-eyed. A headache started like it always did, but I didn't complain.

I held my breath and sat extra still when Mother curled

my eyelashes, remembering the time five years ago when an itch had made me move and she had ripped out a clump of lashes. The pain had been so intense that I hadn't been able to hold in the tears that had rolled down my cheeks and ruined Mother's careful work. I had been sent to my room for the rest of the day and she had not spoken to me for three days.

I pushed out my lips, keeping them open a sliver, while Mother lined my mouth with a scarlet pencil and filled in each lip with scarlet lipstick. She slipped a folded tissue between my lips and I closed my mouth on it and silently counted to three. I opened my mouth and Mother withdrew the tissue and dropped it in the wicker bin beside her chair.

Her eyes scanned my face. I waited, breath held, hoping she would not wipe it off and start again. A moment passed. She gave a nod and smiled.

'You're such a beautiful little doll, Mirabelle,' she said, picking up the hairbrush.

She moved to stand behind me and began to brush my hair with long, slow strokes. This was my favourite part. My shoulders dropped an inch and I concentrated on the wonderful sensation of bristles lightly scraping my scalp, but I could not relax. My question hovered at the front of my mind, on the tip of my tongue, in the jolting beat of my heart.

'Mother?' I said.

'Yes, Mirabelle?'

I hesitated. A hot, dizzy feeling swept across my face. Mother's rhythmic brushing continued, falling in time with every other click of the huge grandfather clock. A few months ago, Mother had painted the walls with brown and orange circles, filling in the patches between each circle with mustard-yellow paint so that no white remained. With the heavy burnt-orange curtains pulled shut over the wooden boards that were nailed over the windows, the room was a pit of gloom. Not a shred of natural light penetrated the darkness, though a little light came from a ceramic mushroom lamp in the corner. The roses reeked. Roses needed light and air to grow. It was no wonder they were dead.

I swallowed and licked my lips.

I had never been outside. I wasn't allowed outside.

My question simmered in my throat. I tried to swallow it back down, but it forced its way up like sick. 'Mother, I've been thinking and, well, as it's my thirteenth birthday, I was wondering if, maybe, at dusk, just before dark, I could go out into the back garden – just for a few minutes or so. Surely that wouldn't be too—'

Mother's hand froze halfway down my back. My head throbbed. For a terrifying second I thought she was going to hit me with the hard plastic side of the hairbrush. I waited, unable to breathe, my eyes fixed on the curtains. Tension made my back rigid.

'No,' she said quietly.

Her brushing resumed but this time the brush did not lightly scrape my scalp; bristles dug in so forcefully that they scraped through the surface of my skin. I winced and tried to breathe deeply, choking back tears of frustration, disappointment, gritting my teeth with anger – angry at myself for asking when I knew what the answer would be – frustrated with Mother for not even considering what I believed to be a great idea, and all the while trembling with fear.

'How many times do I have to tell you?' she hissed. 'It's for your own safety.'

She dragged the brush over my grazed scalp a second time.

'I know. I'm so sorry, Mother,' I whispered quickly, dropping my head.

She placed the brush on the table and walked around to

face me. Her eyes were sad as she crouched down in front of my knees and gently pushed my hair behind my ears.

'You know that I love you – that all I want is to protect you, don't you, Little Doll?'

I nodded and looked at her glistening eyes. She sighed and stood up. Her eyeballs glinted, the wetness gone in an instant. 'I have a special surprise planned for your birthday.'

I tried to smile up at her and blinked back tears. 'Gosh. Thank you, Mother!'

'That's all right. You're to study mathematics this morning. Off you go. I'll be in to check your answers in one hour.'

In my bedroom, I sat on the tiny chair at the small white desk and studied hard. Harder than ever. I wanted to show Mother I was sorry for asking my question. I wanted to impress her with my speed, show her how many questions I could answer in an hour. She'd stopped teaching me last year when she said I'd reached a good level, saying that knowing more than that was useless anyway.

A shudder rocked my body. Black thoughts returned, leaking into my mind like bloody puddles. My hand froze above the textbook and I stared at the mustard and cream paisley wallpaper. Sometimes the print made me feel sick, but I could never work out why.

I pushed myself up from the desk and wandered to the oval mirror.

In my beautiful scarlet dress embroidered with its intricate green and yellow flowers, and with my face painted with such precision and care – my hair as glossy as satin in the weak lamplight – I looked healthy. I sort of glowed. Twinkled. Twinkled like stars I'd never seen, and would never see.

Tears prickled my eyes. I held them back and took a step closer to the mirror. I stared into my own eyes until my vision blurred black. *Mother loves me*, I told myself. My fingers went to my hair, my soft, shiny hair that Mother brushed so tenderly every morning and every night. I touched the sore grazes on my scalp. She had not drawn blood. Mother never drew blood. *That would destroy my flawlessness*, I thought, surprised by the bitter edge to the words.

'Mother loves me,' I said into the silence, to my reflection, to my little white bed, to the frilly pink curtains that hid the boarded window, to the gloom that for ever surrounded me.

A sound outside my room made me dash back to the desk.

'Mirabelle?'

'Yes, Mother?'

'Why weren't you sitting at your desk?'

She moved to stand behind me, placing her hands on my shoulders. Her hands were cold. She was a whole head taller than me, her body long and thin. I craned my neck to peer up at her. She tilted her head to the side and frowned.

'I was admiring my dress in the mirror,' I said quickly, feeling a stab of guilt at the lie.

She held my gaze until I looked away. Picking up a red pen from the desk, she bent over me and marked my work.

'One hundred per cent, like always. Good little doll,' she said, patting my shoulder. She placed an apple on my desk. 'I'm going out. As it's your birthday, you may read for the rest of the day in here or in the living room, whichever you would prefer.'

I gasped and stood up. 'Oh, thank you, Mother! Thank you so much. Is this the surprise you mentioned?'

Mother shook her head. A secretive glint lit up her small eyes. She smiled broadly. She seemed excited.

'I'm going out to get your surprise now,' she said, then she left the room.

Chapter 2

Mother loves me. I listened to the sound of her locking and bolting the front door and bit a chunk out of my apple, careful not to let any juice spoil my face. After tidying up my little white desk, I ran downstairs into the living room.

Mother owned at least a thousand books. Every week she turned up with a couple more. Most of them were adult books that I wasn't allowed to go near, but sometimes Mother let me read what she called the 'not so corrupting' ones. She also liked me to look at her big picture books from time to time – the ones that contained amazing glossy pictures of animals and buildings and cities – so that I knew more about the outside. She said it made me less boring to talk to. And next to the door connecting the living room to the hallway there was a small bookcase that was just for me.

The room was gloomy because of the wooden boards and blackout curtains, the red sofa a murky brown in the darkness. I flicked on the orange lamp beside the rocking chair then walked over to my little white bookcase. I saw the present immediately. There, at the end of the third row of books leaning against *Alice's Adventures in Wonderland*, was a book-shaped object wrapped in scarlet paper. I smiled and plucked the present off the shelf.

In Mother's slanted hand my name was spelled out in capital letters.

MIRABELLE

Underneath my name were the words:

For a beautiful little doll who works so hard and behaves so well. All my love, Mother. P.S. You may open this now!

I tore into the paper and stared excitedly at the book. *The Secret Garden* by Frances Hodgson Burnett. This was Mother's way of giving me a piece of the outside world. I half-smiled and lifted up the front cover. The pages were yellow with age and a little rough. I had a sniff. The book smelled intensely booky; good and musty. It was perfect. I curled my legs beneath me in the rocking chair and lost myself in the story, escaping into another girl's world.

I was at the part where Mary Lennox meets a chirpy little robin, a bird which I had only ever seen in Mother's bird books, when I heard something. My heart seemed to jump into my throat. I held stock-still. The sound was coming from the back of the house, but Mother wasn't home yet. I was home alone. No one else lived in the cottage. Just Mother and me. And, horrid as he was to think about, Deadly, the spider who lived in the bathroom.

Without moving, I trained my ears on the direction the sound was coming from. The sound was strange, unidentifiable. Uneven and raw. It was definitely not coming from the front door and it wasn't coming from upstairs, so it couldn't be the boiler having a tantrum.

I remained where I was for a while, my legs pinned under me, eyes wide. I listened. An idea crossed my mind. *No*, I told myself, *you're not imagining it. You're not a little girl any more. You know what's real and what's not*. But I thought about Polly and doubt crept around my mind like a sneaky rat. As a little girl I'd had an imaginary friend called Polly. Polly had looked exactly like me, but she'd been mute. I had played imaginary games with her whenever the opportunity arose and sometimes we just sat beside one another, keeping each other company. One day when I was six, Mother had said I was too old for her and told me I had to make Polly disappear from my head or she would. Worried about what Mother might do, I had ignored Polly until she had shaken her head sadly at me and vanished. I never saw her again, no matter how hard I tried to.

With a frown, I pushed myself up from the chair. *The sound is real. It's real.*

I had to see where it was coming from.

I tiptoed across the living room and carefully opened the door to the dining room. The noise was slightly clearer here. The oak floorboards creaked underfoot and I cringed and leapt through the door into Mother's kitchen. Again, the noise was louder in here – louder than before. My eyes fell on the Venetian blinds and I froze. The strange sound was coming from outside. Outside in the back garden. I was sure of it.

The blinds remained, as always, shut, drawn down over the wooden boards that had been nailed over the windows. Nailed firmly over the glass so no light could break in.

I had never heard anything like this sound from outside before. Outside sounds to me were the perfect twitter of busy birds, the mad onslaught of hail-beasts and the pitter-patter or hammer-attack of rain – depending on its mood – spooky wind wails, thunder roars and the grumbly engine of Mother's car.

Just as I wasn't allowed outside, there were certain places in the cottage that I was not allowed to go. I wasn't allowed in Mother's room and I had been banned from the spare room a few months ago. I thought about the spare room. Mother had carried boxes into that room and spent a lot of time in there recently, but she wouldn't tell me why. I wanted to know but didn't dare ask.

The strange sound from outside stopped. I stared at the blinds above the dark brown cabinet and listened. Nothing. I scanned the room. Mother had nailed her new pop art print to the wall next to the one she'd brought home last month, which was of a singer called Elvis Presley. The new silkscreen print was of a very pretty lady with curly blonde hair. Mother hadn't told me who she was yet. Like the Elvis Presley picture, it was eye-poppingly bright and colourful. I liked it a lot. It made the kitchen less gloomy.

I glanced at the pop art calendar pinned to the wall above the Formica table. Mother had circled today's date in red pen. In the Friday, 23 April box she had written the words *LITTLE DOLL'S BIRTHDAY – collect second present*. Guilt lifted its hot, prickly head.

I heard something else. Jumped as the front door slammed. Heard the locking and bolting of the door.

Mother's back.

I grabbed a glass from the cupboard and turned on the cold tap.

A moment later Mother giggled and I turned around, my heart thumping hard. Mother stood in the entrance to the kitchen wearing opaque sunglasses and a floppy sun hat. She carried a large black holdall in her sinewy arms. She placed the holdall on the kitchen table and looked at me. A smile spread across her face as she took off the sunglasses and hat and dropped them on the table.

'This is your surprise!' she said, spreading her hands wide.

'What is it?' I said, mustering up as much excitement as I could to conceal the frantic pounding of my heart.

She grinned. 'Open the bag and see.'

I put the glass of water on the counter and reached the table in two steps. Outside, in the other world, everything remained silent.

Mother leaned over the bag as I took hold of the silver zip and tugged, wondering why she had not wrapped the present. *She's probably too excited to*, I thought. The zip caught on the black material. I struggled to loosen it and Mother pushed my hands away.

'Let me do it,' she snapped. She ripped the bag clean open and squealed excitedly, her hands balling into fists against her pale cheeks. 'Look, Mirabelle, look! Isn't she perfect?'

I stared, unable to speak. Inside the bag lay a little girl. She was curled up on her side, her tiny chest rising and falling steadily, her eyes closed. She had long, fair eyelashes that fluttered every now and then as if she was having a dream or a nightmare. Her hair was the same butter-blonde as mine, but curly rather than straight and no way near as long. Like me, her milky skin was freckle-free. She wore a pale blue dress, a white cardigan and sparkly, silver tights. There were no shoes on her feet.

'Isn't she perfect?' Mother repeated, stroking the little girl's cheek.

'Who is she?'

'Her name's Clarabelle. Such a pretty name for such a pretty little doll, don't you think?'

I swallowed with difficulty, my mind racing. 'Where's she from?'

'Utopia,' Mother said dreamily.

I hesitated. There was a fiction book in Mother's bookcase called *Utopia*, which meant it couldn't be real. My textbooks had taught me the difference between fiction and non-fiction, so I knew that much. I swallowed. 'Where's she *really* from, Mother?'

Mother's head whipped around, her hair spraying out like sparks of fire. She glared at me, nostrils flaring. 'Don't you like her? Don't you like your present?'

I took a step away from the table. 'I think she's perfect, Mother, I do. I just want to know more about her, that's all.'

Mother's eyes narrowed and she tilted her head to the side. 'If I tell you she's from Utopia, she's from Utopia.'

I nodded and glanced at the sleeping child, a queer, sick feeling working its way up my throat like thick treacle.

'Thank you for my book, Mother,' I said.

'That's fine. Tell me what you think of her, of Clarabelle.'

Mother watched me intently. I looked at the child's face, thought about how oddly similar our names were. Mirabelle and Clarabelle.

'She's beautiful and, er, really small. She must be quite young.' I paused, telling myself to be brave, 'How old is she?'

'She's five,' she said. 'I rescued her.'

The sick feeling eased a little, 'You *rescued* her?'

Mother nodded. She bent down and lifted the little girl out of the bag. Kissing the girl's forehead, she left the kitchen and walked through the dining room into the living room where she placed the child on the sofa and covered her with the crochet blanket. I watched Mother perch on the edge of the sofa and stroke the child's face over and over again, a faint smile on her thin lips.

'If I hadn't saved her, she'd be dead right now,' Mother said softly.

'What do you mean, Mother?'

'That's enough, Mirabelle,' she said, her tone sharpening.

She picked up the little girl and I watched her carry her out of the room. I listened to Mother's feet travelling up the stairs, heard her turn at the top. *She's taking her to the spare room,* I thought.

The spare room that I haven't been allowed in for months.

Mother came downstairs two hours later. Curled in the rocking chair trying to focus on my book, I looked up at the sound of her footsteps and opened my mouth to speak but she walked straight past the living room door without glancing in my direction.

'Mother?' I said, rushing after her into the kitchen.

She slapped butter onto slices of white bread, added spam then pushed one slice down on top. My stomach grumbled and I waited for her to hand me my sandwich, but she walked past me out of the kitchen with the sandwich in hand.

'Mother?' I repeated.

'I'm busy. You can make your own lunch. You're plenty old enough for that now.'

I felt like I'd been slapped. She left the room and went back upstairs.

Mother always made me my lunch if she was home, which she usually was, and she always, always made me my lunch on my birthday. One year she placed a candle on the sandwich and told me to blow it out and make a wish. That was on my seventh birthday. That year I had wished that Polly would come back, but of course she never did.

On my eighth birthday Mother had brought me a red cupcake covered with the most delicious white cream. When I had blown out the candle, I had silently wished to go outside into the back garden just once before I died. Mother had not given me any more birthday candles, but I had still made the same secret wish when I turned nine, ten, eleven and twelve: to go into the back garden before I died.

My shoulders prickled. A headache hummed in my temples.

I had not made this year's birthday wish yet. There was

no point in wishing for the back garden because Mother had already said no. Perhaps when I was older . . . *if I live that long.*

I drifted towards the blinds. A layer of dust feathered each wooden panel. I drew my finger along the bottom panel and inspected the pad of dust on my fingertip. It was grey and furry. Mother's and my skin and hair and who knows what else was hidden in there amongst the million other particles of dirt and grime. Gross, like the smell of gone-off spam.

I rinsed the dust off my finger, my gaze lingering on the blinds. Behind those blinds lay wooden boards and behind those boards lay glass. Behind the glass lay the back garden, where the strange sound had come from. I listened intently and heard nothing. All was quiet out there right now. Perhaps it had been my imagination playing games, driven wild by my desire to go out there and experience the other world.

I glanced at the kitchen door. It too was blacked out, boarded up, locked and bolted so no light could invade the cottage.

My chest twittered with the closeness of outside. There would be grass and flowers and maybe a lovely, adorable robin showing off, like Mary Lennox's robin. A creature I could talk to besides Mother, even though it could not talk back. Someone, perhaps, who loved me.

Mother loves me.

But now she's got Clarabelle, she won't love you any more.

No. That's silly. Mother rescued that girl. That girl's a stranger and Mother knows me.

'Mirabelle.'

Mother! I whipped my head around but she wasn't there. The kitchen was empty.

I frowned, puzzled, scanning the small shadowy space, the abandoned hallway beyond.

I took a step towards the hallway then stopped. My gaze

fell on the frantically patterned paintings Mother had nailed to the kitchen-hallway door last year to 'brighten up the place'. She called them psychedelic. Said they made her feel alive. They made my eyes sting and my brain cringe, but I didn't dare tell her that. I looked at the floor and blinked away the manic patterns that had painted themselves into my eyelids. My headache was worsening. Stabbing pains set my temples on fire. I needed painkillers, but Mother had the key to the medicine cabinet. Said it was the safest way. She kept my vitamins in there too. I had to take a vitamin pill every day. Mother gave me one each morning. It was called a multivitamin. Mother said it would help keep me healthy. She used to be a nurse, so she knew everything there was to know about things like that. She stopped working when I was born. She said her grandfather left her a lot of money when he died so she didn't need to work any more.

Mother would never tell me what happened to my father. I had a million questions, but I wasn't allowed to ask any of them. Usually, if I tried to bring it up she got very angry and looked like she was going to cry. It made me think he was a horrible man and I didn't want to think that. I wanted to think he was like Sara's father in *A Little Princess*, or Baloo from *The Jungle Book*, even though he was a bear. Sometimes I daydreamed about him, about my daddy. In my mind, he was a tall man with light brown hair and sparkly eyes and the kindest smile . . .

My head was splitting in two. It crumpled up the picture of my imaginary father and stamped on it with dirty feet. I put one hand to my forehead and grimaced at the pain.

Before I could stop myself, I left the kitchen and crossed the hallway. At the bottom of the stairs, I stopped. My skull felt like a cracked egg. I had always suffered from headaches but this was the worst one yet.

'Mother?' I called. My voice came out small and pathetic.

I grabbed the banister, leaned against it as a wave of nausea swirled in my throat. I pulled myself up one step then another.

'Mother?'

Another step and another. Another and another and another. My head was splitting open.

I reached the top of the stairs and dropped my head between my knees, but that made the pain worse. I lurched into the bathroom and threw up in the peach sink, my whole body shaking, head spinning.

'Mirabelle! Are you all right?'

'Am I dying now, Mother?' I croaked.

'No. Hush now, Little Doll. You're not ready to go. *I'm* not ready for you to go yet. Remember our little rhyme?' she said, placing a gentle kiss on my head. '*If dolly has a headache, or breaks an arm or two, just kiss the place to make it well, that's all you have to do.*'

I breathed. The pain withdrew its claws.

It was Mother at my side. Mother who was concerned about me. Mother who was rubbing my back and whispering reassuring words and unlocking the medicine cabinet and giving me painkillers and removing my make-up and helping me undress and running me a bath and tucking me up in bed and smoothing my hair back from my hot, damp forehead.

Mother loves me.

Yes, she does. She really, really does.

After a while, Mother closed my bedroom door softly and I shut my eyes against the pain, which was dying much more quickly than I thought it would. I remembered Mother's reassuring words and soft touch. Her worried eyes.

I slept.

Chapter 3

A mewling sound woke me. I sat up straight in bed and strained my ears. Someone was crying. Someone young. *Clarabelle.*

My head ached but the horrific pain from last night had gone. I got out of bed and crept towards the door of my bedroom. I tried the door handle, relieved to find it unlocked. Sometimes Mother locked me in without any explanation. Usually I heard nothing and remained in my bedroom studying for hours before she came to let me out. The longest she had ever left me was six hours. The little gold clock on my desk had told me so. She had apologized that time and given me a big hug, which had made it all better.

The mewling sound was still there so I crept out onto the landing and tiptoed past more of Mother's psychedelic prints towards the spare room. I felt sure that Mother would be angry if I spoke to Clarabelle without permission, but the temptation was too great. Mother was the only person I had ever spoken to and here was a living, breathing, *different* person. If I didn't take this opportunity, I knew I'd go mad with curiosity.

I hesitated halfway across the landing and listened, training my ears in the direction of downstairs. Nothing. Not even a whisper of Mother.

Go for it.

The brown carpet ate up my footsteps as I tiptoed the next couple of steps to the spare room. Ever so quietly, I knelt down and put my ear to the door.

'Clarabelle?' I whispered.

The crying stopped abruptly. The little girl said nothing, but I could hear her ragged breathing.

'Clarabelle? Are you OK? It's Mirabelle. I live here with Mother . . .'

There was no response, only a loud sniff.

'Clarabelle? Please speak to me,' I pleaded.

Silence. Another sniff.

'Please?' I said.

A few more sniffs.

I turned to go.

'My name's not Clarabelle,' she whispered. Then she started crying again.

A shiver criss-crossed my shoulder blades.

'What do you mean?' I said.

But the little girl would not answer. I repeated the question again and again to no avail.

Feeling strange, I said, 'I'll be your friend. You can trust me.' I looked at the doorknob, thought about trying the door. If Mother caught me I'd be in so much trouble. She'd probably lock me in my bedroom for a day. Maybe longer.

'I'll be back soon,' I promised, hoping another opportunity would come.

Mother was in the kitchen boiling eggs. The bubbly water made a hiccuppy, full sound. I stared at Mother's back. She was humming to herself, her head bobbing along to her tune. It was a lively melody I'd not heard her hum before. She was already dressed in her blue bell-bottoms and orange and brown flower blouse. Her legs sprouted down from the blouse like spindly stems.

Sometimes I felt very glad she could not hear my thoughts.

I watched her for a moment longer, feeling like Harriet the Spy, noticing how light and springy she seemed. She seemed happy. Excited almost.

'Good morning, Mother,' I said.

She whirled around, her eyes widening with surprise. 'Gosh, you scared me!'

'Sorry.'

'Let me just finish these eggs then I'll get my purse. We can't have you looking like something the cat's dragged in, can we, Doll?'

I shook my head, noticing with a stab how she had not called me *little* doll.

We ate our eggs, buttered soldiers and salt in silence. I wanted to talk but sensed Mother would not take kindly to it, so I concentrated on my yummy yolk-dipped soldier and thought about how it wasn't very respectful to call a piece of toast a soldier.

I was about to eat my last mouthful when Mother's eyes focused on mine.

'You look awful, Mirabelle.'

I looked down at my plate to hide my expression.

'You look twice your age,' she added scornfully.

I gulped back the lump in my throat. 'I'm sorry, Mother.'

She tutted, finished the last of her toast and took my plate away before I could finish my last few bites.

'Go to the dining room. I'll be in in a minute.'

Trying not to cry, I left the room and hovered in the hallway. I was used to Mother's comments about my appearance, but they seemed worse than usual today. Almost like she'd enjoyed saying those things and seeing my reaction.

I heard the back door open and peered round the kitchen

door. Mother slipped out of the back door holding my near-empty plate. The door banged shut. I frowned and scanned the empty room, wondering why Mother had gone outside and why she'd taken my plate with her. Mother never fed the birds. She didn't like them. Called them nasty little demons. Said she hated their beady little eyes.

I stared at the back door and it stared back, tempting me over. She hadn't locked it. My feet tingled with the desire to cut across the short space. I took a step and the distant hiss of her voice caught at my ears and I hesitated in the doorway trying to make out her words, but they were too far away. Who could she be talking to out there?

Knowing I shouldn't, I dashed over to the kitchen sink and put my ear to the blinds. There was silence for a beat followed by a bang. I jumped and pushed my ear right up against the slats. The kitchen door clicked. It began to open and I ran out of the room into the dining room, terrified Mother would see me and know I was up to no good.

In the dining room, I waited for my heartbeat to slow down and tried not to bite my nails. The idea that Mother was hiding something from me tugged at my mind, but I was more concerned about the things Mother had said to me. And the look in her eyes as she had said them.

Mother loves me.

Does she?

Of course she does. And you do look awful. Who wouldn't look awful after being so sick?

I stripped off my long white nightdress and knickers, hoping to please her with my readiness to be dressed and made up. Mother walked past the dining room and went upstairs. I waited for her but she did not come downstairs after a minute or five minutes or ten or even thirty. She was probably tending to Clarabelle. *Her new little doll.*

Shivering in the gloomy room that reeked of dead flowers,

I wondered what to do. I eyed the grandfather clock in the corner, neck tingling. It was huge and black and hideous with a gold-rimmed face and spiky gold hands. It was the ugliest clock in the world. I didn't understand why Mother kept it. She said it had belonged to her grandfather. Said it was an heirloom.

My skin prickled as I approached the old clock. Up close, it wasn't so scary. Scratches surrounded the dip in the lower door panel as though someone with long, sharp nails had opened it too many times.

With a glance over my shoulder to check I was alone, I slid my fingertips into the dip and opened the glass door. A squeal of hinges made me jump and I quickly closed the door, darted back and tripped over my own feet. I fell hard on my bottom and rolled my eyes at my clumsiness. Moving onto my hands and knees, I went to push myself up and stopped. A piece of paper was sticking out from behind the clock. I stretched out my arm and tugged on the paper. It slipped out and I stared at it, amazed to see a black-and-white photograph of Mother when she was a girl standing beside a wrinkled old man whose face was all scowl. That must be him. Mother's grandfather. My *great*-grandfather.

In the photograph, Mother was holding the old man's hand. She looked pretty in a frilly dress, her hair tied in sweet bunches, but her face looked sad. Her grandfather wore a suit as dark as his glowering eyes. He looked like a shadowy sort of person and I was glad I hadn't met him.

I brought the photograph closer to my face. Something wasn't quite right. The picture wasn't whole. Someone had clearly been cut out of it, because a small, ghostly hand about the same size as Mother's was tucked into the old man's other hand, and the person that the hand belonged to had been chopped off the photograph.

Mother was an only child and her parents had died when

she was a baby, so maybe the person holding the old man's hand had been a friend of Mother's. Maybe that friend had died in a terrible accident. Maybe that friend had been nasty and Mother wanted to forget about them. There were so many maybes that my mind swirled with them.

I turned the photograph over. On the back in Mother's handwriting, it said *Grandfather and me, July 1946, Village Barn Dance*. Barn Dance. I pictured a room full of people dressed in bell-bottoms and flouncy blouses dancing around mooing cows and enormous bales of hay. A giggle burst out of me.

The stairs creaked and I slipped the photograph back behind the clock and spun around.

Mother stood in the doorway with her face half-covered by shadows.

'Have you taken your pill?' Mother's voice was sharp.

'Yes, Mother.'

'Good doll.'

She handed me a pair of knickers and I pulled them on quickly.

'Arms,' she said.

Obediently, I stretched my arms up in the air so that Mother could pull my dress down over my head and onto my goose-bumpy body.

Today's dress was rich blue with a flouncy, white petticoat sewn in underneath. Mother made all of my dresses. I had worn this one many times before and it was growing a little tight across my chest.

Mother stood back and assessed my appearance. A frown scrunched her forehead into crumpled paper and her small eyes shrank to brown peas. For a fleeting moment she was the spitting image of her grandfather and I drew back and looked down at myself, wondering what I had done to earn such a disgusted grimace.

'Take it off,' she snapped. 'It's too small. You're . . . developing. It's disgusting. You're still a child, for God's sake!'

I wriggled out of the dress with difficulty, ripping several hairs out of my head. Fortunately, Mother was too enraged to notice. Muttering under her breath, she stomped upstairs and returned seconds later with an emerald-green dress embroidered with pink flowers. She threw it at me and I pulled it on over my head, hoping desperately that it wasn't too tight. I hadn't worn this one for about a month. I exhaled, emptying my body of air to shrink my lungs. Mother eyed me suspiciously and tilted her head to the side.

'Yes, that's much better,' she sighed. I could almost see the relief pouring out of her. She smiled and I inhaled a huge gulp of air. The room was silent for a second and then it was shattered by a ripping sound as a side seam tore open. Mother's nostrils flared and she grabbed the collar of the dress and ripped it off me, leaving me standing there trembling in my knickers.

'Run upstairs and put on the dress you were wearing yesterday,' she said in a hysterical voice.

I dashed out of the room and took the stairs two at a time. Tears dribbled down my cheeks and I swiped them away, determined to hold them in. I'd be in even worse trouble if I went back downstairs with tear-stained cheeks.

My dress was in the bathroom in the laundry basket. Deadly was standing on the windowsill watching me. I turned my back on him and pulled out the dress, grimacing at the smell. It was still covered with my sick. I grabbed the bar of soap and ran the hot tap, desperate to clean the dress, but Mother was shrieking at me to hurry up so I abandoned my cleaning efforts and pulled on the damp, stinking dress and ran back downstairs. I lost my footing halfway down and nearly fell, my heart a hammer in my tight chest. The grandfather clock struck eight o'clock, booming the eight hours in a slow, mocking manner that made me want to punch its ugly face.

'I'm so sorry, Mother,' I panted, sitting down at the dining room table.

She ignored me and began to paint my face in a frantic, rough way, holding my chin with fingers like pincers, her jaw clamped shut, eyes narrowed. This was not the tender, careful Mother I knew. This was another person. A person who was changing faster than I could keep up. And I knew what had kick-started this change. Clarabelle.

'Sit still,' Mother snapped.

I wasn't aware I had moved. I sat extra still and focused on the orange curtains and what beautiful things might lie beyond. My chest began to relax and I floated in my imagination, picturing birds and trees and grass and flowers. Pretty, gentle things that I could admire. I pictured the sun and my eyes burned with tears that I could not let drop, my heart heavy with longing; I would never see or smell or touch any of these amazing things because if I went outside my light allergy would kill me. Mother only kept me inside for my own good. Mother always knew what was best.

Mother finished with my make-up. I sat up straighter, eager to feel the slow, tender strokes of the hairbrush, but Mother packed up her purse and left the room without a word. I listened to her mounting the stairs, to her opening and closing the spare room door. The sound of her choosing to be with a strange little girl she'd only just met rather than me. I looked at the hairbrush that Mother had abandoned on the dining room table. I picked it up and began to brush my hair in long, slow, gentle strokes, but it wasn't the same.

That was when it hit me: nothing was going to be the same ever again.

I placed the brush on the table and stared at the hideous orange curtains.

Mother's words came into my head, her voice quiet and sad and ringed with a hateful, black truth.

My heartbeat quickened and I put a hand to my chest. My mind pulsed with Mother's words. Words she had been repeating to me for as long as I could remember.

Dolls live short lives.

Chapter 4

I didn't know what to do, so I went upstairs and opened my grammar book. I had studied mathematics yesterday, so Mother would want me to study English today.

I sat at the desk and stared at the words. The text swam. My chest felt like someone was standing on it and my eyes stung with the effort of keeping salty tears locked inside my eye sockets. Stabbing pains pulsed in my temples. I picked up my pen and began the exercises. A tear dropped onto my page blurring the word 'friend'.

Mother loves me.

Love is supposed to be a two-way thing. Do you love Mother?

My door opened; I jumped and swivelled round, dabbing my wet eyes with my fingers.

Mother stood in the doorway. Her mouth was turned down at the corners and her eyes looked shiny. Over her arm she held one of her blouses. An ear-wax orange one with a huge white collar and large white flowers printed all over. It was very ugly.

'I'm sorry, Mirabelle. I overreacted. I'm just worried, that's all.'

'Worried?' I said.

'Yes, I'm very worried.'

'What about?' I ventured nervously, helping Mother remove the stinking dress from my body.

She sighed and rubbed her face. She looked tired. Old. Her hair was starting to grey at the temples and wrinkles clustered around her eyes and mouth.

'I'm worried about Clarabelle.'

Part of me didn't want to hear about Clarabelle. I didn't want Mother to focus on her any more than she already did. Another part of me, the curious cat part, was hungry to know all about the mysterious arrival of this little girl who I never even knew existed before yesterday.

'Why are you worried?' I said.

Mother handed me the orange blouse and I pulled it over my head, grateful to be away from the stench of my own vomit. The blouse smelled of oranges, like Mother, who wore an orange-blossom moisturizing cream every day. I'd asked if I could try it once but she'd said no. Moisturizer was for grown-ups, not little dolls.

Mother perched on the edge of my bed and I swivelled in my chair to look at her.

'Turn on the lamp. It's too dark in here,' she said.

I switched it on, blinking to adjust my eyes to the sudden in-pouring of light. Mother's shadow loomed larger than life on the wall behind her. Her head looked huge, alien-like. I had read all about aliens in Mother's science-fiction books. Science fiction wasn't my favourite genre, but Mother liked me to read a bit of everything. She said it widened my vocabulary and made me more interesting to talk to. But I knew I wasn't interesting, or Mother would want to talk to me more often. I was about as interesting as a toilet roll.

I waited for Mother to speak, wary of asking too many

questions. If I asked too many questions she could close up or get angry and I would never find out more about the little girl in the spare room.

'There's something I haven't told you about grown-ups in the outside world,' Mother said.

I waited, leaned forward a little, suddenly feeling very grown up.

She hesitated. Frowned. 'Grown-ups can be cruel. *Very* cruel. They can have . . . evil urges.'

I gasped inwardly, struggling to wrap my mind around the implications of Mother's words.

'Clarabelle's father,' she said, '*abused* Clarabelle. He abused his own flesh and blood.'

'That's why you had to rescue her!' I said, latching on at last.

Mother nodded and clasped her hands together on her lap. She sat up straighter and raised her chin. 'If I hadn't taken her away from that evil man, I just know she'd have ended up dead – or worse.'

'How can anything be worse than dead?' I said.

Mother snorted, 'Believe me, people can suffer a lot more if they are kept alive.'

A distant smile touched her lips. A smile that didn't make sense, given what she had said.

I ignored an unpleasant twisting sensation in my tummy and asked, 'How did you know Clarabelle's father was hurting her? Did you see?'

Mother looked off into the distance, perhaps into a memory. 'I'm very intuitive, Mirabelle, and when I saw the way he dragged her around the supermarket, I just knew. You know what I mean?'

I nodded, trying to understand, telling myself to look up the word 'intuitive' in Mother's mammoth dictionary later.

'She reminded me ever so much of you when you were little, and I knew it was up to me to rescue her.'

'What about the police? Did you tell them?' I said, thinking about Sherlock Holmes. If there was a policeman like that, I was sure he'd be able to catch a horrible man like Clarabelle's father.

Mother shook her head. 'They wouldn't do anything. It takes years and years for the police to find all the evidence they need to build a case against bad parents, and by then it's too late.'

'What about her mother?'

Mother frowned. 'The mother's irrelevant. All that matters is that I've taken her away from that evil man. I can take care of her properly.'

'Like you take care of me?'

'Exactly,' Mother stood up and grabbed my wrist. 'Look, I'll show you.'

I let her pull me out of the bedroom and across the landing. She released her grip on my wrist and wrestled with the keys at her belt. I watched her unlock the door, suddenly nervous. Did I want to see what was in that room?

But Mother closed the door behind her, careful not to let me look inside. She came out with a sleeping Clarabelle in her arms. Mother had changed her into one of my old white nightdresses. A bubble of envy surfaced in my heart and floated for a second until stronger feelings of pity and sorrow pushed themselves forward and popped the hateful bubble. The little girl was a victim. An innocent, helpless child who had done nothing to deserve the evil actions of the person she probably trusted more than anyone else in the world. I still wondered about Clarabelle's mother, but I didn't say anything.

Mother laid the little girl on the carpet at my feet and

knelt beside her small body, stroking her cheek. The girl didn't stir at all. She looked peaceful, but I could see dried tear stains on her pale cheeks.

Mother pulled up the girl's left sleeve to reveal a horrible bruise on her tiny upper arm. 'Look, Mirabelle, look! Look what that evil man did to her!'

The bruise looked like fingers – strong, angry fingers that had gripped Clarabelle's arm so viciously that blood had climbed to the surface, pooling under the girl's delicate skin like squashed plums under a piece of paper.

'That's awful,' I whispered. 'But you've taken her away from him now. She's safe, isn't she?'

Mother dragged her hands down her face. She looked like she was about to cry. 'That's just it. I'm afraid the damage has been partway done.'

'What do you mean?'

'I mean, Clarabelle's mind. It's damaged. I think – I *hope* – given time, the damage can be reversed, but . . .'

'But what?'

Mother exhaled heavily. 'She's not making sense. Her name, for example. She thinks her name is Emma, which of course is complete nonsense. It's a brain thing, you see. She's all confused because of what that evil man did to her.'

'Does she need to see a brain doctor then?' I said.

'No, don't be so ridiculous,' Mother snapped. 'All she needs is my love and care.'

I looked down at Clarabelle's small face and murmured, 'I can help too. I want to help make her better.'

Mother patted my arm. 'Best if you stay away from her for now. Too many new faces will be all the more confusing for poor Clarabelle.'

I nodded, trying not to feel hurt.

'Now, off you go back to your studies. I'm popping out to get some fabric to make Clarabelle's dresses. By the time

I get back, I expect you to have completed all of Section B. If you finish before I return, you may read your new book.'

'Thank you, Mother!' I said, excited by the prospect of reading *The Secret Garden*.

'You know, I was rather like Mary Lennox as a child.'

'How do you mean?' So far, Mary seemed spoiled and strange and not very nice to other people at all.

'I was very lonely, I suppose. Even though I had a sister, I—'

'You had a sister?' *Mother told me before that she was an only child.*

Mother's eyes burned. 'Did you just interrupt me, Mirabelle?'

'I'm sorry, Mother.'

She exhaled and nodded. 'It's all right. Don't do it again. Now off you go.'

I walked back to my bedroom and turned to watch Mother pick up Clarabelle then take her back into the spare room. Mother was so kind, so good to rescue poor Clarabelle. She had taken it upon herself to take care of a broken doll and fix her, and the extra burden was clearly taking its toll on Mother.

At my desk, I tried to concentrate on subordinate clauses, but something niggled and gnawed away at my concentration. I wanted to know about Mother's sister and I had more questions about Clarabelle. The questions were attacking my brain and hurting my tummy. I tried and failed to crush them. Finally, I got up and did one hundred star jumps, part of my daily fitness routine. The surge of adrenaline boosted my mood a little and I did another hundred and twenty, stopping when my heart felt like it was going to burst. I went into the bathroom to use the toilet then ran downstairs to grab a glass of water. When I returned to the landing, glass in hand, I heard a quiet voice from the spare room.

'Hello?'

It was Clarabelle. She was awake. Her voice sounded wobbly but at least she wasn't crying.

I hesitated. Mother wanted me to stay away from Clarabelle. She had said 'too many new faces will confuse her'. That meant that, as long as Clarabelle didn't see me, I might be able to help her feel better without confusing her and making her feel worse.

'Hi. It's me again – Mirabelle. How are you feeling?'

There was a long pause. I knelt down next to the door.

'Clarabelle?'

'My name's not Clarabelle,' she stumbled a little over the name. 'My name's Emma. Emma Hedges.'

I frowned. She sounded so convinced. Mother was right. The little girl was very confused.

'Help me,' she said, beginning to cry, 'I want my my my mu-u-mmy.'

I couldn't stop myself from asking, 'Your mummy? Where is she?'

'I don't kn-know.'

'You're safe here. No one will hurt you any more. Mother will take care of you like she takes care of me.'

Clarabelle's crying grew louder. My heart hurt; I hated hearing her so upset.

'We're going to be a bit like sisters,' I said, trying to sound excited.

'I do-do-don't want you to be my sister. I want my mu-u-mmy! I want my mu-u-mmy!'

She began to scream the phrase over and over again. I tried to calm her down but her cries became more and more frantic. Feeling like I'd made her worse, I backed away from the door and shut myself in my room. I sat on my bed, hugged my knees and covered my ears, desperate not to hear the little girl's terrible screams and terrified that Mother would come home any second and realize what I'd done.

After about twenty minutes, the little girl went quiet.

I sighed with relief and carried on with my grammar work.

Chapter 5

At midday I went down to the kitchen to prepare my own lunch, as instructed. Mother hadn't said anything about making lunch for Clarabelle, but I made her a spam sandwich too. I also made one for Mother, cutting off the crusts carefully, just the way she liked. I tossed the crusts in the bin, thinking about when she'd taken some toast outside before. I couldn't work out why she'd done that. She hated birds. And then I'd heard her saying something, like she was talking to someone, but that didn't make sense either. There was no one out there to talk to – except for birds and bugs – and I doubted Mother would talk to animals. I probably would if I ever got the chance, but Mother was different.

Unable to stop frowning, I scanned the room. Mother hadn't wiped down the kitchen, which was odd as she was usually so strict about keeping the house clean. To be helpful, I washed the dirty dishes, dried them and placed them in their cabinet, hoping Mother would be pleased. The problem was that it was hard to predict how Mother would react. I often wondered if all grown-ups were like Mother. In my books some of the adults were straightforward and predictable, but that was made up. That wasn't real life. That was the perfect thing about books: you could turn reality into anything you wanted it to be.

If I wrote a book, every bit of the story would be set outside and the main character would be a girl who lived outside and had lots of brothers and sisters, a mother *and* a father. The girl wouldn't be allergic to the light, and she'd be able to turn into a bird whenever she wanted to and fly all over the world and have wild adventures in all kinds of wonderful places. I sighed and finished wiping the surfaces with a dreamy smile on my lips.

I was carrying Clarabelle's sandwich up the stairs, imagining I was the bird-girl, when the front door rattled. I froze on the stairs feeling guilty even though I could not put my finger on what I'd done wrong. I ought to get out of there, away from the doorway where sunlight would be pouring in any second, but my feet were stuck to the carpeted stairs, my neck craned round painfully, my eyes following the movements of bags as they were flung in through the door, which was open about a forearm's width. I pressed myself flat against the cold wall, my eyes trained on the door, which swung open a few more inches every time Mother threw another bag inside. So many bags were piling up in the doorway that the door opened wider, allowing me a glimpse of light so blinding that I gasped and shielded my eyes. It felt like someone had just held a lit match a hair's width away from my eyes and yet I peeled my eyelids open under the protective shield of my hand and stared at the wonderful array of colours outside. I caught a glimpse of shocking blue – the sky – and green so vivid it stung – grass – and a rich, lush, bunch of dark green – bushes, I guessed. I saw slices of wood poking up out of the grass and I saw golden pebbles on the ground. I drank it all in, lapped it up, cared little that at any moment Mother would step inside and see me bathed in sunlight. I suddenly felt so high that I wanted to throw myself down the stairs, jump over the shopping bags and run outside.

But then reality reared its hideous black skull and pain exploded in my brain. Mother was right. I was allergic to the outside, to the sun, to the lovely, deadly light, and I was going to die soon, sooner than I had to, because I had just sped up the process by allowing the light to touch me.

Dolls live short lives. This is the end. Mother's right. Dolls live short lives. Mother's always said it. My allergy to light means that I won't live as long as a normal girl. That is, I think, why Mother calls me a doll. Because I'm not a normal girl. I'm not going to live to be old and wrinkly like other human beings. My light allergy is killing me. It's been killing me from the moment I was born. I can't believe it's happening so soon. I can't believe I'm going to die today.

Panic and fear tore at my throat and I raced upstairs. Clarabelle's sandwich flew off the plate and landed in a mess on the landing. I knew I would be in trouble, but I had to get away from the light. I jumped onto my bed and grappled with my bedcovers, pulling them over myself until I was submerged in darkness. My body shook and my head pounded. The pain was killing me. I was too hot under the covers. I threw them off and lay back in bed. Nausea swept up my throat but the sick feeling hovered there and my mouth did not turn to liquid so I knew I wasn't going to be sick this time.

Staring at the rough, white ceiling, I counted down from one hundred, slowing my breathing to match every other number. I could hear something downstairs, something amazing. I listened for a while and the pain lessened. Curiosity seemed to make the pain go away and my inner cat won.

Still feeling shaky, I padded out onto the landing and hastily gathered up the ruined sandwich. Tearing it into pieces,

I flushed it down the toilet then went downstairs, trying to ignore a nasty stab of guilt.

Mother was in the living room dancing in front of a huge machine I'd never seen before. The machine seemed to produce the incredible sounds filling the house. The sounds coming out of the machine sounded like the tunes Mother hummed. *So this is what music sounds like.*

Mother had her eyes closed and her head thrown back. A dreamy smile played at her lips as she swayed her long, thin body to the music. I watched, mesmerized by her, transfixed by the peaceful look on her face. For a second, I almost didn't recognize my own mother.

'What's that?' I blurted before I could stop myself, pointing at the machine.

Mother laughed and opened her eyes. 'It's a record player, silly. I got it dirt cheap at the car boot. Got a load of records for it too. Thought the music might cheer me up a bit. Help Clarabelle relax. I'd forgotten how great it feels to dance. I only listen to music in the car these days.'

She showed me a bag full of huge black discs.

'These are records. They have music recorded onto them, then they go in the record player, which makes the music come out. It's the bee's knees, isn't it?'

I nodded. I tried to move my body to the music like Mother, but I felt too stiff.

'How do you do that?' I asked.

'Do what? Dance?' she laughed and grabbed my arms, 'Like this, silly doll!'

She spun me around and around and around. I felt my chest loosen and a smile sprang to my face. It was strange but smiling made my cheeks ache. Maybe I wasn't dying. I couldn't be dying, not if I could feel like this. Not if I could feel so alive.

I laughed and Mother laughed. I felt like I'd been whisked

to a fairyland. Like in *Peter and Wendy*. It was the best I'd felt for a long, long time.

'Who made the music?' I said as Mother let go of my hands and I fell onto the sofa, my head spinning with dizziness.

'Only the best band on the entire planet. The Eagles, of course!'

'The Eagles?'

She nodded enthusiastically.

'What does *take it easy* mean, Mother?'

She laughed and held out her hands to me. 'It means relax, chill out, that sort of thing. Come on! Enough questions. Let's dance!'

I grinned and leapt up from the sofa. Mother grabbed my wrists and we spun and spun, around and around and around, like the spin top I used to play with when I was little. Tears shimmered in my eyes and I didn't know why I felt like crying but I didn't care.

'I love you, Mother,' I said, raising my voice so she would definitely hear me.

Mother grinned down at me. 'I love you too, Mirabelle.'

'Your hair looks funny when we spin!'

'So does yours,' she said gaily and she released her grip on my wrists and I staggered sideways and nearly fell over.

We laughed and I paused to catch my breath and Mother continued to dance and sing along to the song. She was so transformed in her face and body that I hardly recognized her.

'Why don't you dance more often, Mother?' I said, trying to copy her swaying motion.

Mother frowned and stopped swaying. 'That's enough questions, Mirabelle. You always ask too many questions.'

She did something to the record player and a harsh scratchy sound cut off the music.

'I'm sorry, Mother, I didn't mean to—'

Without looking at me, she said, 'Go upstairs and write a detailed description of something. I want to see how your control of tenses is progressing.'

I followed her out into the hallway where she was grabbing up bags and lugging them into the kitchen.

'Can I help, Mother?'

She shook her head and I watched her pace back and forth laden with bags.

'I made you a spam sandwich,' I said, following her into the kitchen, 'I cut off the crusts just the way you like.'

'That's nice,' she muttered.

Feeling desperately confused about Mother's sudden change of mood, I picked up my sandwich and took it upstairs with me. At the top of the stairs I listened for any sound of Clarabelle. I heard a sniffling sound and took a tentative step towards the door. Before I knew it, my feet had carried me to the spare room.

'Hi, it's Mirabelle. Are you feeling any better?' I whispered, careful not to call her Clarabelle in case it upset her again.

I heard Mother's footsteps on the stairs and rushed into my bedroom. I thought about going out to talk to Mother, but I didn't want to upset her any more than I already had.

As instructed, I sat at my desk and began to write, but it was hard to concentrate when all I could think about was whether or not the light was slowly killing me. I couldn't even ask Mother; if she knew I'd let the light touch me, I'd be in terrible trouble.

'Don't throw the crusts away when you cut them off. Leave them on the side,' Mother said, making me jump.

'What? I mean, pardon, Mother?'

I looked up from my robin description and leaned forward in what I hoped was a casual, natural-looking movement.

Mother was standing in the doorway, her eyes fixed on something far away. My arm obscured my work. I didn't want her to see it. Not yet. Not until I had decided whether to show her the description with my drawing or without it. Mother used to let me draw pictures to go with my work when I was little, but I was learning that the rules were different when you turned thirteen. Mother might disapprove of the fact that I had drawn a sketch to go with the description. Then again, she might not. I was beginning to realize that I could never be sure which way Mother would go. It was starting to make me more nervous but more careful too.

I distorted my face into a fake smile, trying to ignore the soft crying sounds coming from the spare room. If Mother heard them, she did not show it. I wanted to ask if Clarabelle had had any lunch but the words dried up on my tongue.

'I said, don't throw the crusts away.'

'Why? Are you going to give them to the birds?'

'That's none of your concern. I need them, that's all you need to know.'

'Oh, OK. Sorry, Mother.' I dropped my gaze, fought tears. Wondered why she needed to keep the crusts. It seemed very odd.

'That's all right,' she said. She took a small step into the room. Her voice soft, she said, 'I didn't tell you about my sister before.'

'Your *sister*?'

'Yes. I had a sister,' she said.

'Really?' I sat up straighter. The fact that Mother was opening up to me filled me with hope that I was not a lost cause. I was not going to die – not soon anyway. *Mother still loves me.*

I leaned forward, drawing forgotten, the mystery of the crusts pushed to the back of my mind.

'Yes. Her name was Olivia. She was my twin.'

'Your twin?'

My mind buzzed with this new information. Why had she not told me this before? If she had a sister, then I had an aunt. Why was Mother talking in the past tense? Was my aunt dead? But I knew better than to blast out loads of questions like bullets from a bank robber's gun. If Mother wanted to tell me stuff, she would, in her own time.

'Yes,' she said solemnly.

'Were you and her identical?'

'You and *she*,' she corrected.

'Were you and she identical?'

She shook her head, her eyes glazing over. 'We had the same blonde hair, but she was a great deal more beautiful than I was. She looked like the most perfect little doll you could ever imagine. Very like you, in fact. Everyone commented on her beauty. Complete strangers would stop in the street and give her compliments. Grandfather loved her for it.'

She moved over to my bed and sat down, beckoning me to join her. I got up from the desk and perched on the edge of the bed and she patted her lap, like she used to when I was little. I lay down and rested my head on her thighs, looking up into her face, thinking about how difficult it must have been for Mother, being the ugly duckling and always being second best.

The knots in my chest loosened and began to unravel as Mother's fingers lightly stroked my forehead. She had not treated me so lovingly for a while now. Tears bubbled up but I suppressed them by focusing on the angular cut of Mother's jaw, the way it moved as she talked.

'Olivia was perfect,' Mother repeated. 'Grandfather thought she was an angel – his angel – and he spoiled her rotten. On the outside she looked so innocent and sweet and lovely, but on the inside she was pure evil. Rotten to her core.'

She went quiet for a while but continued to stroke my head.

'What was he like?' I said. I had asked about my great-grandfather before, but Mother never told me much.

'After breaking his leg fighting so bravely in the First World War, Grandfather went into the oil industry – that's where he made his money. When my parents died in the car crash, he retired and came back to look after us. We were only two years old at the time. We were a handful, but Grandfather raised us all by himself. My grandmother had died ten years previously. Grandfather was a faithless man after that – rare for that time – but he was also traditional, like me. He was very strict.'

'Was he nice to you?'

'He taught me right from wrong. He fed me and clothed me and made sure I wanted for nothing. He was a good man, most of the time.'

'But was he *nice*?'

'Nice. Such a subjective word. Such a meaningless word. I'd rather you didn't use it, Mirabelle.'

'Sorry, Mother. Was he kind?'

'He was a hard man. War had seen to that.'

'I'm sorry, Mother.'

'He spoiled her rotten.' Mother's tone darkened, 'Bought her everything she wanted. Every book she liked, she got. Every doll she liked, she got. I mean, listen to this – one day, when we were very young, perhaps four or five, Olivia decided she wanted my doll. She already had several dolls, but he didn't even hesitate. He just let her have her. Just like that. My sweet, beautiful, little Isabelle. And when I got angry about it and tried to take Isabelle back, he shouted at me and told me I could never have a doll again and Olivia – I still remember the smug look on her perfect face – yes, she *loved* the fact that she could simply flutter her eyelashes at him and he'd get her anything she wanted. She loved the attention too. Craved it . . .'

She trailed off like she was lost in thought. Lost in memories. I felt sorry for her, but I was desperate to know more. Questions scratched at my throat like sandpaper.

I waited a few beats then asked my question, 'Did Olivia . . . die?'

Mother's fingers stilled on my head.

'That's enough,' she said sharply. She looked down at me suddenly. From this angle her eyes looked crossed, her nose knife-sharp, her cheekbones blade-like.

Without warning, she stood, making my head jerk forward then flop back onto the bed. I sat up and watched her walk away, longing to hear all about my evil aunt Olivia and my great-grandfather.

After a moment, driven by a reckless impulse I couldn't understand, I dashed after Mother. I froze in my bedroom doorway and watched her stop in the centre of the landing. She reached up and pulled the bronze knob that was attached to the door in the ceiling. The trapdoor dropped open and she reached up again and pulled down a metal ladder. The silver rungs squealed as she climbed. She disappeared into the attic and I heard the creak of her weight as she walked across the ceiling above me.

I sighed, disappointed, my tongue sizzling with questions, but then an idea popped into my head. I looked up at hole in the ceiling and began to think. I had never been in the attic before so I didn't know what secret treasures lay up there, no doubt hidden beneath dust and cobwebs and other gross, disturbing things, but a tingling feeling in my chest made me feel that at least one answer lay above my head, cloaked in darkness, waiting to be uncovered.

The thought gave me hope and I latched onto it like a leech.

I returned to my bedroom with a plan forming in my head. If I was going to die soon, I wanted answers before that happened and I wasn't going to get them from Mother.

I sat down at my desk and smiled nervously.

Mother had never said I couldn't go up into the attic.

Chapter 6

The front door banged shut and the key crunched in the lock, signalling Mother's departure from the cottage and unlocking the rising hysteria that was gurgling inside me. Mother was gone. Gone shopping for groceries and maybe a few more books and another pop or psychedelic piece of art. Gone for how long, I did not know.

The little gold clock on my desk helped me to track the seconds and minutes and hours that made up a day. I could never be certain, but on average Mother's trips into the outside lasted two hours. On occasion, of course, they hovered around the six-hour mark, but these lengthier trips were few and far between, so I could not bank on her being out for anywhere near that long.

Clarabelle was quiet, which was good. Perhaps she was asleep. I had seen Mother go into Clarabelle's room this morning holding a syringe. Mother loved Clarabelle and she had worked as a nurse, so I guessed the syringe had been full of some calming medicine that would help Clarabelle adjust to her new way of living. I felt sorry for Clarabelle. Even though Mother had rescued her from a nasty family, Clarabelle had been torn abruptly from everything she'd ever known. I wondered if she used to go to school every day. Did she have a best friend who she missed? Did she miss her school teacher? In many of the books I read, teachers were mean. But in some stories, the teachers were lovely. Maybe Clarabelle's teacher was lovely. Maybe her teacher had comforted poor Clarabelle when she had been beaten by her father.

I wondered if Mother had acted a bit too soon by bringing Clarabelle here and making her part of us. Then told myself not to be so stupid. I knew hardly anything about the outside. Mother knew it all, but I only knew little fragments; things that Mother told me; things I read in books. I wanted to know more. A lot, lot more. It was hard to feel full when I didn't know all of the things that made up the other world. But at least Mother told me things. Things she thought I needed to know.

But . . . does Mother always tell you the whole truth?

Yes! Stop being so bad.

I cringed. I shouldn't be thinking these ugly thoughts, especially as I was about to betray Mother's trust in the worst way. Mother had never said no to the attic, but I knew she wouldn't want me up there. Just because she had never said the rule out loud, that didn't mean it did not exist.

Guilt glued me to my chair. I looked at *Othello*, the Shakespeare play I was supposed to be reading. The tiny words blurred into unreadable spiders' legs – thousands of them. Black, spiky, harsh. My heart thumped in my chest and a cold sweat broke out under my arms. I should not go up into the attic. I should be a good doll and do as I was told. I had never gone against Mother before. Not like this.

Dolls live short lives.

No. Go up there. Investigate. Stop being such a scaredy-cat!

I hurried out of my bedroom onto the landing before I could change my mind.

Plunged in shadow, the landing looked more unwelcoming than ever – a cold, brown void that lay below a possible wealth of treasures. I looked up, just imagining, the curious cat scratching relentlessly at my skull. Beyond that small door in the ceiling lay answers, I felt certain of it.

I stood on tiptoe and reached up to the small brass knob. My fingers skimmed cold metal. I was too short, which was hardly surprising. I had nothing to compare myself to, but I only reached up to Mother's chin and Mother told me that dolls usually stopped growing at about thirteen years old. Mother measured me every year. When she last measured me I had been exactly five foot tall. I did not know Mother's precise height. And I never asked.

My tummy started to hurt, low down, and I laid my hand on it. It felt rock hard. I wasn't used to betraying Mother's trust. I knew better than to be so stupid and yet here I was, standing beneath the attic, about to do something I knew deep down was against Mother's wishes. But I had to know more. There were things I needed to know and if Mother was not willing to tell me . . . well, if I was going to die soon anyway, did it matter if I disobeyed one unspoken rule?

The sick, unthinkable feeling that always flooded me when I thought about dying erupted in my chest. It was overwhelming. Terrifying. This fear was worse than the fear of what Mother might do to me, should she ever find out, which I was determined wouldn't happen. If I stopped dilly-dallying, I would be up and out of the attic before Mother came home. I was wasting time. There was a perfect word for what I was doing. It began with a 'p' and hovered on the tip of my tongue and mind. I was p . . . pr . . . pro . . . procrastinating! I was dragging my heels – no – more than that – I was putting off the inevitable. I had already made up my mind. I was going up there.

I dragged the chair out of my room and placed it in the centre of the landing, directly underneath the attic door.

Cramps roiled in my tummy. I ignored them and stepped up onto the chair. I could easily reach the brass knob, so I turned and pulled. The door opened with a loud creak. I glanced at Clarabelle's door and strained my ears; all remained quiet. The end of a ladder was in reach, so I pulled at it tentatively and it slid down and out of the darkness like an uncoiling snake. I jumped off the chair, ladder still in my hands, and nudged the chair out of the way with my shoulder. It promptly fell over, thudding onto the carpet. My heart thundered, but there was no noise from Clarabelle's room; she was heavily asleep. Thank goodness.

Shuffling backwards, I pulled the ladder down until its feet met the carpet and the ladder was fully extended. I gave it a push, checking it was secure. If the ladder was too wobbly and I lost my balance and fell, it would be a disaster. Visions of Mother returning to find me in a heap on the floor, my body twisted like a discarded, damaged doll, flickered in my mind's eye. But if I fell, I fell. I had to know more. I had to go up there.

A steely kind of determination settled itself in my mind, and I ascended the ladder with slow, careful movements. Each rung creaked underfoot and gave way a little, but not much.

I reached the top of the ladder and stared into a pit of shadows. Biting my lip, I braced myself, fearful of creepy-crawlies that might be lurking on the walls, and felt along the wall for a light switch. There was no point going inside if I couldn't see anything. My fingers touched string and I tugged. Something clicked and a naked bulb came on, emitting a low buzz. The bulb was weak but it did the job. I glanced around the attic, my eyes greedy. Attic floors could be unstable, I knew, so I gingerly stepped onto the floorboard in front of the ladder, relieved to feel nothing give way, the wood cool beneath my bare foot.

An unpleasant smell circled me. It was an ancient, mouldy, moth-eaten kind of smell that made me wrinkle up my nose and breathe through my mouth as I stared in horror at the masses of cobwebs that hung between the wooden rafters like Gothic, lace drapes. The roof was not far above my head; if I stretched my arms up, my fingers would touch those grotesque cobwebs, no doubt inviting a horde of hungry spiders to crawl down my arms and underneath my dress where they would feast upon my skin with their tiny, needle-sharp fangs. Big, evil spiders like Deadly.

Ugh. I shivered and turned my attention to the contents of the attic, reminded of poor Sara Crewe in *A Little Princess* who was forced by Miss Minchin to sleep in the attic all on her own.

I counted eight cardboard boxes, one filthy mattress and two leather trunks. There was a lot of stuff to search. It was going to take me all day, maybe longer, to go through everything. But I didn't have all day. I didn't even have two hours.

Testing each part of the floor with an outstretched foot, I made my way towards the closest box. Like all the other boxes in the attic, it was a plain cardboard box, big enough to fit me inside if I were to curl up in the foetal position. It was smothered with dust and contained lots of grubby, dusty, old books. I picked up a few, surprised to find them written in another language. Latin perhaps. I was careful to check for Deadly's friends before picking anything up. I sneezed three times and more dust clouded the air.

One box down, seven to go.

I had been up in the attic only about ten minutes so far, giving me quite a bit longer before Mother came back. Hopefully.

I pulled open the second box and stared. It was full of

photo albums. I picked up the top one and blew off the dust. The moment suddenly felt so big that I stopped breathing. Something tickled my arm and I screamed in terror at the enormous, big-bodied spider on my right forearm. For a moment I was paralysed. It looked like Deadly's bigger, hairier father.

I dropped the album and flicked Deadly Senior off my arm with my free hand. My skin crawled and I rubbed my arm frantically, desperate to be rid of the lingering feel of his spindly legs on my skin. Revulsion pulsed through me. I exhaled shakily and looked down at the album, which had fallen open to the middle.

Taped to the page was a black-and-white photograph of two girls who looked about the same age as each other, perhaps ten or eleven years old, holding hands. One girl was a lot prettier than the other with a rounder, more symmetrical face and a small, delicate nose. The pretty girl smiled at the camera but the other did not. Both girls were dressed in identical frilly dresses and wore their hair in matching bunches. I brought the album close to my face and stared closely. Both girls' faces were painted like mine. I recognized the plainer girl as Mother. The other girl must have been Olivia. Mother's twin sister. My evil aunt. Except, she didn't *look* evil. If anything, it was Mother who looked a bit—

A banging sound interrupted my train of thought. *Mother's home.*

I left the album where it was, leapt over the box, scurried back to the attic door and scrambled down the ladder, heart thrashing. My feet found carpet and I seized the ladder and hoisted it up. It was heavy but it slid up, up, up . . . and then I couldn't push it any further up because I was too short.

I froze, listening for Mother, but all was quiet. Had it been Mother I'd heard, or had I imagined the distant banging sound?

Gently, I slid the ladder back down until it rested on the ground. I tiptoed up to the banister and peeped over. The front door was shut. Mother wasn't back yet.

I exhaled a whoosh of hot breath and rolled my eyes at my own stupidity. I was on edge and had imagined the sound, a bit like I had the other day in the kitchen.

I looked at the ladder. Now that I was on the landing, I found it impossible to make myself go back up into the attic. How long had Mother been gone? It could not have been more than twenty minutes, surely?

I padded into my bedroom and checked the clock. Yes, Mother had left twenty-two minutes ago. She would not return yet. Hopefully.

But my heart still hammered in my chest and my palms sweated. That noise had given me an awful shock. I stood and listened. Nothing. I must have imagined it.

Deciding all was safe, I climbed up the ladder and carefully retraced my footsteps.

I found the album and turned the page.

The next photograph was of the pretty girl sitting on a bed dressed in a frilly nightdress. She was surrounded by dolls. A strange, sick feeling entered my throat. My fingers hovered on the edge of the page. The girl was probably about two years older than she had been in the previous photograph. Her mouth was fixed in a smile but her eyes were wide with what looked to me like terror.

I could not make sense of what I was seeing. The girl's face was painted like mine. She looked like me. I scanned every inch of the image, but there was no trace of Mother in the picture.

An unpleasant feeling slithered in my tummy.

I did not want to turn the page, but I had to.

Slowly, I lifted the page. My hand flew to my mouth. Anger twisted inside me. *No. No!* I knew what that was and it wasn't right. It wasn't right at all. It was horribly, horribly wrong. Mother had warned me about the foul things some men did in the outside world and this was one of those things.

Once, when I was eight or nine, I'd begged Mother to let me go outside at night, begged her to take me for a night-time walk somewhere close by. I hadn't cared if it was right outside the house, I just needed to be out there, breathing the air and looking at something different, even if it was hidden by darkness.

After giving me the silent treatment for a day, she had sat me on her lap – a rare treat – and told me about Sex. Sex was something grown-ups did, she'd said. She'd described how it worked in a matter-of-fact way and then her face had gone very pale and she'd said that sometimes, in the outside, men had evil urges that made them turn their attention to little girls who were too young and too small and too innocent to have Sex. She said there were lots of these men out there, which was why she could not, for one second, consider taking me outside for a night-time walk.

At the time, this had been enough to stop me asking to go outside, but as I grew older, I learned from my books that, in spite of these dangerous men, people took their chance in the outside and never got hurt. I wanted that chance too. I craved it. Even if it was just at night where the light couldn't harm me.

My fingers felt sticky with sweat. They quivered slightly as, unable to stop myself, I flicked to the next photograph. Sick rose in my throat. What Mother's grandfather was doing to Mother's twin sister was awful, and the fear and pain in her eyes . . .

I closed the album with a loud slap and shook my head, trying to vanish the things I'd seen. My mind struggled to process everything. I closed my eyes, clenched my hands into fists. Aunt Olivia could not have been any older than me in those pictures. My great-grandfather had hurt Mother's sister, Olivia. Had he hurt Mother too?

One more question circled my brain like a bird of prey: why would Mother keep these pictures? This . . . *evidence*.

The only explanation was that Mother did not know they were up here. I stared around the attic with new eyes, unable to search any other boxes, unable to forget what I had seen. That poor girl. Mother had warned me about the evil that lurked in men. I thought about poor Clarabelle. How she too had been hurt by her own father. No wonder Mother had rescued her; she had seen the same terrified expression in the little girl's eyes and known what that evil man was doing to her. It was clear now that Mother had also been hurt – but why had she said that her grandfather was a good man? It didn't make sense.

I rushed away from the foul album and tripped over a box. My hands and knees thudded onto the floorboards and I screamed as something sharp dug into my palm. I lifted my hand and gaped at a small hole in my skin, at the blood rising up like water out of a flood hole. How would I explain this to Mother?

Frantically, desperate to keep the blood away from my dress, I searched the attic for a piece of fabric, cloth, anything to stop the bleeding. Then I spotted it. Poking out of one of the trunks was a blue bit of fabric. I picked my way over to the trunk and knelt down. With my left hand, I lifted the lid. Inside the trunk lay a pale blue dress that looked big enough for a toddler. I grabbed the dress and wrapped it around my bleeding hand. I tied the sleeves of the dress into a tight knot around my wrist and sighed, racking my brain for things to tell Mother about how I cut myself. Racking my brain for *lies*. Guilt sliced across my tummy and I sighed again. Poor Mother.

I moved to close the trunk, but something caught my eye. Poking out from beneath a small yellow dress with white hearts printed all over it, was a scrap of newspaper.

I plucked the paper out from under the dress and laid it flat on my knees. My hand throbbed. The blue dress was already blood-soaked but I ignored the pain and stared open-mouthed at the newspaper cutting, blood draining from my face. I looked down at the little blue dress I'd wrapped around my hand. A white label had been sewn into the inner collar of the dress. Black letters had been sewn into the fabric. The black letters spelled out a name. I looked from the newspaper article about a missing three-year-old girl to the name label sewn onto the dress.

I could not move. Blood dripped through the blue dress onto my knees. My dress was ruined. Mother would be furious, but I still could not move.

Chapter 7

Mother, Mother, Mother.

I closed the trunk, switched off the attic light and descended the ladder in a dreamlike state. Standing on the chair, I managed to restore the ladder to its folded-up position inside the attic then I shut the attic door. Mother would never know I had been up there. She would never know what I had seen. I could go on as normal. Mother was still Mother. The Mother I had always known. The Mother who had rescued Clarabelle. The Mother who loved me.

I drifted downstairs, untied the blue dress, put it in a bin liner and shoved it deep into the kitchen bin underneath all the other rubbish. In a daze, I wandered upstairs, sat down on my bed and stared at my hand. The cut had stopped bleeding, but my hand was covered with congealed blood and it really hurt. I had not bothered to rinse it. For some strange reason, the sight of all that blood was comforting.

I heard the front door open and my heart flipped. I folded up the article and tucked it inside my pillow case.

Mother cares about me. Mother would never lie to me.

'Mirabelle?' Her voice floated up the stairs into my bedroom. It sounded so familiar, so *her*.

I curled myself over. Hugging my injured hand to my stomach, I croaked, 'Mother?'

'Mirabelle? Mirabelle!' She was coming up the stairs now, her footsteps heavy and angry, her voice sharp.

'In here, Mother,' I whispered.

The door burst inward and she rushed towards me, 'Mirabelle! What happened?'

'I cut my hand,' I said.

'How? On what? What on earth were you doing?' she demanded, crouching down in front of me.

I shrugged. Tears dripped down my cheeks onto my bloodied lap. I saw Mother take it all in; my spoiled face, ruined dress, torn hand. I could not bring myself to lie to her. But I would not tell her exactly what had happened.

Mother stared at me. A frown creased the space between her eyebrows. I waited, sniffed, tried not to hope too hard that she wouldn't get mad. Her eyes darted all over my face and dress. Her lips pursed and she shook her head.

'Poor little doll,' she murmured. She leaned over and kissed my hand, '*If dolly has a headache, or breaks an arm or two, just kiss the place to make it well, that's all you have to do*.'

She left the room then returned with a laundry basket. She helped me remove my dress and dropped the soiled material into the basket then led me to the bathroom where a hot bubble bath was running. The mirror steamed up and the soothing fragrance of orange-blossom saturated the warm air.

'This is a sign,' she said darkly, whether to me or to herself I couldn't be sure.

She checked the temperature of the water then helped me step into the bath. Immediately, my muscles relaxed and the cramps in my tummy eased.

'Keep your hand out of the bubbles,' she instructed, her tone gentle.

I watched her leave the room. Mother was not furious. She was being loving and kind. Mother would never lie to me.

Mother doesn't lie.

The article didn't mean anything. The label on the dress didn't mean anything. There was no need to say anything or do anything about it. Mother need never know.

She came back in and cleaned my hand with disinfectant, her movements slow and soft, her brow creased with concern.

I watched her bandage my hand. She knew what to do. Mother always knew what to do. She had trained as a nurse before she had me. Nurses cared for people. A nurse would never do anything bad. Mother would never do anything bad.

'There,' she said. 'Now tell me what happened.'

She moistened a cotton wool ball in the bath water and gently removed my make-up.

I closed my eyes, enjoying the sensation of soft, warm cotton wool stroking my face.

'Mirabelle, tell me.'

My eyes snapped open. Mother continued to wipe off the make-up but the pressure she applied was more forceful. Panic nibbled at my insides.

'I, um, fell,' I said, staring at my hand, hoping she could not hear the frantic pacing of my heart.

She carried on wiping my face. The pressure lessened a little.

'You fell?' she prompted.

I stole a glance at her eyes. They were fixed on a space above my head. Zoned out almost.

I cleared my throat. 'Yes. I went to the bathroom and

when I was coming out, I thought I heard a noise, so I ran downstairs and I tripped and fell and my hand slammed down onto something sharp on the carpet.'

There. I'd lied. Guilt exploded in my chest. The bath suddenly felt too hot.

'Mother, can I get out now, please?'

She nodded and left the room without saying a word.

Worry chewed and gnawed at me, but I pulled out the plug and climbed out of the bath. I wrapped a towel around myself and dried my feet on the bathmat before going out onto the landing. Mother was unlocking Clarabelle's room.

'Mother?' I said.

Either she did not hear me or she pretended not to. She went into Clarabelle's room and closed the door. I moved closer to the room. Was Mother angry? Why had she left so abruptly? I made my way to Clarabelle's door and put my ear to the wood. I could hear Mother whispering loving, soothing things to the little girl. In that moment, a sharp pain twanged in my heart. I longed to be that little girl again. That perfect, innocent, unspoiled child who believed everything Mother said and who, in Mother's eyes, was a perfect doll who was not about to die.

I turned and walked back to my bedroom. Dried blood soiled my bedsheets. I slowly removed the sheets and retrieved some fresh ones from the airing cupboard. I did not change my pillowcase.

Exhausted beyond tears, I got into bed and tried not to think about the newspaper article underneath my head and the dress in the rubbish bin.

I woke up, surprised to find that I had fallen asleep. My head felt groggy and my hand throbbed. I pulled on a nightgown and went downstairs as quietly as I could, unsure where Mother was, unsure whether she was angry with me. I did not know how long I had slept; if I had slept against Mother's wishes, she was sure to be cross.

'Mother?' I said when I reached the bottom of the stairs – the stairs I had used in my lie.

There was no sound, no response, so I crossed the hallway and entered the living room, my heart jolting as I took in the scene.

Clarabelle sat at the table in my seat and Mother sat beside her, painting her face. The dead roses were gone, the vase empty.

'Mother? I'm sorry.'

Mother did not reply. It did not even seem as though she had heard me.

I approached the table. 'Mother?'

'Yes?' she said, continuing to paint the girl's face.

Clarabelle's eyes moved to mine. Her eyes looked sleepy.

'I'm sorry I slept for so long. I didn't mean to.'

'That's all right. Sit down and wait your turn. I'll make you up in a second. I've nearly finished Clarabelle.'

Relief burst in my chest and I sat down, happy to wait, grateful Mother still wanted to paint me.

'There!' Mother said, clapping her hands and beaming at Clarabelle. 'Isn't she beautiful? Such a pretty little doll. Now what do you say, Clarabelle?'

The little girl yawned. She looked so strange with all that make-up on.

'Thank you,' she said groggily.

'Thank you, *what*?' Mother said.

'Thank you . . . Mother.'

'That's better. Good little doll.'

Mother proceeded to brush Clarabelle's curly blond hair. I watched, fighting a creeping sensation of unease. Why was Mother telling Clarabelle to call her Mother? I thought about how Clarabelle had insisted her name was Emma. Emma

Hedges. I thought about the similarity between our names. Mirabelle and Clarabelle. Was it a strange coincidence or was the little girl's name really Emma? And why did the child seem so groggy today? Just a few days ago she was screaming for her mummy and now she was behaving like this. So calm and obedient. Was it the medicine Mother had given her in the syringe? Was Mother . . . I could not complete the thought.

'Go back up into your bedroom now, Clarabelle. I'll be up to tuck you into bed soon. I know it's morning, but you need to rest.'

Clarabelle obediently left the room. I watched her go. She moved sluggishly, as if invisible weights were tied to her ankles pulling her down.

'What's wrong with her?' I said.

Mother's eyes narrowed. 'What on earth do you mean?'

I swallowed, regretting my words. 'Nothing, Mother.'

'She's tired, that's all. When you've been through something like she has, you become tired very easily.'

I nodded.

Mother picked up her red purse.

I looked down, feeling something wet between my legs. Mother's eyes followed mine. She screamed and jumped up from the table.

'You filthy girl! Go and wash yourself. Stuff your knickers with a flannel. I knew this was going to happen soon. I just knew it!'

'What? Oh! What's happening to me? Am I dying?' I began to sob. I looked down at my nightdress, at the blood turning the white cotton bright red.

'No, not yet. Don't be so ridiculous. It's only your period, which means . . .' she trailed off, waving her hand at me. 'Never mind. Go on, get out of my sight. I can't bear to look at you like this. I knew your time would come, but I hadn't imagined it would be so soon.'

'But, Mother, please! What are you saying? Am I going to die?'

She buried her face in her hands. Her whole body shook. 'Get out! Get out! GET OUT!'

I stumbled backwards out of the room. I ran upstairs and shut myself in the bathroom, chest heaving, heart pounding, confused and frightened. A period. What did that mean? A period was another word for a full stop. Did that mean my life was coming to an end, like a sentence? Was it another sign that I was dying?

Sniffing back tears, I recoiled as Deadly scurried across the room, heading for the crack in the wall. Once he'd disappeared, I did as Mother had told me as quickly as I could and then went into my bedroom and changed into one of my prettiest dresses, hoping Mother would approve, that seeing me looking like her little doll again would calm her down.

Before I left the room, I checked my reflection. The dress was a bit tight. I chewed my lip, scared the seams might split. I tried to smile at mirror-me and told myself the dress would be fine as long as I didn't breathe too heavily or make any big movements.

'Mother?' I said, hurrying downstairs. 'Mother? I did as you asked. Mother?'

Mother ignored me. She moved away from the record player as the Eagles' music blasted into the room, the volume so loud it hurt my ears. A song about a witchy woman pounded against the walls. I noticed the red purse on the floor in the middle of the room, its contents spilled over the carpet.

'Mother? Mother, please,' I said.

She closed her eyes and swayed to the music. Tears rolled down her cheeks. She held the photograph I'd found behind the grandfather clock against her chest. Without looking at me she pushed me backwards out of the room and shut the door in my face.

Chapter 8

I sat on my bed and stared at the printed wall. Mother refused to talk to me. She would not even look at me. She had begun to act like I didn't exist. I knew I had done wrong by sneaking up into the attic, but Mother didn't know I had done that, so that could not be what was making her so angry at me. In my aching mind, I replayed her reaction to the blood between my legs. That was what had made her so angry, and yet that was not my fault. Earlier in the day, when Mother had been in Clarabelle's room, I had been naughty and looked in her *Medical Encyclopaedia*. According to the big book – which was non-fiction and therefore full of honest facts – every girl's body did that sooner or later. To bleed was natural. It meant I was developing properly. It was a sign that I was entering a thing called puberty and my body was getting ready for pregnancy – which was a weird idea – but was not, I told myself forcefully, a sign that I was dying.

I thought about the evil photographs in the attic and Mother's reaction made sense; I had to be more understanding and kind. If I showed Mother sympathy, maybe things would go back to normal.

I spent the morning trying to complete a really hard comprehension test on *Oliver Twist*. I loved the story, especially the bit at the beginning when Oliver asked for more food, but answering questions on the book wasn't as fun as reading it.

I heard the front door slam and listened to the grumble of Mother's car as it drove away. Even though I hadn't seen her all day, I felt tension whoosh out of me like hot air.

Almost straight away a mewling sound came. I recognized it instantly: Clarabelle. She was crying. She started calling out, her voice high and croaky so I couldn't hear what she was saying.

I left my desk and opened my bedroom door. The landing was a pool of gloom, the air stale and dry.

'Clarabelle?' I said, thinking about the name she'd mentioned before. Emma. Should I use that name? I didn't know. Mother had told me that Clarabelle was confused, that the girl's father's evil actions had damaged her brain and made her think strange things – like the idea that her name wasn't Clarabelle. Was Mother right?

'Mir-a-belle? Mir-a-belle?'

My heart twanged at the wobble in the little girl's voice. I hurried along the creaky landing and knelt outside her bedroom door. 'Yes? You OK?'

'Mirabelle? Is that you?'

'Yes. It's me.'

She sniffed. 'Hi.'

'Hi. Why are you crying? Are you hurt?'

'No. I'm sad.'

'Why?'

'I don't know. My new mummy's nice to me and she says she loves me, but I want to go home.'

My tummy lurched and my heart twisted at the phrase

'new mummy'. I thought about the article and the blue dress. Told myself not to think about them.

'Home? What do you mean?' I said.

'Where my other mummy and my daddy are.' I tensed at the word daddy. Mother had said she'd rescued Clarabelle from her father. She'd told me he was evil. That he'd been hurting the little girl.

Yes, but she also said Clarabelle came from Utopia.

'Where's that? Where's your home?' I said. 'Where are your other mummy and your daddy?'

'I don't know.'

'Oh.'

She began to hiccup. 'Mirabelle?'

'Yes?'

'I miss my mummy and my daddy. Will I see them again soon?'

I hesitated and bit my lip. I was already being bad by talking to Clarabelle without Mother's permission, but I had to know. I had to find out what was going on. Mother was very sad from what had happened to her and her twin sister when they were young. Maybe she had made a mistake. Maybe she had made more than one mistake. If she had, maybe I could put it right. I couldn't bear to hear Clarabelle so upset. She was my new sister. It was my job to look after her. I thought about *Little Women* and *Pride and Prejudice* and how much the sisters in those stories looked after each other, and decided I would do the same. If Clarabelle was upset, I would work out why and try to fix it.

I also needed to find out if Mother had done the right thing by bringing her here.

'Tell me about your daddy,' I said.

'What do you mean?'

'I mean . . . what does he look like?'

She hiccupped and giggled. 'Mummy says Daddy looks like James Bond. But with a big bottom.'

'Who's James Bond?'

'A man in films at the pictures.'

'The pictures?'

She went quiet.

'Clarabelle?'

'I'm Emma.'

'Oh, sorry. I forgot. Emma, tell me about your daddy. Is he kind?' Inside, I winced – she sounded so sure that Emma was her real name. Who was right – her or Mother?

'Oh yes! My daddy is kinder than any other daddy in the world! He buys me presents and he tells me stories from his head and he carries me upside down to bed. He makes silly faces and pretends to pick his nose when Mummy's not looking!' She giggled and hiccupped.

'He's never hurt you?'

'No. Once he shut my hand in the door, but it was an ax-dent.'

I frowned. Her father didn't sound bad at all. He sounded like the sort of daddy I dreamed about. Like Captain Crewe from *A Little Princess*. Had Mother made a mistake?

Is she lying?

'I miss him. I miss Mummy. I miss Mummy's cuddles. I like my new mummy, but she doesn't smile properly and she doesn't cuddle me very much. I want to go home.' She started to cry again.

I tried to shush her and move the conversation on to something else, but she wouldn't stop crying.

Eventually, feeling like I'd only made things worse, I trudged back to my bedroom and got on with my work.

I spent the rest of the day attempting to understand *Othello* and trying not to wince every time I heard Mother and

Clarabelle. They were downstairs together. I think they baked a cake, because the delicious smell of warm sponge floated into my room.

At lunchtime, when I went into the kitchen, it turned out I was right: Mother and Clarabelle were sitting at the kitchen table together eating slices of jam sponge.

'Good afternoon, Mother,' I said quietly.

Mother ignored me. She smiled sweetly at Clarabelle, who stared sleepily up at me. Jam dripped from her lip onto her chin. I glanced at Mother, saw her eyes narrow at Clarabelle's mistake. Clarabelle had ruined Mother's careful work. I poured myself a glass of water, expecting to hear Mother tell her off, but she did not utter a word.

'Mother?' I tried, taking a small sip.

She smiled again at Clarabelle, licked her finger and tenderly wiped the jam off the girl's chin.

'Mother? Please. I know why you're so upset. I—'

'Leave us,' she snapped.

'But, Mother,' I said urgently, stepping up to the table, 'I can help you. I want to help.'

Mother slowly stood up and walked around to stand in front of me with her back to Clarabelle, who stayed sat at the table eating her cake.

In a harsh, lowered tone, she stabbed her finger into my chest. 'I said *leave us*. What, exactly, do you not understand about that simple instruction?'

My chin trembled but I sucked in a breath and whispered, 'I know what he did. I know why you're acting like this.'

'What?' she snapped. She seemed half-angry, half-puzzled now.

'Your grandfather. I know what he did to you. And, and, to Olivia.'

The moment I said 'Olivia', Mother went crazy. She grabbed my hair in her fist and dragged me out of the room.

I saw Clarabelle jump up from the table, her little face pinched with fright.

'Mother, please! I just want to help you. I love you!'

I tried to pull and twist away but I couldn't. Mother hauled me to the front door and pushed my face against the wood.

'Is this what you want? Is it?' she screamed in my ear.

'What? I don't understand!' I gasped.

'You want me to kick you out? Out there? Where the light will burn you from the outside in? You want that, do you?'

'No, Mother, no! Please. I'm sorry. I'm so, so sorry.'

But Mother wasn't listening. She unbolted the door, unlocked it and opened it an inch. She shoved my face towards the opening; I scrunched up my eyes and tried to resist but she was too strong.

'Please don't. I'm sorry!' I sobbed.

There was a moment of silence, then Mother actually laughed. It was a short, sharp laugh. A laugh that suggested she was enjoying this.

Her grip on my hair loosened. She brought her mouth to my ear and whispered, 'If you want to stay here with us, inside where it's safe, you will keep your mouth shut, do what you are told, and you will never, ever mention her name again. Is that understood?'

I nodded. Silent tears streamed down my cheeks.

She let me go and pushed me backwards. I stumbled onto the stairs and fell on my back.

Mother closed and locked the door, threw me a disdainful look then walked away towards the kitchen, singing sweetly, 'Little Doll? Why don't we read a story together? Wouldn't that be nice?'

I stared at her retreating back, lost in a whirlpool of emotions, but there was one emotion battling against the fear, misery and confusion that I had never really felt before.

Anger.

Chapter 9

I shouldn't feel angry at Mother. Mother was coping with things in her own way. She was simply trying to protect me, make me understand. Light was deadly to me. And there were men out there like her grandfather who would want to hurt me. It was no wonder Mother had always told me the outside was so dangerous.

But she laughed at you. She enjoyed tormenting you. And if she really loved you, would she do what she just did to you? Would she threaten to send you outside into the deadly light if it really was deadly? And the light didn't kill you that time when you were on the stairs and Mother started throwing bags through the doorway. Think about the article. Think.

No. Stop it.

I pushed myself to my feet and leaned against the banister. Mother's voice floated out of the kitchen and along the hallway to my ears. She was reading to Clarabelle. It sounded like she was reading *A Little Princess*. A wave of sadness washed over me. Had Mother chosen that book on purpose? *A Little Princess* had been my favourite book since I was eight. It was Mother's favourite children's book too. When I was little she had once told me that she'd often felt like

Sara Crewe as a child but, unlike Sara, she had not been allowed to have even one doll. I thought about the pictures in the attic. Mother's twin sister had been surrounded by dolls. Had all of those dolls belonged to her?

A peculiar thought jabbed at me: was it normal for Mother to paint my face every day? I had never read a book where someone's mother painted them. I had never really considered the fact that it might not be . . . *right*.

No. It's OK. It's Mother's way of showing you she loves you. No one is identical. Look at Sara. She makes friends with a monkey. That's not normal.

I thought about this. Normal people didn't have monkeys for pets, but the Indian man in *A Little Princess* was good and normalish. Being a bit abnormal didn't have to mean being bad. Dogs were a more normal choice and I had always wanted to ask Mother if we could get a dog, but I had never screwed up enough courage to ask.

I frowned and chewed the inside of my mouth. Sara Crewe was the cleverest, gutsiest girl character I knew and she never felt guilty for her actions. But I wasn't clever or gutsy. I was boring and well-behaved, *just how Mother wants me to be. Except . . .*

A smile tugged at my lips and a spark of victory danced across my guilt: the attic. I had gone into the attic. That was really naughty. Pretty gutsy too. And brave.

Stop. Stop being bad. Mother is hurting. Think about what he did to her when she was little.

But I didn't want to think about it. Thinking about it brought images into my head that made me have sick, bitter feelings I'd not experienced before. I was glad he was dead, but puzzled. Why would Mother say he was a good man when he had done those awful things?

Shaking my head, my long hair swishing like a mermaid's, I tiptoed down the stairs and crept along the hallway. The kitchen door stood slightly ajar. Mother stopped reading and explained what had happened in the story so far. Her voice was sweet. Loving and tender. Lilting and expressive. In that moment, I yearned to be her perfect little doll again, to be treated like the only thing that mattered. Special. Her special, perfect little doll.

My heart hurt and my knees buckled. I nearly collapsed. I leaned against the cupboard under the stairs and listened as Mother turned her voice into Sara Crewe's serious, seven-year-old one and said: '"*. . . you see, if I went out and bought a new doll every few days I should have more than I could be fond of. Dolls ought to be intimate friends. Emily is going to be my intimate friend.*"'

Her voice turned now into her narrator voice, a voice I knew as intimately as the position of the tiny mole beside my right eye.

'*Captain Crewe looked at Miss Minchin and Miss Minchin looked at Captain Crewe.*'

Now Sara. '"*Who is Emily?*" *she inquired.*'

Now her low, gentle man's voice. '"*Tell her, Sara,*" *Captain Crewe said, smiling.*

'*Sara's green-grey eyes looked very solemn and quite soft as she answered.*

'"*She is a doll I haven't got yet,*" *she said.* "*She is a doll papa is going to buy for me. We are going out together to find her. I have called her Emily. She is going to be my friend when papa is gone. I want her to talk to about him.*"

'*Miss Minchin's large, fishy smile became very flattering indeed.*'

Mother's voice changed to the high-pitched one she used when she was excited, like when she'd come back with Clarabelle. '"*What an original child!*" *she said.* "*What a darling little creature!*"'

Clarabelle giggled then yawned – a huge, long yawn.

I heard Mother's chair scrape, the fridge open, liquid being poured into a glass. Glug, glug, glug.

'Drink your milk then you're going back to bed for a sleep.'

'I don't want to,' Clarabelle said, her voice small and whiny, 'I want to go outside and play.'

'You can't. I've already told you this,' Mother's voice was steely.

'Why? I want to go play. I always go play.'

'Clarabelle. Look at me. Look. At. Me.'

Clarabelle sniffed.

'You can't go outside because it's dangerous.'

'Mummy never says it's dangerous,' Clarabelle said quietly.

'Well . . . Mummy isn't well, remember? That's why you live here now. I'm your new mummy. I'm your mother and you must listen to Mother.'

There was silence. I heard the grind of object against object and guessed it was Mother sliding the glass of milk across the table.

'Now drink this and then go upstairs. Hurry up now, or there'll be no more stories.'

'If I wear a hat, can I?' Clarabelle persisted.

In my head alarm bells belted out a manic tune. I cringed. This could only lead to disaster. Clarabelle didn't know it yet, but Mother did not like resistance of any kind. Mother always, always got her way.

A horrid beat of silence followed.

'Fine,' Mother said.

I jerked in surprise.

The chair scraped; she was getting up. 'If you want to go outside, go outside. Here, I'll unlock the back door for you.'

'Yes!' Clarabelle squealed. Her chair scratched at the floor. She too was on her feet. I heard her skipping, skipping towards the back door.

The key crunched in the lock, but the door did not open.

'You may go outside as long as you're prepared to feel the most pain in the world,' Mother added solemnly.

The skipping stopped. 'What do you mean?' Innocence. Confusion.

'If you go outside you will get hurt very, very badly. The light will hurt you.'

'But it never hurt me before . . .' Doubt crept into her voice. Fear simmered there too.

'Yes, I know, but you're poorly, just like your old mummy. She got ill and gave her illness to you. So now you can't go outside into the light. Light will hurt you, Clarabelle.'

'But what if I wear a hat and gloves?'

'No. It won't work. The light can travel through clothes and when it does, it will kill you, but first you will go through a huge, horrible amount of pain.'

'What will the light do to me?' Clarabelle said, sounding curious rather than upset.

'It's too horrible to say,' Mother said. She locked the door. I heard the jangle of keys.

'Tell me. I want to know.'

'I'm not sure I should tell you. You might be too young . . .'

'I'm not. I'm five!'

Mother chuckled. 'Ummm . . .'

'Please! Please, please, please, please!'

'Tell you what. You drink your milk, then I'll take you upstairs for your nap and I'll think about it.'

'Does that mean you'll tell me when I wake up?'

'Maybe.'

'Please?'

Mother laughed. 'Maybe. Now, drink up like a good little doll.'

Clarabelle swallowed her milk noisily. She yawned again.

Footsteps headed my way. I darted across the hallway into the living room and hid behind the small bookcase. They walked upstairs slowly, Clarabelle trying to guess what the light would do to her – *will it make my eyes sting? Give me a headache?* And Mother saying *Oh no, worse than that. Much, much worse . . .*

Crouching down behind the bookcase like a frightened rabbit, I stared unseeingly at the curtains. First the name. Clarabelle. Three syllables. Ending in 'belle'. Belle meant beautiful. I knew that from *Beauty and the Beast*. Dolls were supposed to be beautiful. I was Mother's doll. Now Clarabelle.

Read the article. Read it properly.

No. Mother always tells the truth.

Does she?

I dashed over to Mother's gargantuan bookcase. It loomed large and intimidating, full of millions of pages, billions of words. Imagination crammed between slivers of leather. Each row was dust-free, the lip of each shelf glossy and dark. Mother wiped and polished the bookcases every day. Even now the scent of wood polish tinted the air. Mother cared for her books almost as much as she cared for her dolls. Us. Clarabelle and me. In that order now, it seemed.

There it was again: Mother's huge *Medical Encyclopaedia*. This would be the second time I'd looked in it recently to work out Mother's words.

To work out if she's telling the truth.

No.

Yes.

Maybe.

I looked over my shoulder. Mother was still upstairs with Clarabelle. I needed to know. I had to put this devilish uncertainty to bed. If Mother was telling the truth and I was allergic to light – and Clarabelle was allergic to light – it would be in here, in this mammoth book. Newspapers were biased, Mother had taught me all about them. But encyclopaedias were non-fiction. Pure fact.

I wiggled out the large book from the bottom shelf between the *Oxford English Dictionary* and *Roget's Thesaurus*. The book was so heavy that I had to kneel on the carpet and rest it on my knees. My fingers scurried over the pages to the index section at the back of the huge tome. The pages were thin and slippery but smelled comforting. For me, books had a perfume of their own. Warm, musty, exciting.

I'm a bookworm and a booksniffer – a bookdog.

I had a good, long sniff. This encyclopaedia was about ten years old, so quite new, but it smelled good and booky, and I already knew it was full of modern, up-to-date science I could trust.

In the index I found the word I was looking for: allergy. I trailed my finger down the allergy sublist looking for 'light', but it wasn't there. I carried on down and spotted the word 'sun'. Sun allergy, pages 222–225. I flipped to page 222 and immersed myself in information about 'Solar Urticaria' (SU). SU was a rare condition where exposure to ultraviolet radiation or sometimes even visible light brought on a case of hives that could appear in both covered and uncovered areas of the skin. That sounded like the condition Clarabelle and I had! I lingered over the word 'rare' for a few moments – disturbed by the idea that rare meant very few people in the whole world could have the condition. The words *too much of a coincidence* skittered across my brain, but I read on, desperate to know SU's symptoms and effects.

Areas affected are bare skin not usually covered by clothing; however, it can also occur in areas protected by clothing. Skin regularly subjected to sunlight may only be slightly affected, if at all. Those with severe cases will also have reactions to light bulbs that produce a UV wavelength. Sparsely covered parts of the body can also be affected by this form of light.

In some cases, life with SU can present a plethora of difficulties. Some patients experience persistent itching and pain resulting from the rash (a result of exposure to UV radiation). If large areas of the body are affected, the loss of fluid into the skin may cause headache, dizziness and vomiting. In very rare cases, people may experience a stroke or heart attack due to swelling in the body. Other side effects include bronchospasm and glucose variability problems. If a vast area of the body abruptly comes into contact with the sun's rays, the individual may have an anaphylactic reaction. However, away from light, the rash will usually diminish within several hours. In severe and rare cases, the rash can take one to two days to fade.

What on earth were bronchospasm and glucose variability problems? And what was an anaphylactic reaction? I flipped to the back of the book again, found bronchospasm, flicked to the right page. I couldn't really understand what it was, just that it made breathing difficult. I found out that glucose meant blood sugar and guessed that glucose variability meant unstable amounts of sugar in the blood – why that would be a problem I couldn't guess, but I didn't have time to look it up. It didn't sound that bad anyway – definitely not as bad as the broncho thing.

I sensed Mother. Any second now she would come running downstairs and I would have to shove the encyclopaedia back in its place and act normal. Unable to stop myself, I located the page about anaphylactic reaction. That sounded serious. Enough to kill a person if not treated by a doctor straight away. Was this what Clarabelle and I had? Was that why Mother wouldn't let us outside? I swallowed, flicked back to page 222, hesitated, tore it out.

'Mirabelle?'

Footsteps thudding downstairs, moving quickly. Urgently.

Mother was coming. She knew I was up to something. And I was. I was being gutsy for once. Breaking the rules. Mirabelle the gutsy had come out to play.

Thud, thud, thud.

My heart flipped. I stuffed the page down the front of my dress and frantically shoved the huge Encyclopaedia back into its place.

Thud, thud.

It got wedged in, half-sticking out of the shelf.

Thud.

I gave it another push. The book slid in an inch but still protruded more than the books beside it.

I swivelled on my knees to face the small bookcase as she strode into the room, eyes aflame.

Chapter 10

'What are you doing?' She fired out the words, sharp with accusation.

Trying to find out the truth.

'Nothing, Mother. Just looking at my books.'

I could feel the crumpled page against my collarbone, thought for a horrible moment a corner of paper was visible out of the top of my dress.

Her eyes darted away from mine. She scanned the room quickly. I held my breath. Her eyes fell on the immense bookcase and she wandered over, raking her fingers through the hair on my scalp as she passed. The touch was not pleasant but not unpleasant. I wanted her to comment on how silky my hair felt, but she didn't.

'Shall I go upstairs and study?' I said. I stood up, glanced at the *Medical Encyclopaedia*, at its traitorous position. Wished I'd given it a harder shove.

Her fingers danced across the shelf second from top. Tap, tap, tap across Agatha Christie's spine. She hummed to herself – Eagles, I knew – apparently lost in her own thoughts. I was going to be lucky. Her focus wasn't on me. It was on her beloved books. I turned to leave the room.

'Mirabelle?'

I stopped. 'Yes, Mother?'

'What were you really doing in here just now?' Her voice sounded dreamy, faraway, detached. That voice made warning signs bounce off the walls.

My heart skipped. *Be brave. Lie.*

I bit back rising guilt. 'I was looking for *A Little Princess*. I felt like reading it again, but I couldn't find it.'

She turned and walked away from the bookcase towards me, her steps slow, eyes unfocused.

'That's because I'm reading it to Clarabelle,' she said, stopping to stand in front of me.

She reached out and tucked my hair behind my ear. A tender gesture. I wanted to like it but her touch suddenly felt odd to me. Strangely false. Like the touch of someone trying to comfort a stranger.

'It's a great story. I'm sure she loves it,' I said. 'Shall I go to my room and study now?'

Eyes still glazed, she murmured, 'I don't like to talk about my sister.'

I tensed and looked at her. I waited and held in my questions. If she wanted to tell me more, she would.

In a small voice she said, 'He gave her everything she wanted. Me, nothing. Nothing but lessons. I did everything I could to please him. Everything.'

I opened my mouth to ask what she meant and stopped myself.

She drifted away from the bookcase over to the grandfather clock. Her fingers traced the clock's face, leaving smudges on the glass. I walked over and raised a hand to comfort her, to pat her back and soothe her and tell her I was sorry about what she had gone through.

She whirled around and my hand froze in the air.

'Aren't you going to ask me about his lessons? Don't you want to know what she did to me, Mirabelle?'

'Yes, I'm sorry, I—'

'Just go. Go to your room now. I'm tired.'

'Please, Mother, please. I really want to know.' I placed my hand on her arm, gently, ever so gently.

She stared at my hand. A frown knitted her eyebrows together like the curtains in my bedroom. She muttered something I couldn't hear.

'Pardon?' I said.

Her eyes were wet. She shook her head and a tear plopped onto the shiny white toe of her shoe.

'You know, Mirabelle, sometimes I wish I'd never been born,' she said, staring at the space above my head.

'Why would you wish something horrible like that, Mother? If you hadn't been born, neither would I.'

She laughed and looked away, fisting her hand so hard that her knuckles popped out like hazelnuts.

'How can I make you feel better, Mother? I want to help you.'

She yanked her arm out from under my fingers and walked over to the sofa. She sat down and stared at her knees.

'Mother?'

'I'm fine. Go upstairs now, like a good girl.'

I watched her sitting there, so alone. For a moment, she looked like a little girl. Lost and lonely and helpless. I took a step towards her.

Her head snapped up and she glared at me. 'I said *go*.'

With a lump in my throat, I tried to walk normally out of the room and mount the stairs at a steady pace. As soon as my foot touched the landing carpet, I hurled myself into my bedroom and shut the door. My hands shook slightly as I withdrew the page from my dress. I sat down at my desk, slid my textbook out of the way and laid the page out on the desktop, flattening and smoothing out the creases best I could. Solar Urticaria. It sounded more like a planet or a star than a rare medical condition. Rare. That word again. It didn't say how rare – like one in a hundred or one in a thousand – just *rare*. But how rare was rare?

I re-read the symptoms and flashed back to that moment on the stairs. When I had seen the light, a headache had come then I'd thrown up. Those were two of the symptoms of SU. But . . . I read the passage carefully. It was only if light touched you that symptoms developed. You didn't get headaches and sickness from simply seeing the light. Hang on – yes you did – *sometimes even visible light causes a case of hives that can appear in both covered and uncovered areas of the skin.* Did I get hives? What were hives? I guessed hives were some kind of rash. Yes. That made sense. But I hadn't been aware of a rash on my skin. There could have been one, but I was too busy throwing up at the time to notice any weird patches on my body.

Why would Mother lie?

The question made me look up from the page. I winced with guilt.

Read the article again. Think about the dress.

No.

Yes, yes, yes!

Suddenly I knew what I had to do. My heart pounded. *You're going to die soon anyway, so you might as well.*

Before I could talk myself out of it, I turned on my lamp and held my hand directly under the bulb – not close enough for the heat of the bulb to burn as it would burn anyone, just close enough to see if my skin would react oddly. The light illuminated my hand, making it look a sicky, yellow colour. I counted to thirty. Nothing. No redness, no swelling, no burning sensation and definitely no rash. I held my hand there for another thirty seconds. Another thirty. Nothing. No change in my skin at all. No itching or burning or anything.

I exhaled and turned off the lamp. Inspected my hand again, to be sure. My skin was absolutely fine. That meant, according to the encyclopaedia, that I did not have an extreme case, which also meant that I was very unlikely to experience the other awful symptoms I had looked up. I frowned. If I didn't have an extreme version of the condition did that mean light exposure would not kill me? With a sudden jolt, I realized something else: nowhere in the text did it say that SU made you die young. According to the big book, as long as a person stayed out of sunlight, they did not run the risk of dying. So why did Mother always say that dolls lived short lives? Was there something else wrong with me? Some incurable disease she'd never told me about?

I shook my head. *No.*

I nibbled on my nail, realized, stopped. Mother would be mad if I ruined my nails.

Suddenly I felt like screaming and hitting my fists against the walls. I stood and paced the small room, panic licking me like searing flames. My eyes fell on the frilly pink curtains that were nailed into the wall. The centre of the curtains was sewn together in a neat cross-stitch. I had never tried to unpick those stitches, but now I wondered. Were boards nailed over the windows behind the curtains, or was there nothing but glass behind the thick pink material?

Be brave. Find out. But take precautions.

There was a pair of nail scissors in the bathroom. I hurried out of my room, retrieved them from the bathroom cabinet and froze. Deadly was sitting on the door frame at my eye level, poised to attack. My heart raced. I could rush past him and hope he didn't jump at me or . . . I scanned the room.

My gaze landed on the bar of soap on the sink. I picked it up. It was slippery and gross. I took aim, inhaled and fired. The soap hit the door frame above Deadly. He didn't even flinch. I looked at him, wondered what he was thinking. I'd attacked him so he had a right to attack me now, which was probably his plan.

There was no time so I grabbed the flannel from the side of the bath and folded it in half so it was thick but not too small. Keeping my upper body dead still, I raised the flannel and crept towards him.

Deadly remained in his place, bold and arrogant.

I stared at him. My enemy.

I stopped a safe distance away, my heart jittering.

He was so big but so small at the same time. I looked at the flannel in my hand. Looked back at Deadly. He stayed where he was. Was it possible that he was just as afraid of me as I was of him? Too frightened to move, not too evil to be afraid.

I lowered the flannel. Deadly and I looked at each other. He didn't move a leg. His stringy bedroom hung above his head in the corner of the ceiling. There were no dead flies in there. I wondered if he was hungry. If he was hungry, he would be even more tempted to bite a chunk out of me.

I raised the flannel again. My hand shook. I took a step closer, weapon ready in case he attacked.

With a squeal I leapt past him out of the room and ran into my bedroom.

Heart slowing, I stood and stared at the centre of the curtains. If I unpicked the curtains, Mother would see what I'd done next time she came into my room. But I had to know.

I pulled a yellow doll dress out of my wardrobe and laid it on my desk. Trying to steady my trembling hands, I took hold of the centre of the curtains and began to snip through the very centre stitch. There were a good fifty stitches holding the curtains together. I cut open the first one and wiped sweat from my forehead. Good. One down, tons to go. I snipped through the next and the next, biting my lip, struggling to keep from shaking. Every few seconds I glanced at the door, certain Mother would rush in.

With five stitches snipped, the curtains still revealed nothing. Each curtain kissed the other, protecting me from what lay behind. Unsteadily, I placed the nail scissors on my desk and picked up the yellow dress, wrapping it around my hands. I took a breath, shuffled my body to the side out of the path the sunlight would take when I parted the small unpicked space in the curtains. If there was no wooden board behind the material I would be subjecting myself to real light. My heart pounded. I inhaled, exhaled then pulled the curtains apart. My heart sank to my feet. Disappointment curdled with fear. There was no glass, just wood. Mother had made certain I was protected – *or unable to get away.*

My last thought rocked me to my core. I let go of the curtains, grateful to see them fall back together. You couldn't even tell I'd picked some of the stitches out. Mother would only notice if she inspected them closely, and why would she? They had held fast for my whole life. They were a permanent feature of my bedroom. My life. My short, short life.

I wondered if Clarabelle's room was the same. Mother must have boarded up her window too. That must have been why she had spent so much time in the spare room prior to Clarabelle's arrival. And I had heard banging when she'd been in there, I remembered.

Something in my mind clicked. My eyes went wide. My tummy lurched.

Mother had prepared the room for Clarabelle. Mother had known Clarabelle was coming here *before* that day in the supermarket, *before* she had seen Clarabelle and known she was being hurt by her father and known she had to rescue her. Did that mean . . .

I couldn't, *wouldn't* complete the question.

Chapter 11

Mother went out an hour later. The door slammed shut; louder than usual, I thought. Maybe she was still angry with me. Did she suspect I'd lied earlier? Was I going to be punished when she got back? I winced at the thought. Would it be the silent treatment again?

I thought about going to Clarabelle's door, seeing if she was awake. No – Clarabelle needed to sleep and Mother would be cross if I disturbed her.

But Clarabelle was only a delaying tactic. I was never going to go and talk to her. I had already made up my mind.

I left my room and slowly descended the stairs. I knew I was going to go through with it. Dread was unfurling in my chest like a huge black demon hand and I let it. The hand closed on my heart and squeezed and squeezed. I felt like I couldn't breathe but I also felt that if my heart didn't slow down, I would have a heart attack. I imagined Mother coming home to find me sprawled on the floor clutching my heart, my eyes rolled back in my head, froth dribbling out of my mouth. She would be so upset. She'd dash over to me, hold me in her arms and sob. She'd tell me how sorry she was, how much she loved me, how I was not going to die . . .

Guilt gnawed and nibbled at my heart, but a creeping, dreadful sense of certainty lived in my head now, and it was beginning to thrive. I had to know the truth. I desperately wanted to believe in Mother; to believe anything else was to shatter my world as I knew it.

But it will also mean you're not dying. That you're not allergic to outside. And what's so good about a world of locked doors and boarded windows?

They battled: the need to believe her and the desire for her to be lying.

I entered the living room, walked to the rocking chair and dragged it over to the living room doorway to face the front door. I picked up *The Secret Garden* and sat on the rocking chair, setting the swing in motion with a light push of my feet. The chair creaked comfortingly. I'd sat on this rocking chair so many times but never in the living room doorway in the direct path of the front door.

I was in position now. All I could do was read my book and wait for Mother's return. When she opened the door, everything would become clear and I would finally know the truth. Even if it killed me.

Chapter 12

The grandfather clock struck six o'clock, droning the hour in its loud, rough voice. The sound tugged me out of my book. I looked round at its hideous face and wondered where Mother was. She rarely stayed out this late.

I re-read my last paragraph. Mary was about to show Colin the secret garden. I couldn't wait to see Colin's reaction. With a jarring shudder, it occurred to me that I might not live to read on and see it. I might never find out how the story ended. I would never know if Mary Lennox ended up happy.

Then I heard it. A crunchy growl of wheels. A grumbling engine. The slam of a door. She was right outside, right now.

My heart flip-flopped and I placed my book on the floor beside the rocking chair and stood up. It was too late to turn back.

The front door clicked and I jumped as it inched open and a band of light raced towards me across the floorboards. As the door opened wider, the band grew, stretching across the floor and lengthening, running diagonally across the narrow hallway towards the living room door and me. The light was white. My eyes tingled but I fixed my gaze on that ever-growing light.

The door stood open about a hand's width and remained in that state. The light had not yet reached my feet. I looked down at my bare toes. They were an inch away from the band of sunlight. All I had to do was lift one foot and take a step forward and I would know. But fear was my enemy and sucked my courage away. I stood, frozen to the spot. Behind me the rocking chair still rocked, creaking on and on and on as if it could creak on, moved by some unseen presence, for all of eternity.

A bag flew through the front doorway. I stared at the brown paper bag as it tried to stay upright, then flopped onto its side. A red apple rolled across the floor, escaping the collapsed bag, only stopping when it hit the wall to my left.

Mother will kill me when she sees me standing here.

Not if the light kills you first.

Clarabelle's voice came from above sending loud, frightened cries through the ceiling, cries that pierced my heart and gave me courage.

Another bag and another thumped onto the floor and the door drifted open a little further.

It was *now*, and finally know the truth, or *never*, and never know for certain. I needed an end to this uncertainty. That, more than anything else, was the thing killing me. Not knowing was like a disease eating me up from the inside out.

I held my breath and stepped forward.

I felt light on me. Warm, lovely light. I swam in it. I waited for the pain, the rash, the headache, the nausea, the vomiting. My heart pumped hard and fast but nothing happened. I took another step, making sure I was totally enveloped by light. Then another step. Two more bags landed on the floor in front of my feet. I raised my hand, took hold of the door, pulled it wide open and stared at the outside. Sun hit me. My eyes burned with tears. Mother lunged at me, pushed me back screaming and cursing, shocked, but worse – enraged.

She slammed the door shut, locked it, pocketed the key. I lay on the bottom step of the stairs. Other than a bruise on my back from hitting the stairs, I felt fine, giddy in fact.

'What the hell are you doing?' she screamed.

I smiled up at her, too happy to respond.

She slapped me across my face. Hard. Once. Twice. My eyes focused and tears streamed. Mother had never hit me before.

'I'm sorry, Mother – I just – I don't know what got into me! I wanted to know what it was like and I kind of got mesmerized and then my feet were pulling me towards the light and I couldn't stop myself.'

I looked up, conscious of my face, how I must look. My make-up must be ruined. My eyes were probably red from crying.

'You look awful. I expect the light will be working its way into your veins right now,' she said, leaning over and bringing her face close to mine, 'Yes, I can see it. Oh you poor, silly doll.'

My hands flew to my face. 'What? What can you see?'

'The disease, of course, spreading through your body, contaminating your skin. Killing you.'

She sighed and dragged her hands down her face.

'Killing me? No – I feel fine. It doesn't hurt. I'm fine. Look,' I showed her my pale, smooth arms.

She shook her head. 'It doesn't show there, but on your face. And inside. Inside your body things will be happening now. Terrible things.'

'Please – what's wrong with my face? Terrible things – what things?'

'Your organs will be starting to melt into one another, and then even more horrible things will start to happen.'

Her eyes glinted. She turned her face away and I noticed

her lip curling up on one side into a half-smile. A thought hit me: was she enjoying this?

'You need to be punished for what you've done,' she said.

I said nothing. My face felt fine, but I wanted to see what she was talking about. Was she lying or was something happening to my face? Had I just carved my own coffin?

Mother turned away from me completely, waving her hand. 'I can't bear to look at you right now. At what you've done to yourself. You disgust me. Go to your room. I don't want to see you for the rest of the day and there will be no dinner for you tonight.'

I sat on the step, frozen for a moment. She walked away, leaving me alone.

Heart pounding, I scrabbled up the stairs on my hands and feet and ran into my bedroom, flicked the lamp on and faced the mirror. I stared, horrified. Not horrified by a rash or anything like that, but horrified by Mother's cruelty. There was nothing wrong with my face. Other than a slightly pink handprint from where she'd slapped me and two black streaks of mascara, my face was absolutely fine.

The light had not hurt me. I was not dying.

Chapter 13

To my surprise, Mother went out again. I heard the door slam, the car growl away.

Time had passed and nothing had happened to me. I was fine. Absolutely fine. I didn't even have a headache.

My tummy churned as I remembered Mother's meanness. Anger and misery burned like fire and ice in my veins, and hot, prickly confusion pierced my mind like a thousand needles. Mother was wrong about me having a light allergy that was killing me. Had she been lying or had she made a mistake? I didn't want to believe she was lying but I couldn't stop thinking about the article, and fearing that she'd been lying all along, about everything.

I shook my head so hard my brain rattled. There was a way to find out more. Clarabelle. Clarabelle, the little girl Mother said she'd rescued from Utopia. The little girl who thought her name was Emma and said her daddy was the kindest man in the world.

Mother would be livid if she knew I was going to talk to Clarabelle without her permission, but right now, I didn't care. My cheek still hurt from her slaps. She'd slapped me. Twice. And she'd *smiled*. There was a side to Mother that wasn't kind. She could be cruel. Very cruel. And cruel people probably lied.

I thought about Miss Minchin from *A Little Princess* and shivered. There was something about Miss Minchin's character that reminded me of Mother. I'd always felt it but had ignored the feeling until now.

Shaking my head to get rid of such disloyal thoughts, I stroked my bruised cheek and thought again about Clarabelle and what she'd told me about her daddy being a good, kind man. The little girl had no reason to lie. Mother said she was confused but I wasn't so sure, especially not now. Mother had never me hit before. I'd never dreamed she would.

I looked at my bedroom door and snagged my lip between my teeth. I had to know if Mother was lying or making mistakes. I had to know the full truth. About everything.

Fearful Mother might be back any second, I dashed out of my room and hurried along the landing.

Clarabelle's room was quiet.

'Clarabelle? It's Mirabelle. Want to talk?'

A rustling sound came followed by her voice, which was bright and chirpy. 'Mirabelle? Hi! I'm glad it's you. Can we play I Spy?'

'What?'

'I Spy. Can we play it? Please? I'm bored. I'm asposed to do colouring but I don't want to any more.'

'What's I Spy?' I said.

'You don't know what I Spy is?'

'No. Tell me.'

'OK. It's where you say a letter and I have to say a word with that letter.'

'P.'

'No, silly! You have to say, "I spy with my little eye, something beginning with P."' She giggled. The sound made me feel warm inside. I was relieved to hear her sounding happier than before, and less sleepy.

'All right,' I said, 'I spy with my little eye, something beginning with P.'

'Hmmm,' she said excitedly, 'I know! Paper! Am I right?'

'Yes,' I lied, still not understanding the game.

'Can we play again?'

'I need to ask you a question first. When did you first see Mother?'

She was quiet for a while. I heard a clicking sound coming from her room.

'At the supermarket. She told me to come with her. She said she was Mummy's friend and Mummy wanted me to go with her, because Mummy was poorly, but . . .'

'But what?'

'But it was funny.'

'Why? What was funny?' I pressed.

'When I was in the car, Mother gave me a sweetie that didn't taste nice and I heard Mummy shouting my name. I wanted to say bye to Mummy and I waved and then my head went all funny.'

After a beat, she asked if we could play I Spy again, but I couldn't speak.

I mumbled that I had to go back to my room then staggered across the landing. Inside my bedroom, I hurried over to my bed, slid a trembling hand inside my pillowcase, pulled out the newspaper article and read.

Sunday, 5 June 1966

Girl, Three, Goes Missing in Salisbury

Police are searching for a missing three-year-old girl who they suspect was abducted in a supermarket near her home.

Polly Dalton was last seen on Saturday afternoon, standing beside a red car in Sainsbury's car park. The missing girl's mother, English teacher, Jane Dalton, 25, said she realized her daughter was missing when she reached for her hand in the supermarket and she wasn't there. 'I was talking to an old friend and took my eye off Polly for a second. She must have wandered off when I wasn't looking.' Polly's father, veterinarian Peter Dalton, 27, was at home when the incident took place.

Local shop assistant, Rebecca Birch, 16, said she saw a little girl matching Polly's description: 'She was standing next to a red car. I think she was talking to someone in the car, but I couldn't see who it was.'

Police said they were becoming 'increasingly concerned' for the missing child's safety and have deployed a large number of officers to investigate the disappearance. Detective Chief Superintendent Frank Jones said his officers were following a number of lines of enquiry: 'Salisbury police have launched an intensive search and criminal investigation into the abduction of three-year-old Polly Dalton. Polly was last seen in Sainsbury's car park at around 2.30 p.m. We are obviously becoming increasingly concerned for her safety and are asking for anyone with information to please contact us.'

Hundreds of residents were said to have joined the hunt for Polly on Saturday with many continuing their efforts overnight. As news of the apparent abduction broke, around 200 people gathered at Salisbury Cathedral to help in the search for the missing girl.

Petrol station owner Tanya Khan said she re-opened her station on Saturday night to help efforts to find the missing child. Khan said: 'My father called to ask if we would open so people could get petrol to help in the search. Locals are out in full force.' She said some people had returned home overnight, but were planning to resume at 6.30 a.m. 'It just shows the community spirit of the town and how people get together in a crisis to do anything they can to help.'

Police released two pictures of Polly and urged anyone with information about the child's disappearance to come forward. Salisbury residents have also put up posters of Polly around the town appealing for information.

Harry Taylor, who works at the Haunch of Venison on Minster Street, said the pub was empty on Saturday night with many people joining the search. 'All the locals are looking for her,' he said, adding that police officers were 'everywhere' and they were also searching cars.

The air in my room seemed to close in around me, making it difficult to breathe.

I frowned at the black-and-white photograph of the little girl. She was smiling. She looked so happy. Even though the photo wasn't in colour, I could tell that this little girl had fair hair. She also had a small button nose and a heart-shaped face. And she wore the dress with the label sewn into its collar.

Chapter 14

Mother didn't come to see if I was all right. She didn't call me for dinner either, so I had nothing to eat and spent the entire night trying to convince myself that the article and the things Clarabelle had told me meant nothing.

I would not look at the article again. Even thinking about the words on that yellowed piece of paper made my heart drum, yet they were all I could think about.

The next morning I stayed in my bedroom, half-hoping Mother would call me down to paint me, half-hoping she would leave me alone. She didn't call me. At midday she left the house and I snuck downstairs into the kitchen to make myself a sandwich. My movements were robotic, my mind dazed with tiredness and I jumped when the strange sound came. I whipped my head towards the blinds and hurried across the room, heart thudding. There was definitely something out there. Out in the back garden. Mother had driven away, so it wasn't her making the sound, which made me begin to wonder. My mind went to a dark place so quickly I surprised myself. I shook my head and put my ear to the blinds. I listened. The sound was half-banging, half-crowing, like some injured animal was out there in the other world alone and in pain. I looked at the kitchen door, thought about the newspaper article. I thought about the bread crusts. Shook my head again. No. It wasn't what I thought it was. Mother was innocent. She had gone through a horrible childhood, which explained her moods. No one who had a troubled childhood was ever at peace. I had learned that from books. Even though most of what I read was made up, there was a lot of truth in it. I knew that as well as I knew the mole next to my right eye.

The sound stopped. I listened some more. Heard nothing. I looked at the kitchen door again.

No. Trust Mother.

She told you she rescued Clarabelle from Utopia.

So?

She's lying, obviously.

Maybe she made a mistake.

I turned away from the kitchen door, picked up my sandwich and went upstairs. At my little white desk, I ate ravenously, unable to stop picturing the black-and-white photograph of the three-year-old missing girl.

I would have been three years old in 1966.

The missing girl was called Polly Dalton.

The blue dress had the name Polly Dalton sewn into it.

I shuddered and glanced at my bedroom door. An idea was forming and solidifying and making itself hard to ignore. Mother wasn't around, which meant, if I wanted to, I could sneak into her bedroom. Clarabelle was as quiet as a mouse, fast asleep no doubt behind the locked door of the spare room. The cottage was quiet too, unnervingly so.

I stood and left my bedroom. Every step I took sounded like I imagined an elephant's would. The nerves beneath my skin quivered and twitched, quivered and twitched.

I wondered where Mother had gone, how long it would take her to reach the closest house or shop. I pictured her smiling face as she had hit me, then I crossed the landing and stood outside her bedroom. This was forbidden territory. Under no circumstances was I allowed in this room. I'd probably find the door was locked, like the one to the spare room.

Cursing my trembling hand, I turned the doorknob and pushed. Nothing happened. I tried pulling but the door remained shut. Locked. Locked to keep me out. Locked, maybe, to keep whatever she had in there hidden from me.

I stood and stared at the door. I needed to get in that room. Mother wore the keys on her belt, but maybe, just maybe, she had a spare key.

I ran downstairs and darted into the living room. I scanned every part of the gloomy room and latched on to Mother's immense bookcase. With quivering fingers I pulled out every book and looked behind and between them. When I couldn't reach, I dragged the rocking chair across the room and stood on it to search the upper shelves.

The hunt took ages and I didn't find anything.

Next, I hunted high and low in the dining room – again, nothing.

Feeling almost dizzy with frustration, I dashed into the kitchen and searched every cupboard and drawer. I even looked inside the oven, but there was nothing to find.

With a long sigh, I trudged out of the kitchen and stopped outside the cupboard under the stairs. Perhaps she kept a spare set of keys in there . . .

I glanced at the front door and listened. Outside, everything stayed quiet. She wasn't back. Not yet.

I doubled over, pulled open the door and stuck my head inside. It was too dark to see much, so I turned on the hall light and opened the cupboard door as wide as it would go.

Mother kept her cleaning products in there. I scanned the gloomy space, saw a light switch and flicked it. The light flickered on and I spotted a cake tin on a shelf at the very back of the small space. Holding my hopes in one tight breath, I leaned forward and grabbed the tin. I gave it a gentle shake. Something inside rattled and my heart seemed to trip over itself.

Resting on my knees, I placed the tin on the floor and bit my lip. What I was about to do was very bad. If Mother found out I'd been sneaking around and hunting through her things, she'd be angry, but if she knew I was about to look inside this tin – something that she'd clearly kept hidden from my sight – she'd be worse than angry. If that was possible.

I stared at the front door and listened and listened and listened. No sound came.

With a shuddery breath, I wiped my palms on my lap then clawed open the tin.

Smack bang in the centre was a wad of money tied together with an elastic band. It looked like nothing else was in there. I frowned and picked up the money; underneath, lay a key. One key. I grabbed it, replaced the money and put the tin back on the shelf at the back of the cupboard.

I looked at the key – it could open any door in the house – the front door, the back door, my bedroom door, Clarabelle's bedroom door . . . Or Mother's door. The chance was slim but not impossible.

I ran up the stairs and approached Mother's bedroom with a racing heart. Knowing I was running low on time, I slotted the key into the hole and twisted. To my utter shock, the little chamber clicked. I smiled, amazed by this piece of luck.

Trembling, I withdrew the key, turned the doorknob and pushed open the door.

Immediately, the scent of orange-blossom filled my nostrils. I stared at what I could see with the door only partially open: a huge old wardrobe stood on the right-hand side of the room. There was a neatly made double bed whose sheets were pure white. To its left was a small wooden table and to its right a small bookcase. The room was colourless, the opposite of my room. The opposite of the living room with its circles of brown and orange paint all over the mustard walls.

As far as I could see, there were no pictures in Mother's bedroom either. No pop art. No psychedelic prints. It was strange. Unexpected. Almost like there was another side to Mother I'd never seen before. A side she'd hidden away in this room.

I looked back at the bed with its pure white cover. It was bathed in a glorious pool of yellow light.

I stepped into the room, squinting against the brightness: on the far side of the bedroom was an open window, a window that was not blacked out or boarded up. An open window that allowed beautiful, bright, sparkling, wondrous light to pour unfiltered into the room.

My eyes burned and began to water, but my feet transported me, dreamlike, to the shimmering window. I blinked furiously, willing my eyes to adjust and allow me to enjoy this heavenly sight, but they blurred and tears welled, blinding me. Still, my feet carried me on, past the bottom of the bed, towards the warmth of the glorious sunlight. I could hear birds chirping, smell fresh, clean, rich oxygen which broke through the orange-blossom fragrance, beating it away until there was nothing left but the smell of fresh, sun-glossed air.

For a long time – how long I don't know – I stood in front of the open window, eyes shielded by my left hand, salty tears freely flowing down my pale cheeks, taking my fill of the outside.

I inhaled deeply and stared in wonder at the view that stretched so temptingly before my eyes: first there was a small front lawn, wild and overgrown with long grass so green it hurt my eyes almost as much as the sunlight. Through this tangle of grass weaved a stepping-stone path, the stones of which were pale grey and made smaller by the long blades of grass. The garden wilderness was closed in by a wooden fence that must have stood only as high as my waist and which looked broken and battered in places. Beyond the fence lay a dirt road, on either side of which stood masses of tall, looming trees. In Mother's magazines and books – on the rare occasion she had shown me – I had seen these things: trees, grass, bushes, sun, sky, farms, houses, animals. I had pictured them in my mind, but never had I seen them for real. So now I stared and stared, feasting on these sights, delighting in their realness.

The thicket of trees stretched on far into the distance, but beyond the dirt road I could see a road made of some kind of grey stone, and then, far away, a beautiful assortment of different coloured fields which splayed out in all directions, one of which held grazing sheep that resembled little clumps of cotton wool. Beyond the sheep field lay a sea of houses which, from this distance, seemed large enough only to house dolls.

Clouds floated across the sun, giving me some relief. I lowered my arm and stared open-mouthed at the scenery. At those houses in the distance. Eagerness and excitement snapped me into action. If Mother wasn't lying and she'd made a mistake, I could prove to her that I wasn't allergic to light, and one day she might let me outside.

I turned away from the window and scanned the rest of Mother's bedroom. There was nothing unusual at all about the room. The carpet was brown. The bedside table held nothing but a small lamp and a book: *Rosemary's Baby*. No pictures hung from the walls. A second wardrobe stood to my right, the door ajar just a touch, as if it was too full to close properly.

Aware that I had wasted precious time, I walked straight over to the wardrobe and pulled open both doors.

For a second, I thought my mind was playing tricks on me. But as I continued to stare at the frightening display lining the shelves, my heartbeat quickened and my mouth grew dry.

The wardrobe was full of dolls. Every shelf was lined with them – some naked, some clothed. From the clothes rail hung more dolls. Every single one was tied to the metal pole by her hair.

They dangled there lifelessly. There must have been at least twenty crammed in there. Though every doll was different, they all had one thing in common: every single one had a photograph taped over its face – a photograph of a young woman whose eyes had been coloured in with red ink. Some photographs had been coloured in so forcefully that holes had punctured the paper revealing the dead, beady doll eyes that lay beneath. I recognized the dolls from the photographs I'd found in the attic. These dolls had been on the bed with Mother's sister, Olivia.

The air was punched out of me. I was suffocating. I couldn't breathe. Couldn't hear. Couldn't think.

My knees buckled and I fell to my hands and knees. I began to moan. Tears splatted onto the backs of my hands and I gazed at them unseeingly. My teeth found my lip and bit. Hard. Too hard. Blood came and with it the terrible, tearing truth: she was a crazy, mad woman. She had been lying about everything. I did not know her at all.

Chapter 15

I thought back to my earliest memory. It was of Mother and me making a cake together when I was four. I remembered us pretending to be witches and using our wooden spoons as wands and pretending the bowl was a cauldron and the flour and eggs and butter and sugar were lizards' tongues and bats' wings. I remembered her smiling, me giggling, us being happy and playing together like a real mother and daughter.

But it had all been a lie.

An immense wave of sorrow rolled through me and I curled up on my side on the bed and hugged my knees to my chest.

For a long time, I lay there, head spinning. I tried to make sense of everything, but there was no sense to be made. Sense was a thing of the past. The present overflowed with chaos and madness.

I sat up and swivelled around to look at the boarded-up window. I picked up the article and brought it right up to my face. Beside the little girl's right eye was a tiny black dot. *My mole.* In the background was a house. *My house?*

I couldn't get my head round it. She had taken me from

my real parents. She had locked me inside this cottage for the last ten years of my life and made me think I was allergic to the outside. Made me believe I was dying.

The pressure in my chest was suddenly unbearable, as if someone was standing on my heart, yet at the same time an immense sense of relief warmed me. I felt guilty for feeling that way, and part of me wanted to scream and smash my fists into the walls, but I didn't. Instead, I stared hard at the picture of me – innocent, happy me. Polly. I liked that name. No. I *loved* that name. It felt . . . *right*.

I got under the covers and turned onto my side. My body began to shake uncontrollably and my breathing lost track of itself. Short, sharp, ragged breaths wheezed out of me, and I squeezed my eyes shut and counted down from one hundred. I wanted to call for Mother, but she was no longer my mother. It was becoming harder and harder to breathe. I was hot, too hot.

It will pass. It will pass. Just breathe.

I pushed off the covers and counted down from one hundred again and again and again.

Finally, breathing became easier. I opened my eyes and stared at the ceiling. I tried not to think about all that I had discovered, but my brain reeled with it.

I was Polly Dalton. I was not allergic to the outside. If I walked out of the house right now, I would not die. I was not on the verge of dying. That was a lie meant to . . . I swallowed drily . . . *control* me. Everything was so wrong, and yet everything suddenly seemed so horribly right. So *real*.

Horror and grief tied me to the bed. My heart throbbed and my head banged. Staring at nothing, I curled into a ball, dug my nails into my palms and moaned as the agony of loss sank in and ripped me apart.

Chapter 16

I finally dragged myself off the bed and sat cross-legged on the floor in front of my bedroom mirror. My eyes were so swollen I could barely see. In my head, I replayed the moment Mother had slapped me and told myself I should be relieved she wasn't my real mother. A real mother wouldn't do the things she had done to me. A real mother wouldn't tell their daughter they were dying when they weren't. Yet loss wedged itself in my chest, stubborn as a nail, and refused to budge. I had lost the only mother I had ever known. I had lost my real parents, and they had lost me. They had lost me when 'Mother' had taken me away. But why? Why had she taken me from my real parents? *Why? Why? Why?*

The question was on repeat in my head, circling and circling and circling, like the vicious hornet that got trapped in the cottage one summer. It didn't make any sense. I felt like I was going mad. But she was the mad one. She was the one who didn't make sense. People didn't take other people's children. It was wrong. It was worse than wrong. It was crazy and not something a human being did. People were supposed to have their own children and then look after them themselves, not steal someone else's baby.

From my books I knew that animals didn't take other animals' young. Lions didn't take other lions' cubs. Even cats, who could be sly and mean and liked to kill other animals for fun, never stole other cats' kittens. It went completely against nature. Just like someone living shut up behind boarded windows for their whole life.

I'd also read about cuckoos – birds who liked to lay their own eggs in other birds' nests and then abandon their own babies. They did something stranger too, which was to make their eggs turn the same colour as their victims' eggs. They were experts in copying the eggs of their chosen target. The nastiest fact of all was that when the cuckoo chick was born, the mother cuckoo threw the other birds' eggs and chicks out of the nest, so that her own baby would be better fed by its new mother. It was cruel and selfish and crazy. When I had first read about cuckoos I'd cried for the mummy bird and her poor unborn – or only just born – babies. Now, sitting on the floor in front of the mirror, I cried for myself. I also cried for Emma.

The cuckoo killed other baby birds so that her own baby would be brought up by another mummy. Mother hadn't done that. She hadn't killed me, but she had stolen me and shut me inside and kept me in constant fear of dying before I grew old. She had stolen Emma too and now Emma faced the same life as me. A life in the dark. A life full of lies.

I shuddered and stared into my bloodshot eyes. My face looked grey in the unlit room. Kind of dead.

Which was worse? Being killed by another baby's mother when you were too young to know the difference, or being stolen from your mummy then made to live in the dark?

I had been living these past ten years but was I really alive? Mother called me a doll, but dolls weren't alive. It made me think of Pinocchio, the wooden puppet turned into a real boy. Was I like Pinocchio – but in reverse? Had Mother been trying to turn me from a real-life girl into a lifeless doll? Someone she could control?

It was a weird thought. One that made me grow cold from the inside out.

Yes, you are alive. Of course you are. You can breathe and bleed and cry and breathe and bleed and cry some more. It's better to be alive than dead.

But is it better to be alive than dead if I'm trapped in this house for the rest of my life?

The idea made my heart flutter with confusion and fear, yet a thrilling pulse of excitement shot through my veins.

I thought about the outside, about the wonderful things I could see and do, and the heart-stopping possibility of seeing my real mummy and daddy; and then I thought about the dangerous people I could meet. If what Mother said was true, there were evil people on the outside.

But there's a dangerous person in here too. A person who took you ten years ago. A person who lies and keeps you locked up inside. A person who made you think you were dying.

Now that you know the truth, do you really want to stay here for ever, trapped in a prison with someone like that?

My reflection frowned. This was all I'd ever known. *She* was all I'd ever known.

And Clarabelle – no – Emma . . . what about Emma?

As if she'd read my mind, the little girl began to batter her fists against her bedroom door.

'Mirabelle! Mirabelle! Are you there?'

I turned. My heart thumped. Mother was out, but she'd been out for a long time now. How long I didn't know. Too long to be sure she wouldn't return to the cottage any second.

Emma cried out again. She was shut up in her bedroom calling out for me. Me – the only person who knew the truth. Me – the only person who could tell her what was going on. Tell her the real reason she was here.

The question was: should I tell her? If I told Emma that Mother had taken us from our real parents, what would she do? She was only five years old. I was thirteen and I was having a hard time getting my head round it. How would someone so little cope with the fact that she'd been stolen from her parents? People she still remembered and loved.

My throat tightened. I didn't remember my mummy and daddy. Not at all.

I wondered what that meant. I was only three years old when she took me from them, but surely I should recall something. Anything. Like the sound of my mummy's voice or my daddy's laugh or the way it felt to be cuddled and held by them.

Emma called my name again. I looked at the door and listened. Nothing sounded other than her fists hammering against her bedroom door. It was safe, for now, but something held me back from going to her.

'Mirabelle! Mirabelle! Please! I've got something to show you!'

With a thick swallow, I pushed myself to my feet and opened the door. Without leaving the room, I said, 'What is it?'

'Come and talk to me. Please. I don't like being alone.'

'What is it you want to show me?'

'A picture. I drawed it.'

'But the door's locked. I can't come in.'

'Oh. I really want you to see. It's good. It makes me happy.'

'Tell me about it then.' I stepped onto the landing and winced at the creak of the floorboard under my foot.

'OK – oh! I just had an idea! I can push it under the door!'

I looked down. Through the gloom, I saw a sliver of white paper slide under her door.

'What do you think?' she said excitedly.

I leaned over the banister and listened carefully to make

sure Mother's car wasn't grumbling towards the house. Certain it wasn't, I hurried along the landing, bent down and picked up the piece of paper.

'It's lovely,' I said, turning it this way and that to try to work out what she'd drawn.

'It's Mummy – my old mummy, sorry – and my old daddy. Do you like it?'

My stomach twisted and turned like the random colours she'd scribbled across the paper; if Emma told Mother about this, she wouldn't like it.

'It's really good, but . . . don't show it to Mother, OK?'

There was a beat of silence. 'Why?'

I considered telling her the truth. She had a right to know. But if she knew, and I made her promise not to say anything, would she break her promise? Mother couldn't know that I knew the truth. If she found out, she'd be very angry. Maybe too angry to control what she did to me.

'Why?' she repeated, her voice whiny.

'She just wouldn't like it, that's all.'

'Why not?'

'Because . . . because it will upset her that the picture you've drawn isn't of her.'

'Oh. Oh, OK! I'll draw one of her then. Shall I do that?'

'Yes. That's a great idea. That will make her happy, and it's good to make Mother happy.' I almost choked on the words.

An odd silence followed, stretching on for too long. Feeling guilty, I shifted on my knees and thought about going back to my room.

'Mirabelle?' she whispered.

'Yes.'

'Do you like Mother?'

I hesitated. 'Do you?'

The little girl sniffed. Her voice wobbled. 'Sometimes she looks at me in a cross way and I don't like it.'

Again, I fought the urge to tell her the truth.

Emma started to cry. 'I think I want to go home. Mother says my old mummy is poorly, but I don't care.'

'Don't cry, Emma. Please don't cry.'

'You called me Emma!' she gasped.

I bit my lip.

Her crying grew louder. 'I want to go home. I want to see Mummy and Daddy. I don't like it here.'

'Shush. Be quiet—'

I stopped talking. There was rumbling up the gravel path. Mother was back.

'Stop crying. She's back. She won't like it. And don't tell her about your picture. I've got to go.'

The front door clicked. I scurried back to my bedroom, shut the door and sat at my desk, heart hammering against my ribs. Emma went silent, but not before Mother heard her and thundered up the stairs.

Chapter 17

'Clarabelle? Are you awake?' Mother's voice was quiet. Too quiet.

Her footsteps carried her to a stop outside my bedroom. I could feel her standing there, hovering on the landing like a giant spider.

Emma stayed silent. I tensed and dug my nails into my palms.

'Little Doll? Were you crying? It's all right. Mother won't be angry.'

Emma said nothing.

Fear laced my spine. The lie in Mother's words was as clear as water, her anger unmasked by her sugary tone – a tone I knew so well; knew better than the face of the grandfather clock or the grooves of the boarded windows. She was angry that Clarabelle had woken up or angry that she was upset. Maybe both. It must be killing her that her new little doll was finding it hard to accept her new home and new, fake mother.

'Clarabelle, I know you're awake. Answer me. Now.'

Why she didn't unlock the door and go into Emma's room, I didn't know. It was almost like she was enjoying Emma's fear.

'Clarabelle—'

'Mirabelle called me Emma. Why do you call me Clarabelle?'

My eyes widened and my pulse smashed against my temples.

'*What?*' Mother said.

I heard her unlocking Emma's door, heard her open and shut it, heard their muffled voices. I couldn't make out their words.

A sick feeling swirled in my tummy. I wasn't supposed to talk to Clarabelle. I definitely wasn't supposed to call her by her real name.

I glanced around the room, suddenly afraid that Mother's rule of never drawing blood might have changed. Before I knew the truth, I'd believed she would never hurt me badly, but now I wasn't certain of anything. She wasn't the person I'd thought she was. The person I'd believed her to be would never have spoiled my looks, but now that she had Emma, her new little doll to paint and dress, would she care if I wasn't perfect? Would she stop herself from spoiling my face or body?

I heard Clarabelle crying and winced. Mother could be frightening her, or worse – brushing her hair so hard it grazed her scalp, like she'd done to me before. She wouldn't shed any of Emma's blood, but the idea that the small girl was scared or in any kind of pain was horrible. And it was all my fault – I had called her Emma.

Mother's voice cut through my thoughts, sending shudders through me. 'There, there, Little Doll. Mirabelle is very jealous of you, that's why she called you that silly old name. She just wants to confuse you. But don't worry, Mother will punish her for it.'

She was speaking loudly on purpose so that I would hear.

Chapter 18

I sat at my desk and bent over a textbook, but I was oblivious to its words. My head whirled with uncertainty. And fear. Mother stood on the landing outside my room. I could hear her breathing, smell her orange-blossom moisturizer. Part of me wanted her to stand there for ever. Another part wanted her to come in and get it over with. Whatever it was, I could handle it. In the last few weeks, she'd ripped my clothes off me and scraped my scalp and slapped me in the face, and I'd handled it – what more could she do to me that she hadn't already done?

Still, my heartbeat smashed against my chest like it was trying to break out. My hands trembled, so I sat on them and tried to read the book on my desk, but the words were a blur.

I flinched at the creak of the landing floorboards as she moved. She didn't enter the room; she went into the bathroom for a few minutes then headed downstairs, footsteps hurried.

I lay on the floor and pressed my ear to the musty carpet. I could hear her doing something downstairs, moving things around aggressively by the sound of the thuds, bangs and crashes that came through the floor below me.

Stiff with tension, I tiptoed to the door. No sounds came from Emma's room. I wondered if she was OK. I wanted to call out and ask her, but didn't dare risk it – not with Mother in the house. Part of the reason she was mad was because I'd spoken to Emma.

Footsteps hammered up the stairs, making me jump. I leapt away from the door and dashed to my desk, sat down and stared at my exercise book.

Mother pushed open the door and stepped into the room. 'Mirabelle?'

'Yes, Mother?' I said, turning to look up at her, finding her name odd on my tongue.

Her eyes looked like black buttons. She wore a flowery dress that made her look thinner than normal.

'Did you talk to Clarabelle when I went out?' Her voice was cold and thin.

'Yes. She was calling out, so I went to see if everything was all right.'

She looked down at her hands and took another couple of steps into the room, bringing a sickly-sweet smell of sweat with her. Her face was flushed, hair pasted to her cheeks. A vein stuck out of her forehead, pulsing like a snake.

I swallowed, told myself she wouldn't hurt me.

'I was worried about her,' I said.

'She told me you called her Emma. Is that true?'

If a voice could cut, hers would.

I swallowed again. Took a breath. 'When she first got here she told me that was her name. I was talking to her and it slipped out. It was an accident. I'm sorry, Mother.'

'I told you not to talk to her. That you would only make matters worse and that's exactly what you've done. You went against my instruction. You poisoned her mind. She's already confused, and now, because of your selfish, jealous desire to stick your nose in, you've made her worse.'

'I'm sorry. I didn't mean—'

She leaned over and stared into my eyes. 'You've changed. You're not the innocent, sweet, little doll I thought you were. You're just like *her*.'

'Like who?' I said, though I was pretty sure who she meant.

'Olivia,' she spat.

Spittle hit my lip. I flinched and drew back.

She grabbed my upper arm and squeezed. 'She lied and stole and did whatever she wanted. She was selfish too. All she wanted was to see me suffer. I'm beginning to think that's all you want. Is it? Is that what you want, Mirabelle?'

'You're hurting me,' I said, trying to pull my arm out of her grasp. She held on, dug her nails in harder.

'Do you realize how difficult these past few weeks have been for me? Do you think it's been easy, trying to get Clarabelle to see sense? To make her understand? To . . .' She shook her head and trailed off. Tears glittered in her eyes.

I didn't reply. For a split second I wanted to tell her I knew the truth: that I didn't care any more, that she had stolen me and Emma, and I knew she was crazy, but the words died in my throat.

'Answer me!'

'No,' I said, 'I didn't know.'

Her eyes narrowed. 'Liar! There you go, lying again. *Of course* you knew. How could you not? How could you miss it?'

'I, I'm sorry. I—'

'*Enough*. Be quiet. I've had enough of your filthy lies.'

Without another word she hauled me off my chair and dragged me out of the room. I tried to pull back but she was too strong. She dragged me down the stairs so fast I nearly fell. At the bottom, she turned sharply, pulled me along the hallway and forced me to my knees in front of the under-stair cupboard.

I realized what all the banging had been about; she'd taken all the cleaning equipment out of the cupboard. It filled the floor space outside the kitchen. Cloths and bottles and the tin that held the key I'd used to get into her bedroom – all of it had been pulled out – but the light was on in the cupboard, the door open.

She seized the back of my neck and yanked my face up to hers. 'You push and push and push. Is it any wonder I snap?'

I blinked and forced back tears.

'Answer me!' She shook me so hard my neck cracked.

'I try to do everything you ask but it's never enough,' I said, surprised by my own words.

She rolled her eyes and laughed. 'I've done everything for you. Everything, and this is how you repay me? By lying and going behind my back? Well, I've had enough. You need to be punished. I should have done this a long time ago, when I first saw the signs.'

'What signs? What are you talking about?'

'Signs of evil. Signs you're taking after Olivia. Signs you need to be brought back in line.

'Grandfather was good at discipline. Far better than me. For once, I'm going to practise what he preached. You'll thank me for it in the end. If I don't beat this evil out of you, I'll need to—'

She stopped abruptly. She looked miserable, utterly hollowed out, like someone had scraped out her heart and made her look at it. She slumped back onto her ankles. Her grip on my neck loosened. She let go of me and dropped her arms to her sides.

'What?' I said, my voice high with panic. 'What will you need to do?'

Her eyes welled up and she stared at the cupboard blankly like she was in a trance.

Heart pounding, I waited a few more seconds then began to push myself to my feet, but her hand whipped out, her fingers curling around my wrist in an iron grip.

She looked up at me, a cold sneer twisting her mouth. She tilted her head to the side. 'Where do you think you're going?'

'No-nowhere.'

'You haven't received your punishment yet.'

She yanked me back down to my knees; grabbed my head in one hand, my left shoulder in the other.

In my ear she whispered, 'If you disobey me again, next time will be even worse.'

Then she forced my head into the cupboard. Around the corner, standing against the far wall of the small space, was Deadly. Nothing else was in there; just the huge spider.

My heart stopped. Fear made me want to recoil, but Mother thrust my face closer and closer until my nose was three inches away from his hideous, black body.

'Please – Mother, stop!'

I screamed and screamed, but she held me there, saying nothing. I tried again to back out and she held fast, pinning me to the spot. Cold panic spread through my lungs as I stared at Deadly, unable to look away in case he moved. Dread uncurled and attacked as an idea came – she was going to lock me in here, with him.

'Please. I'm sorry. I'll never lie to you again. I promise.'

She loosened her grip a touch. Deadly scurried forward, darting towards me at lightning speed. I screamed and tried to jerk away but her grip tightened. He stopped an inch from my nose. This time, I squeezed my eyes shut and tried to tell myself he wasn't there, but fear made me dizzy. He was there and she was going to lock me in this tiny space in the dark, with him. Hot tears rolled down my cheeks. My breathing came in short bursts. White spots danced behind my eyes.

In a soft voice she said, 'If you ever speak to Clarabelle

again without my permission, I will lock you in here with that spider and turn out the light. Do you understand, Mirabelle?'

'Yes. Yes, I understand.'

'Now aren't you going to thank me for your lesson?'

'Thank you, Mother.'

She sighed as if a world of stress had been lifted off her shoulders. 'Good girl.'

Chapter 19

I stayed in my room for the rest of the day and the whole of the following one. Mother didn't call me down to eat, so I stayed where I was, leaving my room only to go to the toilet or sip water from the sink tap. I tried to focus on reading *The Secret Garden* but I kept reading the same line over and over again, unable to stop myself reliving Mother's punishment and words. She'd been about to say something then stopped herself. It had been something about what she'd need to do to me if I didn't start to be her perfect little doll again. A perfect little doll I knew I could never be, not now I knew the truth.

I felt I knew what she'd been about to say and the knowledge was terrifying – more terrifying than staying in the cottage for the rest of my life and never getting the chance to meet my real parents.

I could have been wrong, but something had woken up inside me. It was like a sixth sense had bloomed in my brain, and this new sense told me she was even crazier than I realized, and that she was getting worse.

I listened intently. The house was quiet. She was out again.

Trembling all over, I wrote a list, starting with the day Mother scraped my scalp.

Horrible Things She's Done

1. Scraped my head brushing my hair
2. Made me think I was dying when I started my period
3. Tore off my dress
4. Forced me into the light
5. Slapped me
6. Told me the light was melting my organs
7. Stopped giving me food
8. Terrified me with Deadly
9. Threatened to lock me in the under-stair cupboard with Deadly

I licked my lips and re-read the list; my senses sharp now, despite the gnawing hunger.

She was getting worse. Much worse. She was losing control. I was in danger. Emma was in danger.

Certainty thrummed in my chest and my palms began to sweat. I thought about the dolls hanging in Mother's wardrobe and my heart wrenched.

I didn't deserve a life like this.

I shuddered and pushed myself away from the desk.

I couldn't stay here any more. Emma couldn't stay here any more. If we stayed here, we would probably die.

I dragged myself up and put an ear to the door. I listened as Mother brushed her teeth. Listened as she padded across the landing and closed her bedroom door.

I was starving and couldn't think on an empty stomach. I crept downstairs, made myself some toast and ate a chunk of cheese. As I ate, my eyes strayed to the huge, wickedly sharp chopping knife on the kitchen counter. My stomach tensed.

I could not, would not attack her.

Mother was crazy. What she had done was evil. If I had to fight to get away, I would, but I didn't want to hurt her. I didn't think I could. She was all I'd ever known. She hadn't always treated me badly.

I dug my nails into my palms and looked at the knife again. I shook my head, felt my hair tickle my cheeks. Exhaling, I hardened my heart against the fear curdling my blood.

There was no ignoring it though: Mother was dangerous. I needed to get away. I needed to help Emma get away. I had to make sure she got back home to her real mummy and daddy. She was too small to help herself and there was no way I was going to leave her here. She shouldn't have to grow up like me, locked in a gloomy house with no friends and no daddy, believing she was going to die soon.

I groaned and rubbed my temples. My heart hurt and my head hurt and I needed all of this to end as quickly as possible. As quickly as possible without anyone getting hurt.

With shaking hands, I washed up the plate and knife and wiped down the surfaces.

I looked at the knife once more then left the room.

Chapter 20

One week later

Though Mother hadn't given me permission, I took a risk and dashed downstairs, determined to get started. For days, I'd sat in my room and tried to work out how to escape, working through situation after situation, idea after idea, doubt after doubt, and fear after fear about what would happen if I tried to get away and was unsuccessful.

Now, finally, it was time to act. If I put it off any longer, I might question my decision to leave, and questioning might lead to doubting and doubting might lead to talking myself out of it.

It was clear Mother had taken great care to keep me a secret. From looking out of her bedroom window I knew that the cottage was far away from other buildings. How long it would take to reach the closest one was impossible for me to guess. Horribly impossible.

Heart thrumming madly, I stood on tiptoe and opened the top kitchen cupboard where Mother kept the tinned food. If my plan was going to work, I might need some supplies.

The last thing I wanted was to escape the cottage then starve to death.

My heart skittered. The thought of leaving the cottage was scary but exciting. For so long, I had dreamed about the outside world. About the wonderful, beautiful, colourful things I would be able to see and touch and smell. I might even see a robin. And the idea of seeing my parents made my heart leap with anticipation and joy one moment then shrink with fear the next. What if they didn't remember me? What if they'd moved on with their lives and wanted nothing to do with me? What if they were just like her?

Mother's voice drifted into the room from the living room, its edges spiky. 'You can't go outside, Clarabelle, Little Doll. It's far too dangerous.'

'Why?'

'I've already told you this. You're poorly, Little Doll, just like your pretend mother. That's why she gave you to me. But don't worry. Mother will protect you. Mother will keep you safe. Mother will never let anything bad happen to you. Mother loves you.'

'Oh yeah – I forgot,' Emma said.

'Good little doll. Come, let's have a boogie together.'

'What's a boogie?'

The Eagles blasted into the cottage. I pulled a tin of beans out of the cupboard. I dropped it into a laundry basket then grabbed a tin of sweetcorn. Laughter reached my ears and my heart burned. I kept putting tin after tin into the basket. When I had eight tins, I picked up the basket and crept over to the kitchen door. The hallway was clear. Another track started to play. This one was about someone's lying eyes. I dashed past the open living room doorway and caught sight of Mother and Emma holding hands and dancing together. Emma saw me and frowned. My heart leapt into my throat and I turned and bounded upstairs, arms burning from the weight of the tins. I kicked open my bedroom door and pushed the laundry basket under my bed. Pulling the covers over the edge of the bed, I turned to see Mother standing in the doorway.

Her face was red, hair wild. Her small eyes took in my unmade bed and messy appearance. I wore her favourite dress but it was uncomfortably tight across my chest and stomach. I had not brushed my hair and wore no make-up. She had not painted my face for a while, preferring to focus her artistic efforts on Clarabelle rather than me these days.

'What were you doing just now? Were you spying on us?' she snapped.

I said nothing. I didn't know what to say. My brain felt like a scrambled egg.

'I suppose you feel left out, do you?' she said, stepping into the room.

I didn't reply.

'Poor Mirabelle. I know it's been hard on you since I rescued Clarabelle, but you can't let jealousy ruin you. Jealousy killed the cat, you know.'

'Curiosity killed the cat,' I said.

Her eyes narrowed and she tilted her head to one side, trailing her eyes up and down my body and face, her lips twisted.

'Are you *correcting* me?'

I shook my head. 'No – I – sorry.'

'Sorry *what*?'

The words tasted sour on my tongue, 'Sorry, *Mother*.'

She stared at me for a long time. Her jaw clenched. A large blue vein throbbed in her forehead.

I looked at the frilly pink curtains to avoid her glare, frightened she was considering locking me in the under-stair cupboard with Deadly.

Finally, she said, 'Good. Now, the kitchen's a mess and

Clarabelle and I need lunch. Go and make us some sandwiches. Don't throw the crusts in the bin. Leave them out on a plate.'

'Yes, Mother.' I fought the urge to ask why she didn't want me to throw away the crusts.

She gave me a curt nod and left the room humming brightly.

As soon as she was out of earshot, I moved the contents of the laundry basket into the back of my wardrobe behind my nightgowns then placed the laundry basket outside her bedroom where I had found it. I hurried downstairs and made her, Emma and myself a spam sandwich, which I gobbled down quickly before taking theirs in to them. They both sat at the dining room table. Emma looked up at me when I placed her sandwich in front of her. I was pleased to see that she didn't look as sleepy as before. Mother ignored me.

Knowing I didn't have much time, I hurried back into the kitchen and grabbed the tin opener and a fork out of the drawer. There was nothing I could do about water because there were no empty bottles and if I emptied one out, she would notice straight away, so I took a mug from the cupboard then ran out into the hallway, past the dining room and past the living room. If I found a stream, I could fill the mug and drink that way. Or Emma and I could just cup our hands together and collect water in our palms. That would be easier. That was what Huckleberry Finn did. I wondered if the water round here would be thick and 'yaller' like Mississippi water or clear like in Ohio. The thought of drinking yellow water was gross but water was water and if Emma and I were dying of thirst, we would need to drink whatever we found.

Realizing that I didn't really need the mug, I turned around and ran back into the kitchen, put the mug back in its normal place then hurried along the hallway and up the stairs.

I deposited my treasures inside my wardrobe along with the tinned goods then hurried back down to hear Mother calling my name.

'Mirabelle! Come and clear away our plates, please.'

Anger and misery bit, making me nauseous, but I obeyed her instructions and cleared away their plates, which I washed up, dried and put back in the cupboards. I left the kitchen, intent on completing the next step in my plan, but Mother stopped me.

'Mirabelle. In here. Now.'

I walked into the room to see Mother smiling sweetly at me. Emma was lying on the sofa fast asleep.

'Yes, Mother?' I said, hating that I still had to call her that, but still used to the feel of it on my tongue.

She stared above my head as she spoke. 'Polish the room then clean the fridge. If you do a good job, I might let you eat with Little Doll and me tonight. Would you like that?'

'Yes, Mother.'

'But if you miss just one spot . . .' she trailed off, eyes glinting.

She picked up Emma and kissed the top of the little girl's head tenderly. Emma did not stir. She looked like a miniature Sleeping Beauty. *And I'm Cinderella.*

Mother left the room with slow steps, holding the little girl close to her chest like she was the most precious thing in the world. I vaguely remembered how she used to hold me like that and felt a stabbing pain in my chest.

I frowned and told myself to get a grip. There was no point dwelling on the past; I had to focus on the now – on getting Emma and myself out of here. Now that I knew what she had done, I realized there was no way to predict the full extent of her wrongness. Her badness.

My eyes fell on the dining room table, to the empty syringe that Mother had boldly left out on display. My knees buckled as an idea that was so terrible but so obvious shot into my brain like one of Robin Hood's arrows: Mother wasn't giving Emma calming medicine to help her feel better about her father; Mother was giving Emma calming medicine to make her easier to control.

I shouldn't have been shocked, but I was. I picked up the syringe and shook my head. Did she drug me too? And if Emma was drugged, how was I supposed to get her out of the house? I could carry her, but not for long. I looked at my scrawny arms, at my bandaged hand. I wasn't exactly muscle girl.

I hurried to the cupboard under the stairs and grabbed a dust cloth and the polish spray. I placed them on the carpet behind me then knelt down and searched the cupboard for a bag, one big enough to hold all of my supplies. I gritted my teeth, worried. There was nothing in the cupboard of any use. Nothing. I reconsidered escaping without any supplies. Would I survive with nothing but the clothes on my back? I didn't even have any warm clothes, but the month was May, so it should not be too cold. The only shoes I had were a flimsy pair of slippers. My feet were much smaller than Mother's, so there was little point in taking a pair of her outdoor boots. But the problem of starving to death was one I had to deal with. I had learned that from my books. Whenever a character escaped, they always had to think about how to deal with hunger. Like in *The Wolves of Willoughby Chase* when Bonnie and Sylvia escaped from the orphanage. That was why I had collected those food tins. Food was essential. Without it, we might die. I had to find a bag to carry them in.

A horrid thought scratched at my brain. Wolves. Would there be wolves outside? I'd never asked Mother about that and now it was too late to ask.

A distant banging sound made me jump. It was the sound from the back garden, the sound I'd heard before.

Mother came running down the stairs, face red and twisted with anger. I grabbed the polish and cloth as she ran past me into the kitchen. I heard the kitchen door being unlocked and hurried into the room to see her disappear out of the back door. What on earth was she doing? The kitchen door was ajar. Light ran down the gap, sucking me forward. It would be so easy to slip out of that door and make a run for it, but I couldn't leave Emma.

I heard Mother screaming something and the banging sound stopped. Was someone out there? Who was she screaming at? I crept towards the door, desperate to know what was happening outside, but the sound of approaching footsteps made me dash back into the hallway.

Mother locked the kitchen door and whipped past me, saying, 'After you've done your chores, go upstairs and take off that dress. I've laid out some other clothes for you. From now on, you're to wear those and only those.'

My question died on my tongue. It would be stupid to ask her about what had just happened anyway.

She disappeared upstairs and I began to polish the dining room table, all the while puzzling over the bag issue. The trunks in the attic were far too large and bulky, so those were out. There were no bags in any of the other rooms in the cottage, except, maybe, in Mother's room. I remembered the big black holdall she had brought Emma home in. That would be perfect. I would have to go into her bedroom a second time.

Chapter 21

I wore the plain, brown, sack-like dress Mother had left out on my bed. I had changed out of my doll dress into the brown one just before she left the cottage. Now I looked like the little slave girl I had recently become. The material of the dress – if you could call it a dress – was scratchy and coarse against my skin, and the fabric smelled musty. Despite the roughness of the dress, there was something wonderful about not having to wear one of my doll dresses, because that's what they were. They were dresses for dolls, not human beings. Mother did not wear silly dresses like that; she wore jeans and floaty blouses. She had left the house dressed in faded bell-bottom jeans and an orange-and-white striped blouse.

I touched the dress, stroked my finger down my cheek. Mother put me in doll dresses and painted my face because she wanted me to be perfect, just like a doll. A perfect, silent little doll that could not answer back. A doll-like girl she could control.

I couldn't believe I had been so blind to her strangeness for so long.

I thought about her car. If only I could drive, I could whisk

Emma and myself far away with speed and ease. If we could get out of the cottage, that was. Also, if I could drive, we could avoid any wolves that might be lurking outside. Huge, vicious wolves with yellow, blood-stained teeth.

I swallowed. Told myself there wouldn't be any wolves.

I forced myself to refocus on searching for the holdall. I glanced around quickly but the bag didn't seem to be in the bedroom. I knew it wasn't in the wardrobe, which was a relief because I didn't want to see her crazy doll display ever again.

I sighed and stumbled away from the bed as the unmistakable sound of a knock on the front door penetrated the cottage. Rushing towards the window, I grabbed the sill and peered out – a man stood down there. A man! A real-life other person! The man wore a green T-shirt. His brown, straggly hair hung around his broad shoulders. A heavy-looking bag was strapped to his back. He knocked again and I hesitated, wanting to call out to him, but unsure whether to trust this stranger. What if he was as crazy as her?

My chance was stolen as Mother's red car grumbled up the dirt road. Unable to believe her timing, I dashed around the bottom of the bed, out of the room. Closing and locking the door behind me, I moved to the edge of the banister at the top of the stairs. I knelt down and peered around the corner, giving myself a view of the front door. My heart raced as I realized this could be my chance – mine and Emma's chance – to escape. The man had looked bigger than Mother, stronger too. If he was a good, kind person, surely he would help us.

The 'if' word hovered over me like some invisible beast; what if he was even worse than her? What if she knew him? What if they were partners? I shook my head, unable to believe I could have been so clueless as to not pick up on her having some kind of evil friend in all of this. I would have seen or noticed something.

I heard voices – hers and his. It was hard to hear their words and I wanted to know – I needed to know. I pushed myself up and ran down the stairs then darted past the front door into the living room where I hid just inside the doorway by the corner wall. I pressed my ear to the cool, hard outer wall and strained to hear their words, but they had stopped talking.

I could not remember a single time Mother had mentioned a man other than her grandfather, who she had only so recently spoken to me about. Once, some years back, I had asked her who my father was. Somewhere deep down, even at six or seven years old, I had known this was forbidden territory, but my inner cat had got the better of me. She had shouted at me for asking such a question then given me the silent treatment for the next seven days. Those seven days had seemed an eternity to me. I had begged her to talk to me, tried to hug her, brought her glasses of water, made her lunch, but nothing worked.

I frowned and wondered if she had treated me like that because she enjoyed feeling powerful. Had she enjoyed tormenting me? If I did not get Emma out of the cottage, perhaps Mother would do the same to her – maybe worse, if Emma was not as obedient as me. As weak and pathetic and gullible as me.

If she is not as weak as me, she'll probably suffer more.

I was weak. For ten years, I had been weak. I had behaved like some kind of toy puppet. Like a stupid, mindless doll – exactly what she wanted.

Not any more.

My hands clenched at my sides and I set my jaw, determined to take advantage of this perfect chance.

The lock crunched, the front door opened and I stepped out of my hiding place into full view.

Chapter 22

'Come in, come in. I'm sure you'll feel much better once you've had something to eat and drink,' Mother said. Her voice was high and happy-sounding. Unnaturally bright.

My first thought was why – why was she inviting the man inside? She was acting like she had nothing to hide. It didn't make any sense, but a lot of things she did didn't make sense. This was yet another one of her odd, unpredictable moves. *Another sign of how mad she is.*

She paused just inside the cottage holding the door half-open, and jumped when she saw me.

'Get back upstairs into your room this instant,' she hissed, her eyes shooting daggers.

I stared back at her and shook my head. 'No. I'm not going anywhere.' I couldn't believe my boldness. I had never disobeyed her or answered back like this. Never. My heartbeat rocketed but I planted my feet, determined to stay.

Shock pulled at her features. She stabbed her finger at me. 'If you don't get upstairs now, you'll pay for it.'

I said nothing, only watched in silence, my eyes greedy with curiosity as the man's face poked through the gap in the door.

'Everything all right, miss?' he said. He had a strange lilt to his accent and he pronounced 'th' as 't' which made me think he might be from another country. I knew a few. I wondered if he was a Frenchman.

She laughed and beckoned him inside, moving into the hallway. 'Yes, everything's fine. Come on in. This is my daughter. Don't mind her.'

She stood beside the door and held it open for him then closed and locked it. She slid the keys into her pocket. The man raised his eyebrows. She smiled and shrugged.

'You can't be too careful living out here in the middle of nowhere,' she said with a girly laugh.

He nodded then looked at me. I saw him take in my odd, potato-sack dress. A flicker of confusion flashed up in his dark brown eyes. He gave me a small, awkward smile. I stared back, taking all of him in, trying to work out who he was. It was strange, but seeing another person wasn't as weird as I'd thought it would be. He was merely a human being. Another member of the human species. A body with arms and legs and a head and eyes and a nose and a mouth and ears. It felt *right* to see another person, even if it was a man.

I stared at him. He had a symmetrical, nice-looking face, a slightly turned-up nose and a square jaw. Spiky hairs poked out of his chin and upper lip. His forehead was shiny with sweat and his skin was a golden-brown shade that reminded me of honey. He didn't have any wrinkles around his eyes like her, which meant he was younger. How much younger, I couldn't be sure. He looked fine – on the outside, but I knew it was impossible to tell what was going on inside somebody's head.

The man looked from me to Mother's retreating back. He seemed a bit uncomfortable, worried maybe, but who was I to guess the feelings of a strange man I'd only just met?

Especially when I hadn't seen one in ten years. Not a living, breathing, sweating one.

I glanced over my shoulder and followed his gaze. Mother was heading towards the kitchen, walking in a weird way, her hips swaying from side to side like the pendulum in the grandfather clock.

She was almost out of earshot, but I couldn't be sure. How could I know he was trustworthy? He could be thinking anything right now. Behind those tired, innocent-seeming brown eyes, his thoughts could be cruel, evil, wicked. That was the horrifying truth; no one could know what was going on in someone else's mind. Thoughts were private. There was no need to make an effort to hide them, because they remained as silent as the dead, voiced only in your own head; right now, she did not have a clue that I was debating whether to ask this man for help or not, just as I had no clue what he was thinking or what Mother was thinking. The fact terrified me. I stared at the back of his head as he turned away from me with a puzzled look on his face. He followed her into the kitchen with slow, weary steps, his bag still weighing heavily on his back.

I followed him, heart thumping, unable to make a decision. To trust or not to trust?

He paused at the kitchen doorway. 'Why're the windows like that?'

'Come in, come in. Take off that heavy bag and rest yourself,' she said, bustling about the kitchen humming 'Take It Easy'.

'The windows?' he repeated with a yawn, still standing.

Mother turned to face him. I noticed her top two buttons were undone, exposing the top of her breasts. She smiled, 'Oh that? That's because my poor little Mirabelle here is allergic to sunlight. Such a shame, but it can't be helped. Poor little thing. Now, what would you prefer, Patrick, ham or cheese sandwiches?'

Her words sounded so false. They were so false. She was false. Everything about her was pretend.

Anger pulsed through my veins and I opened my mouth to say that she was lying, that she had kidnapped me, that she had taken Emma too, but the words melted away as the young man made sympathetic noises, glanced pityingly at me, then dropped his bag to the floor and took a seat at the table, a huge sigh whooshing out of him.

I hovered in the doorway staring at the back of Patrick's head, indecision rushing through me. Patrick. Such a simple, nice name. Could someone called Patrick who looked so normal on the outside be secretly evil on the inside?

Mother handed him a glass of water which he glugged back noisily. Then she turned to me and said brightly, 'Off you go now, darling, up to bed for your afternoon rest.'

She walked over, seized my wrist in a painfully tight grip and dragged me out of the room glaring down at me, a warning clear in her small dark eyes. I did not fight back, though I longed to. She shut the kitchen door in my face and I stood there, small and pathetic in the shadows, battling the urge to cry.

Laughter – his and hers – erupted from behind the door, making my tummy hurt.

I heard a noise coming from above and strained to listen. It was Emma and she was crying. I tensed, fearful that Mother would hear. I glanced from the kitchen door to the ceiling, stuck again. Should I go to Emma and calm her down or should I burst into the kitchen, tell Patrick everything? There was no knowing what Mother would do, how she would react. A small part of me still felt bad for even considering the idea of telling someone what she had done – what she was still doing. It felt like some kind of betrayal, which was ridiculous, because it was she who had betrayed me. She was the one who had stolen me from my parents when I was only three years old. I knew I had to pull myself together. She was dangerous. I had to get Emma and myself out of the cottage. I had to get home, back to my real parents where I would be safe, but could I trust this man to help me? He had turned up uninvited on Mother's door-step with nothing but a big bag on his back. Who did that? Why would someone be wandering around in the middle of nowhere, alone? Was he running from someone? Was he a criminal running from the police? If he was, there was no way I could place my trust in him, not when there was so much at stake.

Rack my brains as I might, I could not come up with a logical explanation for this man's sudden arrival at the cottage. It didn't make any sense. I ran through his actions in my mind. He had sat down with obvious relief, as if exhausted, and gulped that glass of water down so quickly . . . Was he a homeless man searching for a home? Maybe. That was the first idea that made some sort of sense. But then – why was he homeless in the first place? Had he done something bad that had made him lose his home? It was impossible to know.

Emma's crying escalated to screams. The kitchen went quiet. The door opened and I stepped back as Mother froze at the sight of me standing there.

I thought it was only wolves that snarled – like in *Beauty and the Beast* and *The Wolves of Willoughby Chase* – but right then, she snarled at me, baring her small, sharp teeth and yellow-pink gums, her lips curled back, her nose scrunched up. Her eyes looked black in the gloom of the hallway and her body towered over me like a skeletal giant. Her blouse hung loose, revealing the ribs between her small breasts.

I stumbled backwards, sure she was going to hit me, but something changed in her eyes. Her expression softened and she relaxed her face. I could almost see the cogs whirring in her brain as she changed her plan of attack.

'Go upstairs and calm Clarabelle down, please, Little Doll. I'm busy entertaining our guest.' Her voice was soft – and completely fake.

I looked down at her hands, which were balled into fists beside her skinny thighs.

I hesitated, knowing I was taking a risk. She glanced back over her shoulder, her brow creased.

'I'll need the key,' I said quietly.

'The key?' she said.

'The key to her room,' I said, determined not to call Emma by her fake name. 'I can only calm her down properly if I can see her and give her a cuddle.'

The scrape of a chair from the kitchen and Patrick's voice, asking if everything was OK, seemed to force her into a decision.

'Everything's fine – back in a second!' she called, her voice high and girly again.

She lifted the key ring at her belt and hastily removed the spare room key. I noticed her fingers were trembling. The old me would have asked if she was all right, but I wasn't Mirabelle the Weak any more.

'Thank you, Mother,' I said softly.

Before she could change her mind, I turned and walked along the hallway. She went back into the kitchen and shut the door as I ran up the stairs, taking them two at a time, my heart about to burst with excitement and nerves. This was it. This was the first real step.

I knocked on the door. 'Hi,' I said gently, 'it's only me.'

Emma stopped wailing. I unlocked the door and slipped into the room, clutching the key tightly in my sweaty palm, so tightly it made my hand throb.

She sat on the little white bed hugging her knees to her

chest. Her eyes were red and swollen from crying. Snot ran from her nose onto her lips. I looked around the room, not surprised to find it similar to mine, though more colourful as the walls had been painted with pale grey bunnies and enormous red and orange flowers. The bed was covered with a frilly pink duvet. A white bear-shaped rug lay on the wooden floorboards. From the windows hung frilly lilac curtains which had been nailed around the edges into the wall. The middle of the curtains had been sewn together to prevent even the slightest shard of light from penetrating the room. A cute miniature tea set sat on a little white desk alongside a large sandy-coloured teddy bear who wore a scarlet bow around his fluffy neck. Mother had clearly made an effort for her new doll.

'Hi,' I said, perching on the edge of the bed.

She stared at me with her big blue eyes and sniffed. 'My head hurts.'

'Does it? Oh, well, maybe if we go downstairs I can find something to make it feel better.'

'I'm not allowed,' she whispered, her eyes darting towards the door, 'M-M-Mother will be cross if, if, if I go out.'

'No she won't. She sent me up here to see if you were OK, but there's something important I have to tell you first. A secret.'

Emma sat up at this. I noticed she wore one of my old nightgowns. A long white one embroidered with daisies. A strange twinge pulled at my chest. She was my replacement. It was as clear as glass.

I leaned forward and stroked hair out of her eyes.

'What secret?' she said.

'If I tell you, you have to promise me not to say anything. Promise?'

She hesitated, looked at the door again. After a few seconds she whispered, 'I promise.'

'OK,' I paused, trying to think of the best way to explain, 'the woman who is looking after us isn't well. There's something wrong with her. She took me from my real parents when I was about your age and told me I was her daughter. She told me my name was Mirabelle, but my real name is Polly. And now she's doing the same thing to you.'

'I don't understand,' Emma said, wiping her nose with the back of her wrist.

'What's your name? Your *real* name?'

The girl frowned, as if concentrating really hard. She hadn't been here for very long. There was no way she could have forgotten her real name already, but Mother was clever. She skewed the truth, made you think the way she thought.

'My old name is Emma,' she whispered.

'Yes! That's right. Emma is your *real* name. Polly is mine. She stole us from our real parents. She took us because she wanted us, but we have to get away. We have to get out of here and go back to our real parents.'

Emma stared at me. I could see that she was trying to wrap her brain around my meaning. But then she shook her head, 'No. She's nice to me. She loves me. She's my mummy now. She said, she said, that, that . . .'

'She *lied*. She's not your mummy. She took you away, Emma, don't you see? We have to get away from here.'

'But, but, but, I can't. I can't go outside. The light will, will, will . . . hurt me.'

I reached out and took her hands in mine. They were so small, so innocent.

'The light won't hurt you. She lies. It's all lies.'

'Grown-ups don't tell lies,' Emma said firmly.

I sighed. How was I going to get her to believe me? She had to trust me or everything could go wrong.

'Your real mummy and daddy don't tell lies. Most grown-ups don't, but she does. She's different.'

'Why?'

'Why what?'

'Why does she lie?'

I shrugged and tucked her hair behind her ear. 'I don't know. I wish I did, but I don't. All I know is that we need to get out of here, away from her. We need to go and find our real parents.'

'I'm scared,' she said.

'You don't need to be scared. You just need to do everything I tell you to. OK?'

She nodded, but her eyes wandered to the door.

'Promise me you'll do what I say, when I say it? Emma, promise me.'

She looked at me, her eyes wide and wet. 'I promise,' she paused, 'Polly.'

'Good. Good girl. OK. This is what we're going to do . . .'

Chapter 23

'Mother! Mother! Come quick! It's Clarabelle!' I screamed the words at the top of my lungs, standing just outside the spare room. I screamed the words over and over and over, only stopping when Mother's footsteps pounded up the stairs. She turned sharply on the landing, using the banister to propel herself round.

'What happened? What have you done to her?' she screamed, eyes crazed, full of panic.

'I don't know! She's in bed and she won't move!' I panted back. I pointed through the open doorway to the bed. An Emma-sized mound lay beneath the bedcovers.

'Move!' she barked at me, rushing into the room. 'Clarabelle! Clarabelle, talk to me!'

The second she was fully inside the room, I slammed the door shut and frantically jammed the key into the lock. She was back at the door immediately, the ruse blown, twisting and turning the doorknob, screaming and cursing – but the job was already done. I had locked the door. She was trapped. Her fists continued to pound against the door. I stumbled backwards and turned around, unable to believe what I'd just done yet able to keep moving.

'Come on!' I yelled at Emma, who poked her terrified face out of my bedroom door, shaking her head.

'I don't want to!' she cried.

I grabbed her hand. 'You have to. Remember your promise?'

She hesitated then nodded and I tugged her out of my bedroom, across the landing to the stairs. Mother's screams were crazed, her rage terrifying. Her fists pounded and bashed the door with so much force I feared she was going to break it down.

'Run!' I shouted, pulling Emma down the stairs.

We reached the second last step and stopped. Patrick stood at the bottom of the stairs looking concerned. In that moment, he looked huge and almost as terrifying as Mother.

'Hey, hey, hey! Slow down, girls. What's going on?' he said, holding up his hands.

I sucked in a quick breath, knowing I had to get this right, hoping he was a good person. 'Please help us. She's not our—'

Mother's voice cut across mine, drowning me out, 'DON'T LET THEM OUTSIDE, PATRICK! THEY'RE ALLERGIC TO THE LIGHT! THEY'LL DIE!'

Patrick sighed. 'Girls, what's going on?' He crouched down at the foot of the stairs and smiled sympathetically.

I pulled Emma close to my side and tried to sound as mature and clear as I could. 'You have to find a way to get us out of here. We need to leave. She's not our real mother. She's—'

'Now, now, slow down there, girl. You're scaring your little sis.' He reached out to pat my arm but I jerked back out of his reach. His eyebrows shot upwards and he chuckled and shook his head.

'Look, I get it. You have this horrid, rare disorder and it must be mad awful having to stay cooped up inside here all the time, but it's not your mother's fault. She has to keep you inside. It's her job to protect you.'

I tried to stay calm, tried to ignore Mother's ranting from above us. 'Please, you have to believe me. She's *not* our mother. She took me from my parents ten years ago. My real name's Polly Dalton. And she took Emma from her parents not that long ago. Surely you heard about a missing girl? It must have been in the newspaper.'

He looked like he hadn't heard me. His eyes were on the ceiling, his attention on Mother's words, not mine.

I grabbed his arm and tugged. 'Please, Patrick, please. You have to help us. The front door and the back door are locked. All of the downstairs windows are nailed shut, but maybe—'

'I'm not from around here,' he said, looking at my hand on his arm, 'so I don't know about any story like the one you're talking about, but I have to say, it all sounds pretty far-fetched, you know?'

I let my hand drop to my side. 'Emma, you tell him. Tell the nice man what happened to you.'

I looked down at Emma, whose face was buried in my side. Crouching down beside her, I whispered reassuring things and stroked her back, but she burst into tears.

'I wa, wa, wa, want, my, mu, mu, mummy!' she wailed.

Mother heard Emma and shouted, 'Don't worry, Little Doll, Mummy's right here!'

I gritted my teeth and stood up. 'Patrick, please, I know it sounds strange – and it is – I know how strange it sounds. I believed she was my mother until only a few days ago, but I'm telling you the truth. She's crazy. She may seem normal, but she's not. She's insane. She kidnapped me and she kidnapped Emma.'

Tears of desperation streamed down my cheeks. 'Please, Patrick, I'm begging you. Please believe me.'

His face creased with concern. 'Has she hurt you? Does she . . . hit you?'

'No, but, but I want to go home, back to my real parents. I shouldn't be here. Emma shouldn't be here. It's not right.'

Patrick began to nod. He tugged on his earlobe. A frown had etched itself into his forehead making him look older. Finally, he sighed and looked me dead in the eye.

'OK. I've heard you. I'm not saying I believe you completely, but it does seem like one helluva a big lie for such a little girl to make up . . . but I'm not about to go around smashing windows or dismantling them. For all I know, you being cooped up in here could have made you so desperate to get outside that you don't care any more about being allergic to light.'

I opened my mouth to speak but he held up his hands. 'Hang on, hang on. What I'm saying is, I'm going to go upstairs and talk to your mother.'

'She isn't—'

'OK, OK – she isn't your mother – I get that. So I'm going to talk to her, get her side of things, then I'll see about what's best.'

I shook my head. 'No. Please don't let her talk to you. Please just help us get out of here. You could leave right now. Go to the closest town and get the police. Bring them here. They'll know. They'll sort it all out, then you don't have to do anything wrong.'

He frowned. 'Yeah, but you're forgetting one little itty bitty thing: the doors are locked and she's got the keys. How am I going to get out without breaking something?'

The question dangled in the air like a poised blade; he was right.

I swallowed thickly. 'Good point. All right then, but before you talk to her, please wait a second. There's something in the attic that will prove what I'm saying is true. Please? Is that OK? It'll only take me five minutes.'

He sighed. Mother had gone silent. He shifted his weight

from one foot to the other, tugging on his earlobe. 'OK. But be quick. She's gone quiet and it's worrying me.'

'Thank you, Patrick. Thank you so much.'

I pulled Emma from my side and told her to sit on the stairs and wait for me. She resisted a little, but after a few reassuring words she gave in and sank to the carpet with a sob.

Patrick followed me up the stairs. I raced up, taking them two at a time, aware that I had to be quick or he might change his mind.

Standing on my desk chair, I opened the attic door then pulled out the ladder. Patrick helped me lower it to the ground and held it firm as I ascended quickly, my heart thumping against my ribs. I reached the opening to the attic and heard Mother's voice, urgent and low, directed at Patrick. She must have heard us climbing the stairs. I thought about turning around and telling Patrick to ignore her, but knew she would keep talking and he would feel compelled to listen, so I focused on quickly scanning the boxes. With a horrible moment of clarity, I remembered: I had tucked the evidence inside my pillowcase! The newspaper article wasn't up here in the attic; it was down there in my bedroom.

Cursing my forgetfulness, I clambered back down the ladder to hear Mother urging Patrick to get the key to the spare room off me and let her out. Patrick glanced from me to the spare room, clearly torn. Before he could decide what to do, I jumped off the ladder and ran into my bedroom. I shoved my hand into the pillowcase, terrified that she had somehow found and taken my evidence. My hand found nothing, nothing but pillow and cotton, and then – paper – the article. With sweaty fingers, I pulled out the piece of newspaper. Patrick had to believe me now. He *had* to. The resemblance between the now me and my three-year-old self was undeniable. I had barely changed. My face was thinner and I was obviously a lot taller; yet my big, almond-shaped eyes were exactly the same. And the tiny mole was identical. That girl was me. I was that girl.

'Patrick! I found it! Look!' I ran out of my room onto the landing.

Patrick was standing close to the spare room door, his ear pressed against the wood. He was nodding, tugging his earlobe, frowning.

'Patrick?' I said, walking towards him.

He turned slowly. His face looked different, harder somehow. I took a step back, suddenly worried. What had she said to him? Had she convinced him not to trust me?

'Patrick, please, have a look . . .'

'Where's the key?' he said. 'She's having an asthma attack. You have to let her out now.'

'She doesn't have asthma,' I said, thrusting the newspaper article forward, 'Please, just look. This is proof. If you don't believe me after looking at this, I'll give you the key. I promise.'

'Help . . . me,' Mother's voice floated through the door.

'She's lying,' I repeated as his head jerked towards her voice.

He snatched the paper out of my hand. 'What am I supposed to be looking at exactly?'

I said nothing, just watched as he studied the picture of me. His eyebrows rose a fraction and he glanced at me then back at the black-and-white photograph, at me then back at the article. His eyes darted side to side as he read the article. A few moments later, his back straightened and his eyes widened. He slipped the article into his pocket and looked back at the spare room. He put his finger to his lips and pointed to the stairs.

Relief exploded in my chest – he understood! He was on my side. Our side. Mine and Emma's. We were going to get out of here.

I wanted to scream with joy but I kept quiet and followed him down the stairs to where Emma still sat, hugging her knees. I tapped her shoulder and put my finger to my lips. Patrick beckoned us to follow him into the kitchen and we did, hand in hand, Emma looking curiously up at me through wet, swollen eyes.

Once we were in the kitchen, Patrick said, 'I can't believe it – it all seems so far out – but that *is* you. You're her. The girl from the paper. The one who went missing all those years ago.'

I nodded, waited for him to take charge.

He cleared his throat. 'Is there a spare key anywhere? For the front or the back door?'

'I don't know,' I said.

'Let's have a quick look. If we can find a spare key, it'll be a helluva a lot easier to get out of here, and she's not going anywhere, crazy bitch – excuse my French.'

'I'll look upstairs in her bedroom. You two look down here,' I said eagerly. I'd hunted high and low before, so I knew it was unlikely we'd find a spare front or back door key, but we had to try.

He began opening the kitchen doors, directing Emma to look in the dining room for a key. I ran upstairs, making my steps as light as possible and entered Mother's bedroom, pausing outside the spare room, surprised to hear nothing. I wondered briefly what she was up to then refocused on the task at hand: finding a spare key.

I hunted high and low in both wardrobes – the normal one and the crazy, doll-filled one. Nothing. The bedside table drawer yielded nothing. I had a very quick glance under the bed and under her pillows, inside her pillowcases. Nothing.

Sighing heavily, I went back downstairs to find Patrick checking the back of the photograph of Mother and her grandfather. He shook his head when he saw me.

'Looks like I'm going to have to get these boards off the windows. Do you know where she keeps her tools?'

'Cupboard under the stairs, I think.'

He headed out of the room and Emma and I followed him. This was it. We were getting out of here. I began to relax. Patrick was an adult. He was going to help us escape. I smiled at Emma and gave her a hug.

'Patrick's going to help us get out now. We're going home!'

She gave me a small smile and hugged me back. We watched as Patrick charged into the living room with a hammer in his hand.

'Can I do anything to help?' I said, pulling Emma into the room.

He shook his head. Sweat had beaded on his brow. His fingers were trembling and he looked pale.

'Patrick, are you OK?' I said.

'Yep. Just hungry.'

Needing something to do, I dashed into the kitchen and grabbed a piece of ham out of the fridge. I left the kitchen and hurried back into the living room. Using the claws at the end of the hammer, Patrick had managed to prise out two nails. Emma sat on the floor cross-legged watching him, rocking back and forth, sucking her nightgown. I handed him the ham and he gobbled it down with unbelievable speed; I don't think he even chewed it.

There were fifteen more nails to go. I tried to stand still but couldn't. My legs wanted to move. I went to stand behind Emma and stroked her hair in an effort to soothe her.

'Everything's going to be OK, Emma,' I said. 'You'll be able to see your mummy very soon.'

As I said this, excitement stirred in my chest. I was going home. I was going to get away from here. Get to see the outside.

'Patrick, are there wolves in the outside?'

To my relief, he gave me a shocked look and said,

'Wolves haven't roamed England for centuries. No need to fret about that.'

I blew out the breath I'd been holding. 'That's good to know.'

Patrick prised out another nail.

Eleven more nails to go and we'd be free.

I began to smile but my face froze; Patrick, Emma and I turned in the direction of the front door at the sound of it being unlocked. Before any of us could move, Mother slammed the door shut and locked it. She pocketed the key and looked at us with a triumphant smile on her face.

Chapter 24

Blood poured from her knees, soaking through the denim of her jeans. Strands of short blond hair clung like yellow spiders' legs to her sweaty cheeks and her hands were grazed. She smiled but the smile did not meet her eyes, which were wider than normal and distant, like they were not quite in this moment, or even like they were not quite human. Those wide, crazed eyes burned into mine and I took an involuntary step back as Patrick stepped in front of me and Emma, his arms relaxed by his sides, the hammer left on the edge of the window sill. He was only an inch or so taller than Mother, but far broader, far stronger. If it came to it – which I desperately hoped it wouldn't – he would beat her in a fight.

The silence stretched on, infinite and strangely deafening. I thought about speaking, just to break the tension, but I couldn't find the right words. Words seemed to have shrivelled up and rolled deep down into the fuzzy dark part of my mind. Emma's hand slipped into mine and I drew her close, stroking her hair. I wanted to whisper something reassuring to her but again words ran from me, spiralling down, down, down . . .

It was Patrick who finally spoke. 'Let's all calm down and talk, shall we?'

Mother's eyes shifted from mine to his, remaining oddly wide. She tilted her head to the side and smiled sweetly, smoothing down her wild hair. 'What's there to talk about? Mirabelle played a silly little prank because she was trying to show off and everything's got out of hand. Why don't I go and cook us a lovely roast dinner, crackling and all?'

'My name's not Mirabelle,' I said, trying to keep the wobble out of my voice. 'It's Polly. Polly Dalton.'

Mother's whole body jerked as if she'd been shot. Somehow her false smile stayed on her face; she didn't even look at me. She took a small step towards Patrick. 'See, Patrick, she's not well. She's very, very confused. It's not her fault and I try to be patient, but sometimes it really gets to me. She has these strange ideas – did she tell you I'm not her mother? Did she tell you that I kidnapped her? She's very muddled up, bless her, and I know I shouldn't lose my temper and get so angry, but I'm only human and dealing with her on my own has been hard. So hard, really.

'Poor little dot was diagnosed with light allergy disorder when she was three years old. The doctors couldn't explain what caused it or how it came along. I cried for I don't know how many days. I didn't know what to do – Mirabelle's father, bless his soul, died when she was only two so that left just me on my own to cope with it all. Luckily, my grandfather left this cottage to me, along with enough money to keep us going without me having to work, so I've home-schooled Mirabelle ever since. She's such a brave, resilient child, and it shouldn't come as a surprise that not being able to go outside has finally got to her, but, as you can see, it clearly has . . .'

Her eyes shifted to mine, the fire and anger gone in an instant. Now she was all love and warmth and kindness.

'Mirabelle, sweetheart, I'm sorry I lost my temper. Please forgive me, and I should not have focused so much on Clarabelle these past weeks. I know you've been confused and maybe even a little jealous, but everything's going to go back to how it was, OK, Little Doll?'

I didn't say anything. I was too angry to speak. I glared at her, unable to say all that I wanted to, unable to correct her lies.

Patrick put his hand in his pocket and pulled out the newspaper article. With slow hands, he unfolded and smoothed out the paper.

'How do you explain this?' he said, thrusting the paper towards her.

She frowned as if confused and stepped forward to get a closer look at my evidence. A moment passed and another and another. Her head was bowed over the article so I couldn't see her face. I wondered what she was thinking; she must know her lies were blown; she must know Patrick would never believe her now. I tried to predict what she would do now that she knew it was impossible to get Patrick on her side, but she was hard to predict. I had never been able to put myself in her shoes and think forward to her next move. Never. Again I found myself stuck in uncertainty.

Patrick glanced round at me and gave me a reassuring smile. I nodded back and pulled Emma even closer. We were getting out of here soon. I just had to be patient.

Mother looked up, eyes wide with surprise. 'Why that was my friend's little girl who went missing all those years ago. She was the pure image of Mirabelle, so I can see why, in her distress and confusion, poor Mirabelle thinks that's her.' She looked back at me, her eyes welling up with tears, her face crumpling with misery. 'Is that why you've been staying away from me the last few days? You poor little thing – you thought that I . . .' she trailed off, her wet eyes searching Patrick's.

'What about Emma?' Patrick said, although he sounded less certain of himself now.

'Emma?' she said, clearly confused.

At last, I found my words. Rage and fear burst out of me in one hot flow, 'You kidnapped me! You kidnapped Emma! You're lying now! You're insane. Anyone can take one look at that photograph and know it's me!'

Patrick withdrew his outstretched arm. I could tell he was examining the article. Horror crept up my spine – was he doubting it?

Mother lowered her voice, making it sound soft and soothing: 'Mirabelle, sweetie, calm down. This isn't doing your health any good. Come with me and I'll tuck you up in bed.'

I stepped forward and grabbed Patrick's arm. 'Surely you don't believe her? Patrick? Please—'

'Ask Clarabelle,' Mother said quietly.

Patrick looked down at me and shifted his weight. His fingers tugged his earlobe – a habit that I suddenly found the most irritating thing on earth. He shook his head, 'I'm sorry, but . . .'

'No!' I shouted. 'No! She's lying! She's crazy! I can show you – in her bedroom there's—'

'I'm happy to show you my bedroom, if you like, Patrick. I simply want to put all of this to rest,' she said, backing out of the room. 'Follow me.'

Patrick turned away from me and followed her out of the room. I let go of Emma and dashed past him, unable to believe Patrick's stupidity, yet following Mother closely, desperate to stop her from somehow hiding the evidence. It occurred to me that she may have a key for the doll wardrobe. She might run into the room and lock the wardrobe before anyone saw, then claim she'd lost the key or . . . Mother stopped outside her bedroom door and waved me and Patrick inside.

'Feel free to look around. I don't know what Mirabelle's talking about, but please feel free to look – just don't touch!' she added with a light chuckle.

I rushed past her into the room. Patrick followed me. I flung open the wardrobe doors and stood back, 'See!'

'What the he—' Patrick's words stopped abruptly. Out of the corner of my eye I saw him fall, heard him gasp. Blood sprayed all over the bed, the walls, the carpet, me. Patrick fell onto his front on the carpet with a thud. He moaned, one hand on his bleeding side, and swivelled to face Mother, his eyes wide with terror, his other hand held up in self-defence.

'Please, don't,' he gasped. His eyes pleaded with her as she stood over him, a kitchen knife wet with his blood, her head tilted, eyes narrow.

She had *stabbed* him. I looked from the knife to her face, from her face to Patrick lying on the floor. It had all happened so fast. I blinked, trying to make it un-so, but it was real. Mother had a knife and she had used it on Patrick. I couldn't move. My mouth was dry, my stomach like lead.

Mother stared down at Patrick, her eyes bright. 'This would never have happened if you had read the sign – *Private Land* – it says it loud and clear. No one else has ever come here. It's your own bloody fault for being such an ignorant fool,' she spat. 'If you'd left well alone, this would never have happened.'

Patrick's face crumpled. Tears leaked from the corners of his eyes. He squeezed his eyes shut and groaned.

'He's going to die. We have to help him,' I said in a small, weak voice, eyeing the knife in her hand, too aware that it had sliced through Patrick's skin like butter only moments ago.

'And *you*,' she said, turning to face me, jabbing the knife in my direction, '*you* disobeyed me, Mirabelle, didn't you? *You* went into the attic when I was out, didn't you? DIDN'T YOU! You're just like her. You're just like Olivia!'

I stared at her, unable to believe I had been blind to her madness for so long.

'Answer me,' she said.

I took a deep breath, 'Yes. I went into the attic.'

'Why?' She almost sounded hurt.

'I wanted to know more about your sister, but I found the newspaper article. I didn't want to believe it at first, but . . .' I trailed off as she switched her focus to Patrick, apparently bored of me.

'You're spoiling my lovely carpet,' she said, narrowing her eyes. 'Mirabelle, grab his legs. Help me carry him downstairs. Now.'

'But—'

'*Now*, or . . .' she flicked her head at the knife in her hand, and I believed her. I believed she would hurt me too, or worse, if I refused to do what she said. She didn't need me now that she had Emma. Emma was little and sweet and perfect. I wasn't like that. Not any more.

Heart pounding, I moved to crouch behind Patrick, whose face had gone sickly white. I gently lifted his hand away from his wound and picked up his other wrist, surprised to find his skin cold.

'Three, two, one!' Mother said, and we heaved and picked him up.

He groaned as blood oozed from the slice in his side. His face contorted with pain and he bit his lip as we half-dragged, half-carried him out of the room, across the landing and down the stairs, stopping every two steps to get our breath.

'You're heavier than you look,' she said with a strange smile.

Emma appeared in the hallway chewing her nightgown. Mother snapped at her to go up to my bedroom and stay there.

'It's OK, Emma,' I murmured, my eyes following her as she slipped past me and ran up the stairs.

'What are you going to do?' I said.

We had carried Patrick into the kitchen leaving a trail of thick, gooey blood in our wake. Patrick looked like death. He was losing too much blood. A sweet, metallic scent drifted around the kitchen.

Mother placed the knife on the counter and told me to sit down. I did as she said, though I perched on the edge of the chair, ready to move if a chance came. She leaned against the counter watching Patrick, her head tilted to the side, eyes glazed, her expression almost bored. A zigzag of dried blood smeared her right cheek and her nostrils flared as she struggled to regain her breath. Her tongue flicked out of her mouth to wet her thin, dry lips.

Chapter 25

'What are you going to do now?' I repeated.

'This mess is *sickening*,' she said, ignoring my question, her voice raw. 'Clean it up.'

She grabbed the dishcloth and threw it at me. It hit me in the face. I hesitated. She glared, snapping at me to fetch the bucket from under the stairs.

I hurried away and slipped on Patrick's blood. I fell onto one knee and she tutted. Ignoring her, I left the kitchen and opened the cupboard under the stairs. My eyes found the bucket immediately. I grabbed it, pausing at the sight of Mother's toolbox. There were no pockets in my dress, nowhere I could conceal anything.

'Hurry up!'

I snatched up a small screwdriver and put it in the bucket. If she saw it, I was done for, so I rushed into the kitchen, passing her as quickly as possible. With shaky hands I lifted the bucket into the sink and ran the hot tap.

'Add bleach,' she said.

Obediently, I bent down and opened the cupboard under the sink, picked up the bleach and added a tiny amount to the hot water.

'More than that,' she snapped.

I added two drops and looked at her. She nodded sharply telling me to add more. I kept on adding more until she held up her hand to indicate that I should stop. Within seconds the harsh odour of bleach permeated the small room, overwhelming the metallic zing of blood and making my nostrils burn. I gazed into the now steaming water, realizing that if I was to plunge my hand into the liquid to retrieve the screwdriver, I would burn my skin. I sneaked a look at Patrick as I turned off the tap. His body was utterly limp, his face ashen. Was he dead? It was impossible to tell in one quick glance. Mother was gazing down at Patrick's body, leaning her weight against the counter, her fingers inches from the knife.

Hoping she would not notice, I turned on the cold tap and watched the water gush in, cooling off the steam.

'Not too cold,' she said, whipping her head round to glare at me.

I turned off the cold tap and, with difficulty, lifted the bucket out of the sink onto the bloodied tiles.

'Can I have some gloves please, Mother?' I said.

She seemed not to hear me, so I stood up, opened the cupboard and rifled inside.

'No. No gloves. Hurry up.'

Gritting my teeth, I got back down on my hands and knees and dipped the dishcloth into the top of the water in an attempt to keep my fingers dry. I could feel her watching me as I crawled towards a small droplet of blood to her right, nearer the back door. The blood was still wet and I was able to wipe it up in one swipe. I crawled back to the bucket and rinsed the cloth, again conscious of keeping my fingers out of the water. With only two thirds of the cloth wet, I moved to the second furthest droplet of blood and began to clean it, my hands trembling, my fingers beginning to tingle as bleach made contact with my skin despite my efforts.

There were no more small droplets. My mouth went watery. I dipped the dishcloth into the bucket for a third time, keeping the part I was holding as dry as possible. I turned with the dishcloth raised and stared at the huge black-red puddle of blood beside Patrick, fighting a sudden surge of pointlessness. I watched his chest to see if he was breathing. If he was dead, what was the point in trying to fight her now? I should wait for a better opportunity . . . a moment when I wasn't crawling around on my hands and knees with her standing over me and a knife close to her hand.

'Do it,' she snapped.

I inched towards the puddle, my eyes fixed on Patrick, on his face and chest, looking for the slightest hint of movement. *Breathe. Breathe. Please breathe.*

There! There it was! His chest – rising and falling – minutely – just enough!

In that instant, I plunged the whole cloth into the thick puddle of blood.

'Good girl. That's it,' she said, almost breathless.

I fought the urge to throw up and focused on letting the cloth absorb as much of the blood as possible. It took only seconds for the cloth to become heavy with blood.

'I can't! I can't!' I cried, glancing over my shoulder at her, begging with my eyes.

Mother's eyes revealed only excitement. 'Do it,' she said.

'No. I'm going to be sick.'

She stepped towards me, finger jabbing, 'You *will* do it or I will make Clarabelle do it. Is that what you want?'

I shook my head and whispered something.

'What did you say?' she snapped, coming closer.

'Nothing,' I murmured.

'Tell me!' she demanded.

'No!' I screamed, staring at the cloth in my hand.

She froze, shocked by my defiance, and I spun around and

thrust the blood-soaked cloth into her face. She screamed and clawed at the sodden cloth. At the same time, I plunged my hand into the bucket, barely feeling the burn, my fingers scrabbling for the screwdriver, but she was there, grabbing my hair, yanking me back, throwing me down on top of Patrick. I rolled off him onto my side and turned to face her. She reached down with both hands to grab my legs and I kicked and pushed myself up and stabbed the screwdriver into her thigh. She screeched and stumbled, falling into the counter, her hand scrabbling for the knife, eyes aflame, but she knocked the knife, sending it spinning onto the floor under the fridge.

She fought to stand but fell, grabbing her thigh, screaming and cursing.

I darted to the counter, opened a drawer and pulled out a knife. 'Keys,' I said, pointing the knife down at her, careful to keep my distance.

Tears poured from her eyes. 'I'm so sorry, Little Doll. Please, please don't do this! If you go outside, you'll die – I love you – I never wanted any of this to happen.'

'Keys,' I said.

She continued to sob and wail, clutching her injured thigh.

'*Keys*.'

She looked up at me and I could see her noting my determination, seeing how strong I was for the first time. With a shaking hand, she pulled the keys out of her pocket and tossed them weakly onto the floor.

'You'll die,' she said, closing her eyes and sobbing into her chest, 'Clarabelle too. You'll both die.'

'Don't move,' I said, backing up to stand behind Patrick. Placing the knife on the floor beside me, never taking my eyes off her, I grabbed Patrick's upper arms and used every ounce of my strength to drag him out of the room into the hallway.

'Stay where you are!' I shouted, darting back into the room and picking up the knife, relieved to see she was still lying in a heap on the floor sobbing into her chest.

I backed out of the room slowly, the knife pointed in her direction. 'Goodbye, *Mother*.'

I shut the door and placed the knife on the floor by my feet then opened the cupboard under the stairs, listening for any sound of movement from the kitchen, hearing none – not even sobbing, which unnerved me. I quickly found what I needed: an old washing line that I remembered seeing there earlier. I picked it up, tied it securely around the kitchen doorknob then trailed it to the banister at the bottom of the stairs where I stretched the line tight and tied the other end around the top of the banister. It was now impossible for her to open the kitchen door. The only other exit was through the back door, which was locked, or the kitchen window, which was securely boarded up. Mother was trapped. She wasn't going anywhere and I had the keys.

Relief sang through my veins like water through a parched vine, but I didn't slow down. I ran upstairs into my bedroom where Emma lay curled up, her eyes wide and terrified, her nightgown in her mouth.

'Get up,' I said, 'we're leaving now.'

Emma got out of bed, sensing my no-nonsense tone, and watched me grab my pillow and bedcovers, which I dragged down the stairs. I placed the pillow under Patrick's head and covered him with my blankets. He was unconscious but still breathing. There was no way on earth Emma and I could carry him anywhere fast enough, so we would have to leave him there while we went to get help.

'Is the man OK?' Emma whispered.

I nodded and dashed to the front door, hesitating. We had no supplies – I hadn't been able to find the holdall I needed to stash my collection of tins in. How far was it to the nearest house? I didn't know.

I grabbed Emma's hand and pulled her after me back upstairs.

'Go to the toilet then drink as much water as you can,' I said. She followed my instructions and I went into her room to find her slippers or, if possible, any outdoor shoes Mother may have bought her.

In the spare room, I saw how Mother had escaped. She had hacked through the sewn-up middle of the curtains – with what I couldn't be sure, but possibly the kitchen knife – then smashed the glass – so *she hadn't nailed boards over Clarabelle's window* – and jumped out. The drop was big; she had been extremely lucky not to break any bones.

In the wardrobe, I found a pair of black plimsolls which I slid onto Emma's feet. I pulled a blue doll dress on over her nightgown, hoping the two garments together would be enough to keep her warm.

Emma stayed as quiet as a mouse, watching me with her huge, bleary eyes while I emptied my bladder then drank as much water from the tap as I could. We had to stay hydrated. If necessary, we could go without food for a while, but water was essential. I looked down at my slippers – they would have to do. At least they had hard soles. Mother's feet were bigger than mine, so wearing her shoes would only slow us down, and we had to move as fast as possible for Patrick's sake.

We ran downstairs and I tried a couple of keys before finding the right one. With a deep, shaky breath, I slotted the key into the keyhole and unlocked the front door.

Chapter 26

Outside. I was outside, in the other world. I was outside for the first time in ten years. I thought my cheeks would break I was smiling so hard. Greens and browns and blues and light – so much light. Natural light that was warm yet fresh, so fresh it made the fine hairs on my body tingle. I shivered with pleasure, wincing against the sun, though it remained hidden behind a white frosting of cloud.

I wanted this moment to last, wanted to feel, taste, smell, hear every atom of it. I inhaled the air, filling my lungs with the stuff, savouring, relishing, loving everything. Even the red car was a wonderful sight to behold with its gleaming scarlet brightness, its bonnet shimmering with light. Most of the ground was hard earth; natural, not man-made, but a lot of white and golden bits of stone sat beneath the car. And the trees that loomed larger than the cottage – which I did not want to turn and see – the trees were magnificent. So tall and green and full of colour and life. I could hear birds chattering to each other, see ants on the ground, clouds in the sky. My head ached with the brightness, but I was not in any real pain. My skin was not melting off or beginning to burn or peel or do any of the many other horrible things

I had imagined. My eyes were not bursting, my body was not on fire, my lungs had not exploded in my chest. I was alive and breathing and healthy. I grinned down at Emma and she gave me a small smile.

'Can I go home now?' she said.

'We have a little way to go, but yes, we're going home.'

Hand in hand we strode past the car, taking the dirt road, following the tyre tracks that Mother's car had so recently created. We walked quickly along the dusty road, me shielding my eyes with my free hand and scanning the distance, unsurprised to see nothing more than dirt road, trees on either side of us and far, far in the distance, a bright green field. I had seen some of this from Mother's bedroom window.

After about five minutes, a sheen had worked its way onto my skin, Emma's too.

'I'm tired. How long 'til we get there?'

I shrugged. 'I don't know, but we can't stop. Patrick's not very well. We need to find someone who can help him as quickly as possible.'

'What's wrong with him?'

I hesitated, unsure how much to tell her, whether to lie or tell the truth. I'd had enough of lies to last a lifetime – but Emma was only five years old. She had been through so much already. Too much.

Unbidden, the sight of Patrick grasping his side, appealing to Mother, blood soaking through his T-shirt into the carpet, flashed into my mind's eye. I shivered despite the warmth, unable to believe all that had happened. Unable to believe I had managed to escape.

I dropped my arm to my side and looked at the bunch of keys in my palm. I was holding them so tightly that they were cutting into my hand. I loosened my grip and glanced at Emma's damp hair.

'Patrick got hurt,' I said.

'How?'

'Mother hit him and he fell over.'

Emma looked up at me. 'Oh. Is she a bad lady?'

'Yes, but she can't hurt us any more. We're free. Everything will be OK now. Shall we go a little faster? Remember, Patrick needs us to find someone to help him.'

Emma nodded.

We picked up our pace, breaking into a half-run. The clouds drifted off the sun, which beat down on us, making sweat drip down our faces and backs, but we kept up the pace, Emma's sweaty hand in my sweaty hand, which burned and throbbed from the bleach and my unhealed wound.

The dirt road seemed to go on for ever, as did the woods on either side. I considered branching off the road into the woods to look for a footpath of some kind that might lead us to a house or farm, but the woods looked dense and the fear of getting lost or coming across an evil, witchy woman like Hansel and Gretel did in the fairy tale prevented me from following that idea. Instead, I urged Emma to keep up our half-run and tried to ignore the pains in my thigh muscles. My body was not used to this sort of exercise. Emma seemed to be bearing up better than me.

'Polly, can we sing a song?' she said, smiling up at me.

I was panting now and my instinct was to say no but the keenness in her eyes stopped me.

'Which one?' I said, knowing that I did not know many songs.

'Twinkle Twinkle Little Star,' she said and she began to sing.

Mother had sung this song to me before bed when I was little. The thought was disturbing. Memories of Mother reading me bedtime stories drifted into my head and I crushed them, fighting the strange, sick feeling that accompanied the memories. Sometimes she had been so loving, such a good mother. It had been easy to believe her lies when I was younger, when I was her perfect little doll.

I joined in with Emma's song and we ran hand in hand along the dirt road, Mother's keys jangling in my free hand, my head aching from the light and my toes blistering from my loose slippers. I dropped the keys. I wouldn't need them any more.

After a while, we slowed to a walk to catch our breath and Emma sang a song that I had never heard of before which she said was from *Chitty Chitty Bang Bang* – a book of children's songs or nursery rhymes, I assumed. She let go of my hand and skipped away singing, her tiredness suddenly gone as if the song had given her a burst of energy and happiness. She clearly didn't know all of the words, so she kept singing the same couple of lines over and over again. I found myself smiling as she skipped ahead, wondering if I would ever feel that kind of happiness again. Would I find my real parents? Were they even still alive? If they weren't, what would happen to me?

'Emma – can you hear that?' I said, stopping and straining my ears. Emma carried on singing.

'Emma! Stop!' I said sharply.

She turned around, wide-eyed, chest heaving.

I could hear something in the distance. Something coming from behind us.

'Can you hear that?' I said.

Emma nodded. 'Yes. It's a car.'

'A car?' I turned around and looked back the way we had come, heart slamming against my ribs.

Speeding towards us was a red car. Mother's car.

Chapter 27

My first thought was *how did she get out?* My second thought was *run*. I grabbed Emma's wrist and dragged her to the left, towards the woods, thinking quickly: the car would not be able to go into the densely packed trees, which meant Mother would have to leave the car and follow on foot.

I glanced over my shoulder to see the car stop, skidding slightly, pale brown dust puffing into the air. Emma and I ran down a steep, grassy bank into the trees. The slam of the car door told me Mother was not going to give up. In my mind, I pictured her sprinting after us, her face twisted with rage, blood covering her clothes, a knife glinting in her hand. I could not be certain she held a weapon, but my gut told me she would not have come unprepared. If she caught up with us, a knife would be the perfect way of persuading us to come along quietly.

At my side, Emma slipped and stumbled over a thick root. She gasped and cried, slowing down, forcing me to pause to pick her up. Her face was pale and sweaty, her eyes wide with terror.

'Hold on to me with your arms and legs,' I panted. I was already short of breath and though Emma weighed very little,

I was not strong. She clung to me so tightly though that she felt like a second skin. Her small body trembled and vibrated with tension against mine and I could feel her heartbeat thrumming against my chest. I wanted to reassure her that everything was going to be OK, but as I opened my mouth to speak a scream tore through the air behind us.

'MIRABELLE! STOP!'

Emma jumped in my arms and clung on even tighter, making herself lighter but compressing my lungs. Panting for breath, I darted between the towering trees and leapt over a fallen tree trunk and ran on, using my right arm for balance, wrapping the other around Emma. Obstacles appeared out of nowhere. The woods were as horribly unpredictable as Mother. A huge, random hole appeared in the ground a little way ahead. It was very deep and very wide. Like a large grave. If I hadn't been looking at the ground, I would have fallen straight into it and I would probably have broken my legs. Or my back. Or Emma's back. The thought made me even more breathless but I ran on.

Thorn bushes and spiky leaves scratched and tore at my bare arms and legs and dress. My slippers were long gone, lost when we rushed down the bank. I knew my feet were cut and bleeding. I dreaded to think of the grime being crushed and pressed into my bloodied feet, but my adrenaline surge seemed to have made any kind of pain vanish. That was one piece of luck at least.

Clouds covered the sun, submerging the woods in shadows and giving my eyes the chance to stop watering. Everything turned a few shades darker and a few degrees cooler. My breaths came in ragged gasps. I knew I could not keep up this pace for much longer. Emma's arms and legs loosened and she grew heavier, her body dipping towards the ground, her hands pulling on my neck, her body bouncing up and down with every stride I took.

'Hold on – tighter,' I gasped.

She responded but not as well as before. She was weakening and so was I. But I could not stop. I could not let her catch up with us. I thought about Patrick and pushed harder. My legs were heavy. I wrapped both arms around Emma and held her against me. My arms protested from the weight as she sank into them. I was going to have to put her down soon and hope that she could run fast enough.

A low branch came out of nowhere and I ducked just in time, then tripped and fell, throwing out my hands to stop myself from hitting the ground face first. Emma cried out but clung on as we fell. Her back hit the ground though not hard. My arms jarred with the force of the fall. I gritted my teeth and told Emma she'd have to run now. She let go of me and pushed herself to her feet, slotting her hand into mine. We ran. In the distance I could see light penetrating the trees. The woods were coming to an end. Beyond the trees lay a field. A field would be easier to run through – for us and for Mother. But maybe someone would be in the field. A farmer perhaps.

My lungs burned. Emma was too slow. I considered carrying her again but that would mean stopping to pick her up. Was Mother still following us? Since that last, terrifying scream, she hadn't made a sound.

Unable to resist, I glanced back. Mother was nowhere to be seen. I frowned and faced forward. Had she given up? Had she fallen over? Twisted her ankle?

The thought was like the feeling of hot water on aching muscles but I fought the urge to slow down and carried on running, pulling Emma along behind me. And there was the light – more light – shining through the gaps between the trees. And green – so much green. I could see the field. Not long now until we broke out of the woods into open air.

But at the edge of the woods we reached a fence topped with silver thorns of wire which ran as high as my waist. I stopped, picked up Emma and heaved her over the fence, lifting her as high as I could to avoid the thorns.

'Keep running,' I said. She didn't move. I shouted at her to go and she jumped. Tears sprang to her eyes and her chin wobbled.

'I don't want to leave you,' she said.

I nodded, not wanting to waste time arguing, and carefully placed my hand on a small section of wire between the knots, noticing further up the fence a clump of white wool snagged on a thorn. My heart leapt; wool meant sheep or goats; sheep or goats meant farmers or shepherds or goatherds, like kind young Peter, the goatherd in *Heidi*; farmers, shepherds or goatherds meant help.

I swung my leg over the fence, pushing down on the wire with my hand. The fence wobbled and I fell, tearing my other leg on a thorn as it followed my body onto the grass. A sharp pain speared my calf. I looked down, wincing. The vicious metal had ripped a three-inch cut down my leg. Blood dribbled out and down my leg like water out of a tap.

'Are you OK?' Emma said.

I nodded and grabbed her hand. The pain was bad, but not bad enough to stop me. I glanced behind me, saw nothing but trees. Emma looked around too.

'She's gone,' Emma said quietly.

I could hear the hope in her voice, almost like she couldn't believe our luck. For me too, the idea that Mother had gone was too good to be true, and I knew that we had to keep on running until we found someone. If we stopped for too long and she was still around, she might catch up and grab us. I couldn't – *wouldn't* – go back to that place. And Patrick needed help.

'We need to keep running,' I said to Emma, 'OK?'

She nodded bravely and we ran through the ankle-high grass towards the burning sun.

Chapter 28

We ran through the green field into another field and another. The third field was brown and all churned up into one gigantic stretch of dry, hard, rippling soil. Did this mean a tractor had been used on it? Did this mean we were close to making human contact?

My heart leapt and I thought I might die with hope – and fear. What if the person we met was insane too? How many people in the world were like Mother? If she was crazy, there had to be others. I felt my hope sink as a realization set in: we had no choice. We would have to place our trust in the first person – or people – we saw. I knew this and it frightened me badly. But Patrick had been good. Slow to come round, but kind. He had tried to help us, even though he had struggled to believe my story. Would others think I was making it up too? Would they take us back there? Back to that secret house in the middle of nowhere? I shuddered. Just thinking about it made me want to scream.

Emma stumbled on the uneven earth and I held up her wrist, preventing her from falling.

'Thank you, Polly,' she said, looking up at me through misty eyes.

'We're going to be fine. I promise,' I said, trying to make my voice calm.

I had to stop thinking the worst.

It seemed like Mother had given up. We had escaped the cottage. We were outside. Free. I wasn't dying any more – not that I ever had been. I was alive and well and going to find my parents and live happily ever after, like they did in fairy tales. Emma was going to go back to her parents and forget all about this. One day she would look back on it all and it would feel like one really bad nightmare. She was so young that she would forget all about this horrible experience. She wasn't physically hurt. Mother had never harmed her, except for that bruise on her arm the day she took her from the supermarket.

My heart calmed a little. I pushed damp strands of hair out of my eyes, pasting them to the sweaty hair on top of my head, and shielded my gaze from the sun. Up ahead, at the end of the next field stood a few buildings. I blinked several times, desperate to believe what I was seeing, to clear the stinging tears from my eyes. Was it a dream or was it real?

Emma jumped up and down pointing, 'Look, Polly! Look!'

'I know,' I said, beaming down at her. It was real. A real, bricks and mortar farm. Just like the ones I'd read about.

Emma grinned at me and squealed. We ran over the mud ripples using the last dregs of our energy, the sun doing its best to slow us down and losing as we flew across the dirt, carried by hope and excitement, driven by need. Anticipation blasted away some of my concerns and I felt my face relax – we were going to find someone who could help us, help Patrick. Someone grown up and sensible and responsible and full of knowledge about what to do in a situation like this. They would call the police and the police would go to the cottage and they would find Patrick and he would still be alive and they would rush him to a hospital and the doctors at the hospital would save him, and then, when I had been reunited with my parents and Emma with hers, Emma and I would go and visit Patrick in the hospital and take him a present to thank him for helping us get away. And Mother would be locked up in a prison and I'd never have to see her ever again . . .

We slowed to a walk when we got within yards of the farm. There were three buildings in total. The first building was a small house with a low, tile-topped roof and pebbly walls that were an unhealthy off-white colour. We approached from the back of the house and entered an open patch of barren land upon which stood two other buildings and a big metal cage. There were two large, black dogs in the cage which immediately stood up and pressed their faces against the metal wire, baring their teeth and snarling. A third dog lay on the ground chomping on a huge bone. The dog was attached to the biggest outbuilding by a long, thick, metal chain. It was sturdy and muscular with a sloping face and white fur. It paid us no attention other than a couple of glances, too interested in its bone to bother with us. I couldn't take my eyes off the dogs. They were fascinating. So real. So alive, so . . .

Emma hugged my side and shook her head. 'I don't like it here.'

I dragged my gaze from the dogs and stared where she was staring. The building opposite had a strange, zigzag roof and it was locked, a heavy-looking chain and padlock keeping the doors tightly shut, but the door of the building that the dog was chained to stood open a few inches. In and out of the opening buzzed hundreds and hundreds of flies.

'What's in *there*?' Emma whispered.

'I don't know,' I murmured, turning to the small house.

The door was painted dark green and the paint was peeling.

A brass door knocker in the shape of a horse's head stared at me. Next to the door on the wall of the house, scrawled in black pen, were the words *Knackers Yard*. I hesitated, then raised my hand and banged the horse head three times. We waited, Emma's hand trembling ever so slightly in mine. Clouds blocked the sun, pooling us in shadow. I knocked again. Louder, more urgently, straining my ears for the sound of footsteps behind the door.

'Let's go,' Emma whined.

'No,' I said, knocking a third time.

'Hello!' I called.

I tried the door, barely touching the doorknob, and the door swung inward with a long, high-pitched creak. I took a tentative step forward and peered into the gloomy interior of the house.

'Hello?' I tried again.

'Maybe we can find a telephone,' Emma said, her voice smaller than ever.

I looked at her. Mother didn't own a telephone but I knew from my books that lots of people did. 'Yes – where will it be?'

'What?'

'The telephone?'

'We keep ours in the lounge at home.'

'OK, great. So if we can find a phone, we can talk to someone who might help us. We can call the police.'

Emma nodded. 'Yes. The numbers are nine, nine, nine. Mummy and Daddy teached me them.'

'That's brilliant,' I said smiling at her. 'Come on.'

I pulled her into the house, leaving the door open behind us. We were in a small kitchen. The counters were a mess; covered with dirty plates and dirty saucepans and mugs, filling the room with an unpleasant smell a bit like sour milk. I flicked a light switch but it didn't come on.

'The telephone won't be in here,' Emma said.

We left the kitchen and crossed a hallway. I opened one of two doors that led off from the hallway and we entered a room with a bed in it. The bed was unmade and a few pairs of men's underwear dotted the floor. The room smelled like bad breath and sweaty armpits. There was no window in the room. I grimaced, backed out and shut the door. We tried the next and final door in the house and I smiled, pleased to see a living room of sorts. A black box with a window in it sat on top of a table at the back of the room. A television maybe. Like telephones, I had read about televisions but never seen one. Facing the black box was a brown sofa. Drink cans littered the floor around the sofa and magazines lay on a table in the centre of the room. On the table beneath the window sat a black, square object with numbered buttons on. It had to be the telephone.

Emma let go of my hand and ran over to the odd contraption. She picked part of it up and waved it at me.

'Telephone!' she said.

I walked over and took hold of the black thing she was holding.

'Hold it to your ear and I'll do the numbers,' Emma said excitedly.

I did as she asked, feeling strange, uncomfortable, not sure I was doing it right. Emma nodded at me as I placed one of the round end parts to my ear and the other round part to my mouth. She stabbed the number nine on the machine three times and I heard something beep. Then I heard a ringing sound. Then a voice, but the voice wasn't coming from the telephone; it was coming from behind me.

Chapter 29

'Who the hell are you?'

I jumped and dropped the telephone. It fell to the carpet with a thud, a black, curling wire snaking up from the ground to the machine on the table. Vaguely I registered a crackly voice coming from the ground, but the voice in the room seemed to echo inside my skull.

I spun around, inhaling sharply.

A man with a large, round stomach stood just inside the living room doorway. He was dirty-looking, his white vest stained and too tight across his belly. He wore badly fitting jeans and no shoes, only dirty socks with holes in the toes. Long hairs poked out of the top of his vest. Even in the gloomy room I could make out dark circles under his eyes and red blotches on his bulbous nose. His hair was long and stringy and he had a thick, bushy beard. Down by his side he clutched a bulging carrier bag.

'We – er – we—' I tried to speak, but the man held up one large hand.

'Give it me!' he barked, lurching into the room.

'Give you *what*?' I said.

'Whatever you've stole,' he said.

'We haven't stolen anything,' I said, pushing Emma behind me. 'Please, we just want—'

'Come here!' he shouted.

I froze and clamped my mouth shut. He swayed visibly. He let the bag drop to the floor then cursed and bent over, scrabbling to pick up cans as they rolled across the carpet.

'Please, sir.' I said. 'Please may we use your phone? That's all. We weren't stealing. I promise.'

He didn't seem to hear me. Still swearing, he lurched upright clutching a can and tottered out of the room. I looked down at the telephone piece that lay on the carpet, its twisty chain spiralling upward like some kind of bizarre umbilical cord. I could hear a faint dead-sounding tone coming from it and wondered what that meant. Before I could do or say anything, Emma crouched down and grabbed the telephone bit then replaced it on its machine on the table.

'We can try again,' she whispered, tugging me round.

'No,' I said. 'We need to get out of here.'

I pulled her out of the room into the hallway. We crept up the short, narrow corridor towards the kitchen. The man was behaving in a weird way so there was no telling what he might do. I knew a little about alcohol and it was enough to make me wary. Mother had told me everything I knew about it, but I felt quite sure, having now seen this man and the way he was acting, that what she had told me about alcohol was the truth. Not everything she had told me was a lie. Most of it, but not all. A strange pain squeezed my heart. I frowned, told myself to concentrate. We had to get out of this place, find someone who was capable of helping us. This man was not trustworthy. Not in the slightest bit.

He had his back to us when we reached the kitchen. I could see the crack in his bottom. It was gross. He stood in front of the oven humming to himself. A tune I had never heard. It didn't sound anything like the Eagles.

I tried to think straight. We had to get away. If we were quiet and quick, we could creep past without him seeing us and get out.

I hesitated a second, another second, and another, then yanked Emma into the room and towards the door that led outside. Emma tripped, making a scuffling sound. He whirled around, a wooden spoon raised in his meaty fist, a cry bursting from his lips. He reached out and grabbed my shoulder as I pushed Emma forward.

'Go!' I yelled – but she didn't. She stopped and turned around, tears welling in her eyes.

'Come here!' the man bellowed, grabbing Emma's arm. He pulled her towards himself and pushed us out of the kitchen back into the hallway.

'You're not going anywhere yet,' he said with a gurgling cough.

He pushed our backs, forcing us into the living room, shouting at us to sit on the sofa. We did as he commanded. He whirled around and headed back towards the kitchen. I pulled Emma onto my lap and hugged her close, whispering reassuring things in her ear, trying to keep the tremors out of my voice. The fear and worry.

What was he going to do to us? Why wouldn't he let us go? Mother's talk of evil men crawled into my mind, and for a split second I found myself wishing the most unimaginable thing: that I'd never discovered that she wasn't my real mother. If I hadn't learned the truth, we wouldn't be here right now; we would be back in the cottage, our food, beds and clothes provided for us . . .

But not-knowing *wasn't* right and she was dangerous. I knew that. I did. Even so, right now, I would rather be in Mother's company than this man's. If he wanted to, he could do worse to us than Mother. Much worse . . .

My body began to shake. I couldn't help it. Couldn't stop

the tremors from taking over my limbs. Emma was trembling too. I pulled her closer and she buried her head in my shoulder and began to cry.

Think. Think.

A greasy meat smell wafted into the room.

I looked at the window above the small table. The window was small, but I wasn't exactly huge. Emma would definitely fit through. I glanced at the door to the living room. He wasn't back yet, but we didn't have much time until he joined us.

'Get up!' I whispered sharply, pushing Emma.

I ran to the window and unlatched it. It opened about a hand's width. Emma would fit through, but would I?

I hoisted her up and helped her slide herself through the narrow space between the window frame and the window itself. She fell to the ground on her hands and knees and looked back at me, panic making her eyes wider than ever.

'Polly?'

'Go,' I said.

She stared dumbly at me, still on her hands and knees. I pulled myself onto the sill and tried to slide through, but my chest was too wide. I couldn't go with her.

'Go!' I screamed.

She shook her head and grabbed at my hands.

I pushed her away, looking into her eyes, 'Run, Emma. Get help. Find someone. Tell them where I am. And about Patrick. Go!'

Tears spilled down her cheeks. She hiccupped. Her face scrunched up into an unrecognizable version of itself, then she turned and fled.

Chapter 30

I immediately regretted what I'd done. If Emma couldn't find anyone she would die of dehydration or starvation. She wouldn't know how to find water or food in the wilderness and it was hot out there. Too hot. What if the heat became too much and she fainted and a wild dog came along and . . . I bit my lip so hard it hurt, unable to complete the thought, fighting the horrific scene that pushed its way into my mind. Other images collided with each other: Mother finding Emma, dragging her back to the cottage, punishing her for running away, or, worse still, someone as awful as the man in this house finding her, taking her back to his house, torturing her, murdering her . . .

For a second I thought I was going to be sick. I bent over and focused on breathing. Working myself into a state was pointless. I had to think.

'Hey! Where's the other one gone?'

I spun around. In one hand the man held a plate piled high with slabs of fatty meat and steaming potatoes. In the other hand he held a can. He took a long swig from the can then entered the room, elbowing the door closed behind him and nearly losing his balance.

'Hey! I asked you a question!' he barked. He made his way to the sofa, kicking empty cans out of his path.

'She's gone. Out there,' I said softly.

He eased himself down, groaning as he did so and took another swig of drink then placed the can between his right knee and the arm of the sofa and began to shovel meat and potatoes into his mouth, barely chewing before swallowing down the food noisily. He followed every couple of mouthfuls with a swig from his can.

'Gone has she?' he chuckled, then burped.

'Please, sir,' I tried, 'please can I use your telephone?'

'Who're you so desperate to call?' he said, not looking up from his plate.

I paused. Should I lie or tell the truth?

I swallowed, wiped sweat off my forehead with the back of my trembling hand. 'My parents. Emma and I got lost in the woods . . .'

He nodded and looked at me. His eyes looked strange, like jiggling marbles. A memory of Mother and I playing with marbles entered my head followed by one of us playing with conkers tied to string. Sometimes she had been fine. My heart hurt and then I thought about how she had treated me the last few weeks – how she had lied to me for so long – made me believe I was dying. Anger tore through me and I stared straight at the man.

'Let me use the telephone or let me leave,' I said as confidently as I could, crossing my arms and lifting my chin, trying to stand tall.

He shovelled the last mouthful of his meal into his mouth and drained the can. He burped again and wiped his mouth with the back of his hand.

'All right, all right. You can use the phone – after I check something.'

He put his plate on the floor beside the chair and stood

up, swaying slightly. The can fell to the ground, the last couple of drops oozing onto the carpet.

'Come here,' he said, slurring his words. He curled his finger at me and beckoned me towards him.

'Wh-wh-why?'

''Cos I've got to check you ain't stole nothin'. Come here.'

'I haven't stolen anything. I already told you that.'

'COME HERE!' He bellowed the words so loudly that the ground seemed to quake. I jumped and obeyed, walking slowly, fighting tears.

'What's this stupid thing you're wearin'?' he said, waving his hand at my brown sack dress.

I didn't reply. I stopped a little way from him.

He stepped forward, bringing us so close that his foul body odour enveloped my whole body. From here, I could see an intricate network of spiky red veins on his nose and cheeks. Black hairs sprouted out of his bulbous nose above dry, cracked lips.

I hesitated. A mad thought seized me and I kicked him as hard as I could in his groin. He roared with pain and doubled over. I ran for the door, yanked it open, darted up the hallway into the kitchen, opened the other door and sprinted out of the house.

The black dogs snapped their jaws and barked viciously as I ran past, but they were caged and I was free. I didn't spare them a second look as I ran past the man's rusty blue truck and headed in the direction Emma had gone.

Chapter 31

The sun blinded me, my leg throbbed and my feet left bloody prints on the pale, cracked earth. Every few seconds, I glanced over my shoulder, convinced I was being followed by the man from Knackers Yard. I had made it to the next patch of land, which was more a desert than a field. The ground was hard and rough with the occasional clump of sprouting vegetation, so dry and hot beneath my sore feet that it felt like I was running on baked sandpaper. My soles were burning and the pain was becoming unbearable. Not too far away though, beyond this bare stretch, I could see a bright yellow field. Surely the ground there would be cooler, damper.

I looked around me. Heard no one. Saw no one. But I couldn't stop shaking.

'Emma!' I shouted her name over and over again until my voice cracked.

There was no sign of Emma anywhere and I realized with creeping dread that anything could have happened to her. She could have tumbled into a ditch and been knocked unconscious or fallen and broken her ankle. She might have been shot by a farmer, angry that someone was on his private land. Anything could have happened to her. Anything. And it was my fault. I never should have pushed her out of that window.

I slowed down and put my hands on my knees, sucking in huge, warm, pollen-scented lungfuls of air. Tiny flies buzzed around my head and I waved them away and took another moment, one hand shielding my eyes, the other shooing off the pesky little beasts. I scanned the horizon. Saw nothing but fields – and then, far away, five fields away in a north-east direction, a patch of red caught my eye. Was it another farm? A house? It was definitely a building of some kind.

I should have started running towards it, but I didn't. I froze. Spun around, suddenly certain I could hear a car coming. I listened and listened, but all I heard was the whiny cry of the flies pestering me. There was no one chasing me. Not any more. The strange man was probably still lying on the ground writhing around in agony. A naughty sensation of satisfaction rippled through me as I remembered the shock and pain in his eyes. I didn't feel guilty. He'd deserved it, and if he came for me I would do it again.

My breath was back. Wincing, I ran on, climbing over a wooden gate into the yellow field, which smelled so strong it made my head fuzzy and my nose run. The yellow plants were as tall as my waist but not so tough that I couldn't run through them. They were so bright and beautiful. I wanted to stop and admire them, touch them and look closely at their different parts, but I didn't want to stop.

The ground was softer and cooler here, offering my feet a little break. I ran through the field and climbed over another wooden fence into the next field, which held five brown cows and one calf that could not have been very old at all. It was so scrawny and cute. But the big ones weren't. They stared at me with their huge, widespread eyes like they were trying to force me to go away with the power of their stare. Though I was dying to stare back at these incredible creatures and unpick them with my eyes, I stared off to one side. I had learned about the way animals acted around their babies in one of Mother's nature books. I knew that mothers might attack if they felt someone was going to approach their baby, so I took a wide berth, steering clear in case they thought I posed a threat to the little calf. I smiled as the calf tried to gambol over to me and one of the adult cows blocked its path.

I dodged a pile of dung and climbed over another wooden gate. I was now only three fields away. Countryside stretched out on all sides of me and I found myself admiring how beautiful and glowing the landscape was; colours so vivid they hurt; colours so vivid they brought happy skips into my heart. This field was another grass field and easier on my feet. I ran faster, flying over the grass, pumping my arms and legs and feeling like the bird-girl in my made-up book.

I reached the end of the field which was edged by another thorn wire fence. I remembered there were photographs of this type of wire in Mother's Holocaust book. The only reason I'd seen them was because I'd peered over her shoulder when she'd been reading it. There had been some other disturbing photographs too. Ones I didn't like to remember because they made me think about how much evil there must be in the world.

Taking more time than before, I climbed carefully over the fence and paused for breath on the other side before walking forward. This was another grass field, abandoned, I thought, until I saw it: a bull. Bulls were dangerous. And really strong. I'd read about them. In Spain, it was a tradition to put a bull in a big ring and taunt it with a red cloth to make it mad.

There was no way I was going to try to make this bull mad. It was black and unbelievably huge. Scary but amazing. It had its back to me, which meant I might be able to sneak past it and get to the other side of the field without it noticing me. If I was lucky.

I didn't have any time to waste, so I took a few sharp breaths and ran straight up the middle of the field, wincing at the pain in my feet.

Glancing back, I saw with horror that the bull had turned around and was staring at me. One hoof scuffed the ground. With a frantic gasp, terrified it was about to charge, I lunged forward and threw myself through the middle section of a different kind of fence, crying out as it electrocuted me. Needles of pain stabbed all over my hands and arms from where I'd made contact with the wire, reminding me of the time Mother had electrocuted herself changing a lightbulb.

I thudded to the ground and exhaled heavily. I was on the other side of the fence, safe from the bull. That was what mattered. I glanced back to see the bull nosing around in the grass, acting like I didn't exist.

I scrambled to my feet and limped through the last field, relieved to find the stabbing pains in my arms and hands gone after a few seconds, and happy to see that this field held nothing but sheep and lambs, who all skittered away when I approached.

And there it was: a red-brick building. A very big house by the look of it. An expensive, well looked after house. A house that was completely different to the one I'd come from. Did that mean the owner would be completely different? Despite everything, hope flared in my chest. I was so tired, so in need of rest. My feet were in shreds and I could barely walk another step. I felt tears sting my eyes; this could be the end of it all. The pain and fear and danger could finally be over.

But I had to be careful. A shiny black car sat parked on a white, stony drive facing the front of the house. On the other side of the car was a big patch of grass with a white horse standing in the centre. The horse was watching me. Its musty smell wafted in my direction on the warm breeze. I'd seen pictures of horses, but in real life the animal took my breath away. There was something so strong and sturdy yet fine about its body that made me want to keep looking at it, but I couldn't. I wondered if there ever would be a good time to take in all the things out here that I'd missed. I really hoped so. But more than that – more than anything – I wanted to see my parents.

My breath hitched as a series of sickening questions attacked – were they still alive? Would they remember me? What if they'd moved on with their lives and forgotten all about me?

The idea scraped an even bigger chunk out of my heart and I rubbed my chest and told myself to focus on the present and how I was going to get help.

I looked up the drive and saw that it led to a road. A real road, not a dirt road. I had reached civilization. At long last I might be near a town – a place where I could find a policeman.

Crouching low, I pushed open a large swing gate and darted through. I dashed over to the car and hid behind it, peering round at the house, trying to work out whether it was safe.

The house had a large white door and red-brick walls. A pretty white and black sign reading Greenfield House had been attached to the wall beside the front door. Two pots of beautiful flowers hung from either side of the door, making the place seem warm and kind. It looked so nice. So posh. So *light*. Curtains were drawn open in all four windows: two downstairs and two upstairs. There were no boards, no tape, no attempts to hide anything. This was a nice, happy, normal home, I felt almost sure of it.

Exhaling to steady my nerves, I left my hiding place and hobbled to the front porch.

I raised my hand to knock but someone opened the door, making me jump.

Chapter 32

'Oh my!'

A very old woman with short white hair that curled neatly under her chin answered the door. She was small and thin, wearing a floaty, mint-green dress. Her skin was so wrinkly it looked like a scrunched-up paper bag. A white shawl was draped across her narrow shoulders. I could smell something sweet and thought it must be her moisturizer. Her wrinkled hands flew to her mouth as she took in my appearance. I stared back at her, wondering what she saw when she looked at me. What she was thinking. She gripped the door frame and for a moment I thought she was going to slam the door in my face.

'Harold! Harold!' she shouted, turning round, her voice hoarse.

She turned back to me and said gently, 'Wait here a moment, dear. I must get Harold.'

'Who's Harold?' I said, feeling a stab of fear, but she had already retreated into the house leaving the door wide open.

Beyond the door was a dark wood floor and a few steps away was a staircase with a white banister. There was nothing on the floor. No drink cans in sight. Only a clean, flowery smell, like roses before they died.

A grey cat with pale green eyes appeared in the doorway. It stared at me for a few seconds then clearly decided I didn't pose a threat. I watched in wonder as it curled itself around my ankles, purring, its body vibrating as I bent to stroke its silky-soft fur. I suddenly felt light-headed. The urge to lie down was overwhelming. I leaned against the wall beside the front door and closed my eyes.

A sound made me look up. I shrank back.

A tall, grey-haired man with a long face and bent body eyed me up and down. He wore grey slacks and a short-sleeved white shirt which looked clean. He smelled clean too and his eyes didn't jiggle; they looked directly at me. These eyes were a twinkly, light blue and right now they were wide with what I thought was concern.

'Come in, child, come in,' he said, stepping back and beckoning me into the house, his voice low and serious. 'Dot, go and make her a glass of milk and something to eat.'

I didn't move, just stared at him, trying to work out if he was evil or good.

'What's your name?' he said.

I had to think for a moment. I hesitated. Should I tell him my real name? What if he knew Mother? What if they were friends? But then I pictured Mother in this room talking with these old people and the picture didn't make sense.

He shook his head. 'It's fine. You don't have to tell me. Come on into the living room. Let's give those feet a rest.'

Numbly, I followed him into the house, flinching as he shut the door. He didn't lock it, which I took as a good sign. He led the way into a large room with a green and orange-patterned carpet and matching curtains. The walls were white and they looked clean too. Clean and light. I wanted to tell the man – Harold – that I liked his house. Before I could speak, the old lady – Dot – rushed into the room holding a tray. I sat down on a squishy cream sofa, immediately relishing the lack of pressure on my feet.

'Drink some milk, dear,' Dot said, passing me a glass.

I did as she told me, spilling milk down my chin and onto myself and not caring. The cold, fresh milk felt wonderful against my dry throat and I smiled at her gratefully.

'Thank you,' I said.

'Oh dear. Look at your poor feet. I'll fetch something to clean those, shall I, Harold?'

Harold nodded, his eyes never leaving me.

'You need to call the police,' I said, taking a small bite of the sandwich that Dot had made me.

'OK,' he said, scratching his chin. 'Can you tell me why?'

I took another bite of sandwich, chewed it quickly. It was amazing what a little milk and bread could do for energy levels. I felt more awake and sat up straighter.

'There's a man. Patrick. He's hurt. He needs help. And there's Emma. I don't know where she is and it's my fault – I never should have told her to go. I—'

'Take a breath,' Harold said, 'Tell me who Patrick is first.'

'He's this man who showed up at the cottage and then I got him involved and she stabbed him and—'

'Who stabbed him?'

'Mother. I don't know her real name. She's not well. She needs help too but not as much as Patrick. He's dying.'

'OK, OK. What about Emma? Tell me about her.'

'She's only five. She's out there alone, all alone and she's so little, so scared – and it's all my fault!'

I started to cry, tried to stop, knowing I needed to explain better, but completely unable to fight the sobs that took over my eyes and mind and body. I tasted salt. My tummy lurched and saliva flooded my mouth. I jerked forward and threw up. I trembled as another wave of nausea built in my throat, and tensed, expecting it to overwhelm me, but it rolled back down into my stomach. With a shuddery breath, I sagged against the sofa and closed my eyes.

There was a hand on my shoulder. Someone taking the plate out of my hand. A gentle voice saying soothing things. I felt myself being made to lie down, being covered with crochet blankets, someone saying they were going to drive to the police station. I was so tired and the sofa was so comfortable and the blankets so warm and my eyes were heavy, so heavy.

Someone was stroking my forehead.

Saying nice things.

Stroking and soothing and stroking and soothing and stroking, stroking, stroking.

Chapter 33

I woke with a start, heart hammering, thinking I was back there, with Mother, trapped in the darkness of the cottage. I sucked in sharp breaths and stared around, my mind slowly piecing things back together. As my eyes adjusted to the gloom and my nose picked up a flowery scent, I remembered where I was: Harold and Dot's house. I wasn't in the cottage any more. I jerked upright – I hadn't spoken to the police yet – told them about Patrick or Emma! I had let myself fall asleep and now it might be too late to save them. I dreaded to think what might have happened to little Emma. Out there all alone, just five years old.

I pushed back the bedcovers and climbed out of the bed, wincing as my feet took the weight of my body, surprised to see my feet clean and bandaged. Dot. She must have cleaned them while I slept.

The swirly curtains were drawn tightly together. Panic ballooned in my chest; what if they were sewn shut? What if boards had been nailed behind those curtains? No. Dot was kind. She was a good person.

I tugged the curtains apart. They opened with ease and I

saw a starry, navy sky. I marvelled at the glittering dots of light, moved to tears by their prettiness.

I wanted to stare at them for longer but dread erupted in my tummy: the sun had set. It was night. How long had I been asleep? How long had Patrick been lying on the floor bleeding? How long had Emma been wandering around in the wilderness?

I looked down at myself. I was still wearing the brown sack dress but my arms and legs had been wiped clean. The wound on my leg had been bandaged too. Dot had cleaned every inch of me that she could without taking off my dress. I couldn't believe how kind she was.

A glass of water sat on the bedside table. I drained the whole glass then walked to the bedroom door and twisted the knob. The door opened and I slipped out onto a landing which had a green and white flowery carpet. Up here, the lights were off so it was dark. Trailing my hand on the banister, I descended the stairs, pleased to see soft light coming from downstairs. Dot and Harold must still be awake. I remembered suddenly that Harold had driven away to get the police, and realized that Harold and Dot must not have a telephone.

I turned right at the bottom of the stairs and hovered outside the living room. The door was shut. I could hear Dot murmuring to Harold, but no other voices. Alarm crept up my spine. Where were the police?

I hesitated, my hand on the door. Dot and Harold were good, kind people. Maybe the police were on their way. Maybe Harold had told the police then driven back here with the police following him and the police car had broken down. Yes. That must be why the police weren't here yet. I knew that if the police were here, I would hear loud, male, bossy voices. And someone would have woken me up. Someone would be questioning me right this second, desperate to find out everything they could in order to save Patrick and Emma.

Reassured, I pushed open the door and walked into the living room.

Dot was sitting on the sofa, wringing her hands. 'Harold ought to be back by now . . .' She looked up and saw me, stood and rushed across the room.

'You're awake! How are you feeling?' she said gently.

I didn't speak. Couldn't speak. Another woman was in the room sitting on the sofa with her back to me. I couldn't breathe. I knew that body. That long, bony back. That short, blonde hair.

I watched, unable to draw breath.

Mother stood up and turned around, a smile pasted to her thin lips. A smile that did not match the triumphant brightness in her small, dark eyes.

'Mirabelle! Thank heavens you're alive!' She rushed forward and I staggered backwards, putting Dot in between us.

'Mirabelle? Darling, what's wrong? Aren't you happy to see Mummy?'

Dot turned around, her brow crinkling in confusion and concern. 'We thought we'd let you sleep a little while longer. Your mother arrived only a few minutes ago. She's been looking all over for you. She's told me all about your father, but don't worry. He's gone now, isn't he, Mrs Stone?' Dot looked at Mother then back at me.

'Oh yes. That evil man's gone now. After you ran away, I threatened to call the police and he drove off. You can come home now, Little Doll. You're safe now.'

Mother stepped forward, reaching out a hand to me. I darted around to the other side of Dot and held Dot's hand.

Dot looked down at me, a question in her eyes.

'It's OK now,' she said, her eyes flicking from mine to Mother's. 'You can go home with your mother now, OK?'

'She's not my mother.'

'What? I don't understand,' Dot said.

I looked up at the old lady, meeting her eyes, willing her to believe me. 'Please make her leave. She's not my mother. She kidnapped me a long time ago. That's why I look like this. That's why I was running away.'

Mother laughed and grabbed my free wrist. 'What a lot of silly nonsense. Come on, sweetie, you've been through a great ordeal. You—'

'NO!' I shouted, tearing my wrist out of her grip.

Dot pulled me behind herself. She stared at Mother and said in a low voice, 'Please, Mrs Stone. The child clearly doesn't want to come with you. The police will be here shortly. Please leave.' She opened the living room door, still shielding me with her thin, frail body, and gestured with her head towards the front door.

Mother stepped towards us. 'I'm not leaving without Mirabelle.'

'I'm not going with you,' I said, trying to hide the fear in my voice.

'Oh yes you are. You are mine. You're coming with me whether you like it or not.'

She lunged for me, pushing Dot out of the way. Dot stumbled and fell, hitting the ground hard, her hand slipping out of mine. I turned and ran out of the room. Mother grabbed my shoulder and yanked me back, wrapping her arms around my body, holding me to her.

'Stop being so ridiculous, Mirabelle. We're leaving.'

I struggled and twisted and turned. She held on tighter, choking the air out of my lungs.

'STOP IT!' she screamed.

I bit her forearm, tasted blood, and she cried out and loosened her grip. I pulled away and stumbled out of the room across the hallway into a large yellow kitchen. I opened the first drawer I could see and grabbed a rolling pin. Turning to face Mother, I raised the block of wood and glared at her.

'Come closer and I'll hurt you,' I warned, panting for breath.

Dot appeared in the doorway behind Mother holding a shotgun. The gun looked huge against her tiny, frail form, but Dot's voice was as strong as iron. 'Please leave, Mrs Stone. Now.'

Mother turned slowly. Everything seemed so unreal all of a sudden. The room fell silent.

'The police will be here soon,' Dot said, pointing the gun at Mother. 'You need to leave.'

'I'm not leaving without my daughter.'

'I'm not your daughter,' I spat, lowering the rolling pin.

'Yes, you are. Mirabelle, you're not well. You are sick. Very sick, and the last few hours' light exposure have made you delirious. I need to get you back home where you'll be safe.'

'What's she talking about?' Dot said to me, her eyes leaving Mother.

'She's lying again. She's always lying. She's been lying to me for ten years.'

'Oh my God. Ten years?' Dot said, eyes widening.

I nodded. 'She took me when I was three years old.'

'Shut up!' Mother shouted. She swivelled round to face me. 'Where's Emma? What have you done with her?'

I twitched at her use of Emma's real name. It was the first time she'd made that mistake.

'Emma?' Dot said, struggling to catch up. 'Is that the little girl you mentioned?'

'Yes. She took Emma too. On the twenty-third of April.'

Dot gasped. 'Emma *Hedges*?'

I nodded eagerly and glanced at Mother, whose face had softened. She suddenly looked a lot older and utterly miserable. Her face seemed to have crumpled in on itself. Her voice turned whiny and pleading and she fell to her knees and clasped her hands in front of her.

'Please, Mirabelle, please, Mrs Bancroft. Please, I'm not well. Please don't tell. I just needed her. I love her. I only want to look after her. Make her safe. Make her safer than I was when I was a little girl.'

She dissolved into sobs and buried her face in her hands. Her bony shoulders crumpled forward and shook violently as she sobbed.

'But she's not your daughter and neither am I,' I said.

Dot lowered the gun and stepped forward. She mouthed the words 'You OK?' to me. I nodded. My whole body sagged and I leaned against the counter.

'Harold will be back soon,' Dot murmured.

We watched Mother sob. She rolled onto her side on the kitchen floor still hiding her face in her hands. I felt a strange desire to comfort her and resisted it. I looked at the clock on the wall. It was midnight. Where were the police? Where was Harold? Why wasn't he back yet?

As if reading my thoughts, Dot muttered, 'Where is he? What's taking him so long?'

She turned to look at the front door and Mother launched herself at the gun, ripping it out of Dot's grasp and pulling Dot onto her hands and knees. She smashed Dot around the face with the barrel of the gun. I heard a crunch as Dot's jaw broke and she toppled onto her side, unconscious.

With a scream I threw myself at Mother, raising the rolling pin over my head in both hands. But she was too quick. She hit my tummy with the gun, winding me. I staggered to the side and she tore the rolling pin out of my hands and tossed it to the ground. She wrapped her arm around my neck, still gripping the gun in her free hand and forced me out of the kitchen.

'Open it,' she snapped when we reached the front door.

She tightened her grip on my neck and I opened the door, gasping for breath.

Mother's car was parked on the drive where the black car had been earlier. She bundled me into the passenger seat, pointing the gun at me as she hurried around to the driver's side and got in behind the wheel.

'Strap in,' she said.

I did as she said. She stabbed a button and the doors clicked.

'Sit on your hands and don't move. If you move, Mirabelle, I will drive back here and kill that old lady.'

She put the gun on her lap, strapped herself in and started the engine.

Silent tears rolled down my cheeks as the tyres crunched over the drive and we reversed away from Greenfield House. Away from hope.

Chapter 34

We drove in silence, and I bit my lip, forced myself to stop crying and huddled over to the door, curling my body as far away from hers as possible.

In the closeness of the car sour sweat radiated off her in one, great, disgusting swell. My hands ached with the desire to grab the gun off her lap, but what would I do with it if I actually managed to grab it? I couldn't shoot her. She had been the closest thing to a mother I had ever known. I could never shoot her. And yet the notion zigzagged across my thoughts like volts of electricity. Returning to the cottage filled me with a kind of dread that was as intense as thoughts of dying. If I did go back to that place, I was as good as dead. I felt sick with panic at the thought. What kind of life was a life behind locked doors where the one person you got to interact with was her? I thought about all of the times I had behaved like her perfect little doll, sat there so quietly and dutifully as she painted my face . . . I could never go back to being that person. I would rather die.

'You've been very badly behaved recently, Mirabelle,' her words sliced the stillness in two, jarring my thoughts. 'You're usually such a good doll. I don't know what's got into you.

I'm just relieved you're alive. The light must not have been strong enough to hurt you.'

'I'm *not* allergic to light. I never have been,' I said, teeth chattering despite my defiant words. I wanted to be brave, to stand up to her, to fight.

Mother fell silent. My stomach cramped. She accelerated up the road faster and I fought the urge to throw up.

'Slow down. Please,' I said as we swerved round a bend that sent me crashing into the side door.

'I can't. We need to find Clarabelle before something happens to her. Where and when did you last see her?'

Nausea billowed in my throat. 'I'm going to be sick. You have to stop.'

Mother shook her head. 'Hold it in. I'm not stopping. Where did you last see her? Tell me or I'll drive straight back to that house and shoot that woman in the head.'

'You wouldn't,' I said. 'You're not a murderer.' As I said the words, I tried to believe them, and a series of images pirouetted around my mind's eye like a deadly dance; Mother marching up to the house, opening the door, looking for Dot, standing over her, smiling and pointing the gun at Dot's face, pulling the trigger, Dot's face exploding, blood and flesh dripping off the walls. Blood and flesh. Dot's headless body.

'You saw what happened to Patrick,' she said, glancing at me.

I clenched my fists. 'How is Patrick? Is he . . .' I couldn't finish the sentence as another series of gory images attacked.

She shrugged. 'I don't know. I didn't stop to check. I've been out here searching for you two all day. You don't know how worried I've been. Now, tell me where you last saw Clarabelle. This is your final chance before I turn around and go back to that house.'

Up ahead I could see houses and tall lights on the side of

the road. Were we in a town? My heartbeat jackhammered. I sat up straighter, staring at every house we passed, pressing my nose to the glass. One of those houses could be my house. My real parents' house. I looked at the car door. It was locked, but maybe . . .

'You have three seconds to tell me. Three, two—' She slowed the car down.

I turned to her, thoughts of trying the door vanishing, and blurted, 'You need to turn around. Go back the way we came. I last saw Emma at a farm a few fields away from Dot and Harold's house. I left her there. I can tell you how to get there, just please don't hurt Dot.'

She smiled at me. 'Good doll.'

She spun the car around, tyres squealing, and sped back up the road.

For a second I hoped that someone had heard the squealing car and decided to follow us, see what the hurry was all about. But it was night-time and no one sped after us. Heart sinking, I stared out of the window at the last of the houses as we pulled away from a town. I thought about Emma wandering around alone in the middle of the night. I didn't think Mother would hurt Emma. Couldn't believe she was that far gone.

I ran over everything I had told Dot. Had I told her my real name? I had definitely told her about Emma and the fact that I had been kidnapped ten years ago. I gritted my teeth; I had not told Dot anything about the cottage, about where it was. Would the small amount that I had told her be enough for the police to go on? She had told Dot that her name was Mrs Stone. Could that be useful information? Was that the truth or was it another lie?

My stomach began to settle, grown used to the bumpy journey. I looked at the gun on her lap. I could easily reach it.

'Where now?' her voice cut through my thoughts.

We were edging past Greenfield House. The large, white door was still open, the lights still on. No black car sat in the drive. Harold wasn't back yet.

'It's five fields in that direction,' I said, pointing.

Her eyes lit up. She smiled at me. 'I know it. The knacker's yard. Good doll. You don't know how relieved I am. I was beginning to fear you were as bad as Olivia. Always lying. Rotten.'

I licked my lips nervously. Emma wasn't there but Mother didn't know that. Somehow, if I could work it, maybe I could get away when she went into the man's house to look for Emma. Maybe I could get away, find Emma on my own and get to the police before Patrick died. Maybe not all hope was lost.

Swallowing thickly, I tried to work out what to do, discarding idea after idea. The main problem was the gun. I didn't think she'd shoot me, but she was crazy and angry. What if, in a fit of rage, she pointed the gun at me and pulled the trigger before she could stop herself?

Mother turned off the main road onto a bumpy side road. Not far away, the light from the strange man's house glowed like the entrance to Hell.

Chapter 35

I'm going to die. I'm going to die.

I couldn't stop the four-word sentence rotating around my brain. It was because I had decided what to do when we reached the farm. I had made my decision.

Mother slowed the car down, jiggled a stick in the middle of the car directly between us and yanked up another, straighter stick. The car jerked to a stop. The engine cut out. For a moment, we sat in the dark pool of the car, staring out at the light coming from the small house. The dogs in the cage had not barked. Neither had the dog chained to the building. Either they were asleep or they were not bothered by the car's arrival. I could hear her breathing. She sounded wheezy, out of breath, despite the fact that we had been sat down for a while now.

'She's in there?'

Her question sent a shiver down my spine. Her voice was so cold and calculating. She had lost something and she wanted it back.

She called us dolls. I had never thought how strange that was until recently, but a real mother with real love would never call her child a doll. A doll was dead. I was alive. Emma was alive. We could hurt. We could bleed.

I will bleed.

Mother slapped me around the face. 'Answer me!'

I stared at her through the gloom, glad that the darkness hid the tears in my eyes. 'Yes. I left her here.'

I held my breath, certain she would hear my lie. She reached out and I flinched away, thinking she was going to strike me again, but she stroked my hair back from my forehead, her touch gentle.

'You're a good doll. I'm sorry I hit you. I'm just anxious about Clarabelle, that's all.'

I wanted to scream – to yank her hand away from me and give her a taste of her own medicine, but I couldn't move. I couldn't raise my hand to her. Instead, I stared at her lap. At the gun, which looked like a dead, black snake in the darkness. I imagined myself snatching it off her lap, turning it around and pointing it at her. I pictured her reaction: shock, dismay, anger. Pictured her running away . . .

It all played out so perfectly and I began to believe I could do it. I could beat her. I could win. I could regain my freedom, save Emma, save Patrick, live a normal, happy life.

She grabbed my chin. 'If you try to leave, you know what I'll do.'

She opened the door and got out of the car without another word. I gawked at the car door as it banged shut. She had taken the gun with her. I scrabbled with my door handle, but the door was locked. I tried her door, the two back doors: all were locked.

Mother marched up to the house and hammered on the door with her fist. In her free hand she held the gun down by her side. She didn't even try to hide the weapon. She looked back, her eyes warning me. I watched, fearful for the man even though he was a pig. He didn't have a clue about Emma's whereabouts.

When there was no answer, she pounded on the door

again. Five times, louder than before. She waited, foot tapping the ground. After only a short wait, she raised the gun and smashed the door with the thick end. The door held despite her efforts, so she aimed the gun at the door and fired. The explosion made the car windows vibrate. If the man was asleep before, he had to be awake now. Mother staggered back, reeling from the shock of the gun, dust and debris flying into her face. She coughed and dragged the back of her hand across her eyes. Without a backward glance, she kicked down the door and strode into the house.

I heard distant shouting. A man and a woman. Him and Mother. I looked at the window beside my face then at the back seats. Mother's winter coat lay in the back. I grabbed it, wrapped it around my right elbow, turned to face the headrest and knelt up on the seat. Raising my elbow high, I pulled my arm back from the glass, gripping one fist in the other, took a deep breath and rammed my elbow as hard as I could into the passenger window. Pain ricocheted up my arm and I cried out. Breathing slowly and deeply, allowing the pain to ebb a little, I drew my arm up again, counted down from three then smashed my elbow into the glass again. This time a tiny crack the size of my thumbnail splintered the centre of the window. Fighting waves of pain and nausea, I turned around, wrapped the coat around my other elbow, closed my eyes and aimed my left elbow into the crack. Groaning with pain, I gritted my teeth and hit the window again, but it didn't shatter. I sank down onto my knees and hugged myself, breathing through the stabbing pains in my arms. My eyes fell on the door, on a handle of sorts. I grabbed the handle and pushed it down and around; the window slid down a notch. My heart leapt and I turned the handle again, unwinding the window some more. I turned faster, unwinding the window as far as it would go. I unravelled the coat from my elbow and threw it onto the driver's seat. Stealing a glance at the broken front door of the house, I crawled through the window head first, the top of the window digging into my stomach. Stretching out my arms to the ground, I wriggled forward, lowering my upper body and performing a hand-stand of sorts in an effort to extract the rest of my body from the car.

Before I could get to my feet, Mother's voice rang out: 'Mirabelle, stop.'

I turned. Mother pushed the man to his knees in front of her. He looked at me through swollen, bruised eyes. Blood poured out of his nostrils onto his stained vest. He swayed on his knees then threw up over his own lap. The stink of vomit filled the air.

'You saw this girl,' Mother said, waving the gun at me, 'and another one. A smaller girl. Emma. Where is she now? What have you done with her?'

She pointed the gun at the back of his head. His eyes rolled. He groaned and wiped his mouth with his hand.

'Tell me, Derek, or I'll put a fucking bullet in your thick head.'

Derek tried to turn to look at her and she kicked him hard in the back, sending him forward onto all fours. He grunted and shook his head. Saliva dripped from his mouth onto the dirt. With difficulty he pushed himself onto his knees.

'Please don't hurt me, Mrs,' he slurred, 'I've got a kid.'

'Tell me about Emma.'

There was nothing I could do but stand there and watch. Derek seemed to be trying to find the right words. He frowned and wiped his nose, smearing blood across his cheek. Tears dripped down his cheeks.

'I don't know no Emma.'

'The little girl *she* left here a few hours ago. You know exactly who I'm talking about. Tell me or I *will* shoot you.'

Derek dropped his head and closed his eyes. He went very still and for a terrifying moment I thought he was dead, thought fear had killed him. Stopped his heart. Then his whole body jerked and he threw up again.

The air swelled with the sickly-sweet scent of vomit. My insides recoiled and I shifted my gaze from Derek to Mother. In the dimly lit yard she looked like a scarecrow, her straw-coloured hair sticking out at disturbing angles, her dark eyes staring blankly, unseeingly, and her skeletal body looking as if it had been frozen in time. For too long she stood there, unmoving, unblinking, the silence stretching on and up into the eternity of the space above our heads, into the stars, beyond the stars. She was all-powerful in that moment. Derek and I were nothing. She abruptly tilted her head to the side. Her eyes caught the light from the house and glinted. She smiled a smile that did not meet her eyes and then she fired a bullet into Derek's head.

I didn't scream. I was too shocked to scream or move or breathe. I stared as Derek's face exploded into a million pieces and his body dropped to the ground like a stone. I stared as she walked over to me and guided me to the car, opened the passenger door, reached inside and placed the shotgun on the back seat. I stared as she sat me down. Stared as she strapped the safety belt around me then got behind the wheel. Stared as she drove away, face calm, hands calm, movements fluid. I stared the whole drive back to the cottage, unable to think anything except for the same four words over and over and over again.

Chapter 36

Mother was a killer. She'd shot Derek in the head and not even winced when she'd done it. She'd driven back to the cottage with the radio on, humming along to an upbeat song with a queer smile on her lips as though nothing had ever happened. As if Derek was still alive. As if both she and I weren't covered with his blood. As if we were a normal, happy mother and daughter going for a drive in the dark.

She hadn't said anything to me when we'd pulled up outside the cottage. She'd turned off the engine, exited the car, opened my door and lifted me out. I hadn't protested as she had carried me like a baby into the cottage. Hadn't protested when she'd injected me with some kind of drug and put me in my bed and locked my bedroom door.

Morning had come and gone. I lay on my back in bed, head and limbs heavy. I stared at the ceiling, glanced at the door. She'd left the house about an hour ago.

The silence and gloom seemed to consume me. I lifted my arms, let them drop back onto the mattress. Everything felt so heavy, so difficult. Pointless.

Patrick needs your help.

There was that nagging voice again. From behind that

voice came a stranger's voice. The voice of a person called D. H. Lawrence who had written the poem 'Self-Pity', a poem that I had found in one of Mother's poetry books. The voice was harsh and angry: *I never saw a wild thing sorry for itself. A small bird will drop frozen dead from a bough without ever having felt sorry for itself.*

I said the words out loud, testing them on my tongue. Then I screamed Patrick's name as loudly as I could and listened. There was no response. How long had it been since Mother had stabbed him? I couldn't work it out. The mathematical part of my brain seemed to be wading through the drugs, unable to perform as well as normal. I shouted his name again and again and again, listening in between each call and hearing nothing in return. I pushed myself out of bed and swivelled around to touch the floor with my bandaged feet. My entire body ached. I stood up and walked to the door, tried the handle. It was locked. She would be more careful from now on. Now that she knew I could not be trusted. Perfect, obedient Mirabelle was gone, replaced by naughty, rebellious Polly Dalton. In Mother's mind, I was untrustworthy and crazy, but *she* was the crazy one. She was the killer.

Needles trickled across my shoulders. I forced my thoughts away from Derek's headless body onto the here and now. If Patrick was still alive I could not just sit here and do nothing. Mother was out. This was my chance.

I turned my back to the locked door and surveyed the small room, looking at it with new eyes. I had no tools with which to prise the wooden boards from the windows and no weapon of any obvious kind. I walked over to my desk. A small black pot held my pens and pencils, a sharpener and a ruler. I picked up a pen, made a stabbing motion with it. I imagined stabbing Mother and my insides clenched.

Despite the warmth of the room, cold chilled my bones.

I pulled off the bloodstained brown dress and changed into a black doll dress with scarlet roses embroidered over the chest. I hated to wear one of her doll dresses again, but I had to get away from the blood.

The dress was so tight that I could barely draw breath, so I reached up behind my neck and ripped a tear down the back of the dress. The tearing sound was intensely satisfying. I stood in front of the mirror and craned my head round to look at the damage I had done to the dress. Mother would be mad, but if things went my way, she would have little chance to react to what I'd done. I pulled on a fresh pair of knickers and a pair of black tights that I found in the back of the wardrobe. My body grew warm. Panic fluttered in my chest as I turned my attention back to the pot of pens and pencils.

I sat down at the desk and began to write a letter to my real parents, Jane and Peter Dalton. I wrote the word 'Dear' then paused, unsure what to call them. They were my mother and father, but it seemed odd to use those words. It seemed too familiar, yet they were my family. They were my real mother and father. I thought about the police. They would probably be first to find the letter, which meant I had to make it very clear who the letter was addressed to. I scrunched up the paper and grabbed a fresh sheet. This time I began 'Dear Jane and Peter'. Tears filled my eyes. I told myself not to over-think the words.

I wrote for two hours. Wrote until I heard the car pull up to the cottage.

I folded the letter up and tucked it down inside my tights, wrapping it around the bandage on my right foot.

She was back.

I grabbed my fountain pen, lay down on the bed and dug my teeth into my left wrist, tasting blood.

Chapter 37

I heard rather than saw Mother open the door. She stepped into the room. The door creaked and knocked against the wall.

Mother didn't move towards the bed. I caught a faint whiff of orange-blossom moisturizer.

'Mirabelle?' her voice was quiet.

I managed not to flinch when she took a step forward. I kept my eyes closed and focused on listening to her movements.

'Mirabelle?'

I tried to breathe with as little chest movement as possible. She took another step closer and a small cry burst from her lips. She mumbled something about blood. So much blood. She was crying. She was crying for me. My resolve wavered. I reminded myself what she had done to Patrick, Dot and Derek. How she had kidnapped Emma and me. How she would never stop unless someone made her stop.

Something clattered to the floor and I jumped. Keys. She had dropped her keys.

'Mirabelle? Mirabelle!'

She rushed forward suddenly. I opened my eyes and sat

up as she bent over me. Bringing my right hand over her arched back, I stabbed the fountain pen into her left shoulder. She screamed. Her eyes widened and she grabbed at me as I crawled past her. I fell to the floor and she seized my ankle and dragged me backwards as I fought to claw forward. I kicked out and caught her in the face. She roared but released my foot, and I pushed myself up and ran out of the room.

I flew down the stairs and tried the front door, which was locked. I ran into the kitchen. Patrick's body was gone. The floor was clean too. I opened a drawer, but hands seized me from behind. I cried out as she threw me into the kitchen table. My stomach smashed against wood, and fire exploded in my tummy. I dropped to my knees and began to crawl away, blinded by tears of pain, not knowing which way I was headed.

Mother grabbed a handful of my hair and pulled me to my feet. She yanked my head back, exposing my throat, and smiled down at me. Blood soaked her blouse and the ends of her hair.

'You conniving girl,' she spat.

She seized the wrist that I'd bitten and looked at it then threw my hand away and shook her head bitterly.

'You're nothing to me any more. I've given you chance after chance and now this!'

She yanked out a chair and shoved me onto the wooden seat.

'Don't move,' she said, nostrils flaring.

She opened a drawer and pulled out a knife. Turning around, she glared at me. She sat down opposite me and lunged forward, positioning the knife behind my right ear.

'What do you do with a broken doll?' she said, tilting her head. Her eyes looked black. They had taken on that faraway look.

I didn't move. I stared at the table. Shakes overtook my body; I shook so violently that the table vibrated.

Silent tears ran down her cheeks and she looked at me with something like pity. 'Don't worry. I'm not going to kill you. I'm going to give you what you've always wanted.'

Hope flickered in my chest and I glanced up at her.

She smiled. 'I'm going to let you go outside. You'd like that, wouldn't you?'

All hope vanished. She was smiling the smile that didn't meet her eyes and it struck me that she was enjoying herself. She smoothed back my hair from my face. I flinched but she didn't seem to notice.

'Get up,' she said softly.

I did as she said, watching the knife, which she moved out of the way to allow me space to stand. She stood too, grabbed my hand and pulled me towards the back door.

The door was unlocked. She opened it and we walked out together, hand in hand. The day was overcast and muggy. I stared at trees and overgrown grass and mottled, grey sky as she pulled me round to the back of the cottage.

'This is the back garden you've always wanted to see,' she said, gesturing with the knife to a jungle with a large brown square in the centre.

'My grandfather spent many hours out here, you know,' she said dreamily. 'He made me and Olivia come out here too.'

We walked forward into the overgrown garden. The grass was as tall as my waist and so bright it made my eyes sting. Enclosing the garden was a fence and beyond the fence stood the woods.

'We spent a lot of time out here as children, you know,' she said.

She stopped and stared down at the brown square on the ground. I followed her gaze and frowned, confused. The brown square looked like two rusted, metal doors. Two doors *in the ground.*

Mother pushed me onto my front on top of the door. She knelt down, resting one knee on my back to keep me still. Holding the knife between her teeth, she pulled a key out of her pocket and unlocked the door.

I suddenly realized what she was going to do. I struggled to get up but she crushed me against the ground with her knee.

'I'm only giving you what you've always wanted,' she said in a sing-song voice.

She flung open one of the doors and a foetid stench filled the air. She seized my shoulders and pulled me onto her lap, holding the knife to my cheek. I stared down at the hole in the ground, unable to believe what was happening.

'Be a good girl and you'll get all the food and water you need,' she whispered.

'No! Please – don't!' I screamed and swivelled round, pleading, begging her with my eyes.

With a distant smile she pushed me off her lap. I rolled through the doorway down some steps. Above me the door slammed, and I was swallowed by darkness.

Chapter 38

It was the kind of blackness where it was impossible to see anything, even the faintest hint of your own hand an inch from your face. I had known darkness but never darkness this thick. Like tar. Like a demon's blood. I lifted my hand and held it in front of my face. Nothing. Just black. Black and an awful smell of grime and poo and urine and mould and rot all rolled into one gut-wrenchingly hideous stench. A smell so revolting that I retched continuously for about five minutes, but brought up nothing. My tummy was empty. Horribly so.

When my stomach felt calmer, I sat up. Trying to breathe through my mouth, I felt the step around me. It was made of bricks. Dust or sand or dry crumbs of soil lay on the brick surface. Steps meant man-made, which meant this was not a simple hole in the ground. This hole was more than that. But what was it? Why would someone dig a hole in the ground, build steps leading down into the earth and place doors on top? *The Wizard of Oz* jumped into my head. When the tornado had struck, the characters had hidden in the ground. Perhaps this hole was like that. A place to escape terrible weather. But I had never known weather bad enough to destroy a house. England didn't have tornadoes. I would have heard a gale of that force even through the wooden boards that blocked every window in the cottage.

So what was it?

If I could understand what kind of place I was in, maybe I could find a way out.

Stretching out one foot, I felt the ground in front of me. It was another step. I slid onto it, staying on my bottom. I slid down another three steps until I felt hard, solid ground. To my surprise, the ground was smooth, like plastic. Another clue, yet I still couldn't work out what type of cage held me its prisoner. Fearful of bumping into something, I got down on all fours and edged forward an inch at a time, feeling the ground with my hands. Every few inches I stopped and felt the air around me, searching for more clues.

My stomach grumbled. Dot's sandwich was the last thing I'd eaten, but I hadn't managed to digest that – I had thrown it all back up. My heart began to race; what if Mother forgot to bring me something to eat and drink? I hadn't drunk anything for ages either.

Telling myself she would remember, I crawled on, feeling the ground. I felt brick. My hands moved upward, trailing up a solid, brick wall. I rose to my knees and reached up. The wall continued upward. I stood up slowly, worried I might hit my head if the ceiling was too low, but I was able to stand up. I felt for the ceiling, but couldn't reach it. The hole was deep.

Relieved to be able to stand up straight, I moved to the right and reached another brick wall, which I followed round until I came to the steps that led down here. I retraced my steps, moving back round to the left, hands trailing the brick wall. My feet collided with something hard and I jumped at the unexpected object. It was a bookcase. I felt the spines of books, my heart lifting a notch. If I could persuade Mother to bring me a light of some kind, at least I could read until I could work out a way to escape.

I didn't let myself consider the possibility of never escaping. I told myself that Mother would let me out eventually or I would escape. I would get out of here, one way or another. I had to.

Emma's big eyes flashed into my mind. Emma was still out there somewhere. Hot shame swept over me. It was my fault she was out there all alone. Mother would never have put Emma down here. If I had helped her find Emma, Emma would be safe and sound in the cottage – as safe as she could be with a kidnapper.

I closed my eyes, forced myself to focus on now. Focus on where I was, what I was doing.

The air was warm and thick. Too warm. I yanked on the collar of the stupid doll dress and blew air down my front, but my breath was hot and did little to cool my skin.

Tears welled up, but I gritted my teeth, determined not to give up.

I edged past the bookcase and felt the wall again. Nothing. I sidestepped to the left, trailing my fingers across the bricks. My hands bumped into something else – something metal that rose as high as my waist. I moved my hands from the wall to the metal object and quickly worked out that it was a metal bed frame. Bending over, I felt bedcovers, a mattress and a sheet. There was a bed down here. At least if Mother did leave me here for a while, I would have somewhere to sleep. A dirty bed was better than a dirty floor.

I felt my way to the end of the bed and my hands landed on a thin pillow. Kneeling down, I tentatively felt under the bed, but there was nothing there except for dust and grime. Wiping my hands on my dress, I stood up and turned. Again, I felt brick wall and trailed my hands along the rough surface as I inched to the left. I bumped into a small table. There were no chairs near the table and nothing on the table.

Using the tabletop as a guide, I edged round the table until I came to the wall again. When the rough texture of bricks beneath my fingers changed to the smooth feel of wood, I realized I was standing in front of a wooden door. Hurriedly, thinking I'd discovered an escape route, I felt for a handle. Finding one, I pushed down and pulled. Pulling didn't work so I pushed the door open. I gagged as the stench increased tenfold. Still, I edged forward and felt all around me. My hands touched brick wall on either side and my leg collided with something hard. I was in a tiny room. I reached down, my fingertips outstretched. My fingers touched a brick table of some kind. I trailed my fingers along its surface and they fell into a hole in the brick. This was where the stench was strongest. A fly buzzed around my head. Another fly landed on my hand.

Unable to bear the smell any longer, I turned and shuffled back towards the door using the side walls as my guide. I reached the doorway, hurried through, turned and grappled for the handle, pushing the door shut, desperate to put a barrier between myself and the stench.

So the small room was a bathroom of some kind. My whole body jolted. If the bathroom smelled that bad, the stench so fresh . . . someone was using it.

I leaned against the wall, the wind knocked out of me.

I wasn't alone.

A stranger was down here with me.

Chapter 39

In the total darkness I stood still and listened. Listened for the sound of someone's breathing. If I was right, and I was sure I was, a stranger was sitting in the darkness listening to my movements. This stranger must have heard me. They must have heard Mother push me down here. They must have heard me tumbling down the steps, getting up, moving around the space like a blind girl. This stranger had listened to my terror and said nothing. Why? Were they too afraid to make themselves known? Did this stranger expect to remain unknown to me – was that what he or she wanted? Did they want to attack me, take me by surprise?

Scenarios whizzed around my head like bees in a box, my imagination frantic. Spiders were down here – huge ones – vengeful spiders like Deadly with fangs and eight beady eyes and a savage hunger for human blood. And rats. There were bound to be lots of rats. Rats were attracted to foul, reeking places and this place reeked. And the stranger – the stranger would be worse than Mother. They would be rabid with starvation. To them I would be nothing more than a way to keep themselves fed.

My hands found my head. My temples throbbed against

my palms. Dizziness danced behind my eyes. My stomach rippled with anxiety.

Stop it. Think. A wild bird never feels sorry for itself.

I listened hard. I could almost picture my ears perking up, twitching at the ends. But I heard nothing. The silence was as contained and absolute as the dark. All-consuming. I remembered a day Mother and I had played hide and seek. We had laughed and chased one another. Mother had caught me and tickled me. There had been few days like that. Few moments when Mother had relaxed and let me behave naturally, but those moments had been the best . . . and now she had locked me in a hole in the ground in complete darkness with a stranger. Had this always been coming? Would things have stayed the same for ever if Mother had never taken Emma, or would she have taken another girl later on? Was I going to die down here?

A wild bird never feels sorry for itself.

I took a deep breath. Counted to ten. My breathing slowed.

If she wanted me dead, she would have killed me instead of putting me down here. And if the stranger wanted to hurt me, they would have acted by now.

I told myself this but I didn't believe it.

Time stood still. I opened my mouth to speak then shut it again. If I was quiet and hid, I would be safer – unless the stranger was some kind of supernatural creature – which of course they couldn't be – they were as blind as I was down here, which meant silence was my weapon.

Mentally, I retraced my path, recalling the table I had bumped into. I wanted to get back to the bed. The space underneath had been wide enough for me to fit. If I could hide there, I could wait him or her out. They might even give themselves away if they needed to cough or sneeze.

Using the wall for guidance, I turned around and inched back the way I had come. Trying not to think of spiders or rats or the stranger in the room, my fingertips scraped brick and I hoped, even as I tried not to think about them, that any spiders or dungeon-type insects would sense my fingers coming and dart out of the way.

Sweat trickled down the side of my face as I eased myself around the table and edged in the direction of the bed. I closed my eyes against the blackness and willed myself to believe it was black because of my choosing. I had *chosen* to rest my eyes, to plunge myself in inky darkness. My eyes had been dazzled by the sun and they needed a break . . .

But I could feel a strange heaviness dragging down the space behind my eyes. Blinds were being pulled down. Boards were being nailed over the gap between the backs of my eyes and my brain. It was such an overwhelming sensation that I opened my eyes and almost gasped. How long had I been down here? I couldn't work it out. An hour? Five hours? Or was it only minutes? Panic made my insides crawl and my breaths grow ragged.

Trembling, I silently repeated my saying over and over as I edged, inch by inch, towards my goal.

A wild bird never feels sorry for itself. A wild bird never feels sorry for itself.

Then I realized the stupidity of what I was saying: I was not a wild bird; I was a caged one. I was not free. I had never been free, not really, not even when I left the cottage.

My leg hit the bed and I almost cried out. Hastily, feeling like it was the only thing that would save me, I got to my knees and felt the bed frame with my hands then the space between the frame and the floor. Yes. I would fit. I would definitely fit.

I lay down on my front, turned onto my back and shuffled sideways under the bed, cursing the faint scraping of fabric against ground.

I had moved about three inches into the space when I

smelled something odd. A different smell. A smell like bad breath.

And then I heard it. Breathing. Low, ragged breathing. Breathing that wasn't mine.

A hand squeezed my arm and I screamed.

Chapter 40

'It steals from you. The darkness.'

The voice was harsh. Fast. A woman's voice. A voice that produced hot fumes of the grossest kind.

I pursed my lips together and held my breath. Our faces could not have been more than an inch apart. If she wanted to, she could bite off my nose or push her fingers deep into my eye sockets, into my brain. She could kill me in a heartbeat if she chose to.

Her fingers dug into my arm, holding on too tightly – so tightly I wanted to ask her to let go, but I didn't. I couldn't breathe, couldn't speak; I ought to have been relieved the stranger was female, but I wasn't. The craziest person I knew was a woman; a woman had shut me down here in the dark; kidnapped me and Emma; shot a man in the head. A woman I had known for most of my life had rejected me, turned on me, locked me in a black hole in the ground. If Mother could treat me like that, what could this woman do to me?

'I see things. Lights. In the corners. Lights in the corners,' she sounded rushed, like she had to get the words out or they would choke her.

'Then blackness. Nothing else. Just a tunnel. Are you really here? Are you?'

Her hand clenched, squeezed tighter, dug in to my skin and she began to shake my arm. My heart felt like it was going to explode out of my chest. I tried to pull my arm out of her grasp, but she clung on, grabbing at my chest, my face, my hair.

'Are you real? Speak! Speak to me!'

'Stop!' I blurted as she shook harder.

Abruptly, taking me by surprise, her hands stilled. One hand still gripped my arm while the other lay flat against my cheek.

'Say something,' she whispered.

I hesitated, took a breath. 'Let go of me.'

I waited, tense, readying myself for another attack. Her breaths were ragged, louder than mine. A bark of laughter escaped her lips and spittle landed on my cheek. She patted my chest then removed her hand from my pounding heart. Her other hand loosened on my arm, but remained in contact with my skin. With one hot finger, she stroked my arm. I longed to move out of reach but feared what she might do if I moved suddenly.

'Are you *really* real?' she breathed.

'Yes.' *The sounds I'd heard from the house. They came from here. From her. I hadn't imagined them.*

'Hah! Prove it.'

'What?' I said. 'How? I'm already talking to you, aren't I? And you can feel me, can't you? You can probably even smell me.'

She didn't say anything for a long time – just breathed against my cheek and stroked my arm, drawing a figure of eight on my skin with her finger. It was creepy and weird but kind of soothing at the same time. I listened to her breaths grow steadier and felt my own heartbeat slowing.

After a while, she stopped stroking me and removed her hand from my skin. Her breathing quietened and for a few seconds, I thought she was dead.

'Miss?' I said. 'Are you OK?'

She began to cry, quietly at first, then loudly and wretchedly. Beside me, I could feel her body shaking. Her sobs swallowed me whole. She sounded so lost and hopeless that I felt for her hand in the dark and slipped my hand into hers.

'You're not alone any more,' I said, 'I'm real. I promise.'

She allowed me to hold her hand, though hers was floppy in mine. She sniffed and cried, sniffed and cried. For a long time, I said nothing. Sometimes it was good to cry. I tried to think of a word that meant letting out all of your emotions, but my mind felt heavy and blank, as blank as the darkness around us. I stared into the black air. After a while, her hand responded in mine.

'Thank you,' she said softly.

'Come on,' I said. 'Let's get out from under here. You can lie on the bed and rest.'

'Yes, yes. You're probably right.'

I slipped my hand out of hers and shuffled my body out from under the bed. Glad to be off the hard ground, I stepped back to give her enough space then felt for the bed frame and guided her onto the mattress. Through the thin material of her clothing I felt a bony rod on her back, which I assumed was her spine. I couldn't help wondering if she had always been so skinny or if being down here had turned her into a skeleton. Had Mother been starving her? Would she starve me too? Mother had said that if I was good, she would bring me food and water. Had she said that to the lady too?

'I need to sleep,' she said, her voice thick from crying.

I nodded, then realized I had to speak or she wouldn't have a clue about my response.

'Of course. Lie down and have a rest. I'll sit on the edge of the bed, if that's OK?'

'Tell me again,' she said.

'What?'

'Tell me you're real.'

I swallowed, mouth dry. How long had she been down here all alone?

'Please,' she said. 'Tell me.'

'I'm real. I promise. I'm real and my name's Polly.'

'Polly . . . that's a nice name . . .'

I wanted to ask her a million questions but her breathing told me she was already asleep, so I sat on the bed in the pitch black and tried to take comfort in one fact: I was not alone.

Chapter 41

My brain was black. Burnt toast. My eyes were black. Coals, soot, death. My body was black. Mother's eyes. Black was evil. A colour that murdered other colours. But it wasn't just a colour any more. It was a killing force. A force that murdered hope – stole from you. I knew what she meant now. Knew something – however small – of what she'd gone through.

Open-eyed I stared into the nothingness that was somehow all there was. Blackness rolled over me like a never-ending wave. I was trapped inside a belly of black where tar oozed down the walls and slithered across the ground like a giant, black eel.

Darkness. Black. Too much black.

The Eagles' witchy woman song played in my head. Over and over again the same tinny lyrics rotated. With every passing second, my body seemed to float away from my mind, and the only thing that stopped me believing it gone was the mattress under me. If not for that hard slab, I would have thought that I only existed in my head.

I fought to remember images of the woods and the fields, the greenness, the cows and flowers, that beautiful white horse, but black was a fierce enemy. A thief. A murderer. Like Mother. She was the reason I was here. She needed to . . .

'Who's there?' The woman's voice cut in. Shrill. Afraid.

'Me. Polly,' I said quickly, startled into a response.

'Polly? Oh yes . . . I remember. I'm sorry. Your voice woke me.'

'My voice?' *Had I been speaking? Saying my thoughts out loud?*

'You were talking really fast. Saying the word "black" a lot.'

I heard the mattress springs squeal as she shifted her weight. Felt dizzy with relief. She was awake. Together. We could get through this together.

'I'm glad you're awake,' I said, tearful all of a sudden.

She laughed softly, but there was no humour in it. 'I'm glad you're still here. For a moment I thought I'd dreamt you.'

'How long . . .' I hesitated, frightened by what she might say. 'How long have you been down here?'

'I don't know.'

'You don't know? How can that be?'

'Time slips away here. There's no sense of morning and night. Minutes feels like hours. I sleep a lot, but I never feel rested.'

I swallowed a lump of mucus. It slithered reluctantly down my throat. 'I'm so sorry. I can't imagine what you've been through. What you're still going through.'

She didn't say anything, so I gave her time. I shifted my weight. Numbness had started to creep in.

'How old are you, Polly?'

'Thirteen.'

'Shit.'

I jumped at the curse.

'Sorry,' she said.

'It's fine. Shit,' I said, testing the word. It felt good somehow, 'Shit, shit, shit!'

She laughed. This time her laugh sounded more real.

'SHIT!' she shouted.

'SHIT!' I shouted back.

We giggled. After a short while, we fell silent.

'Will you hold my hand?' I said.

'Of course I will.'

Our fingers found each other's and we held hands in the darkness, silent for a time.

'I've never said a swear word before,' I said.

'I hadn't when I was your age. I've said a lot since then though. Sometimes I scream and curse until my throat's raw.'

'How old are you?' I said.

'I was forty when she put me down here.'

Her answer reminded me that she had no idea how long she'd been held captive. It was a horrifying thought. Would I still be here when I was twenty? Twenty-five? Thirty? Forty? Would Mother really do that to me? I couldn't bear to think about it.

Her stomach grumbled. I rested my free hand on my own hollow stomach.

'When did you last have something to eat?' I said, fear trickling down my spine.

She sighed. 'I don't know. Sometimes I think she's trying to starve me to death – then she'll open the roof and put a cup of water and a few scraps of bread on the step.'

'Does she ever talk to you?'

'No. At first I tried to reason with her, but I don't bother any more. She's a cold-hearted monster. Totally insane.'

'Have you ever tried—'

'Escape? Yes. And I nearly died trying.'

'What happened?'

'I must have been here less than a week. I spent my time

working out where everything was. Feeling for anything I could use as a weapon, but there was nothing except for a small table. Back then I was still strong enough to lift it above my head – but only just. I hadn't eaten anything for days and by that point hunger was making me weak.

'I positioned the table on my lap and sat at the top of the stairs for God knows how long, waiting for her to come. I didn't even know for sure that she would come. I was terrified that she was going to leave me here, let me starve.

'But finally she came. I heard scraping above my head, so I grabbed the table and the moment she opened the roof fully – because that's what she used to do – I threw the table as hard as I could through the opening, straight at her.

'But her reactions were too quick – she put out her hands, so the table bounced back into my face. The force sent me tumbling down the steps. I landed awkwardly – *really* awkwardly – and for a while I didn't dare move, thinking I'd broken my neck. She slammed the roof shut, leaving me nothing but a cup of water.

'I lay there sobbing. I was in agony and too scared to move. After a long time, I got up the courage and managed to pull myself into a sitting position. My neck was very sore but not broken.

'She didn't bring me any food for a really long time. I thought I was going to starve to death. Since then I've thought about trying something again, but I'm so weak and I keep having visions of breaking my neck for real.'

'Shit,' I said.

'Yeah. Shit.'

'Did she say anything when she brought you food?'

'Yes. Before she opened the roof she shouted in that she was holding a knife and that if I tried anything, she'd stab me to death then leave me down here to the rats.'

'Rats?' I said, a sick feeling crawling up my throat.

'Yeah. They mostly leave you alone. They frightened me at first, but I'm used to them now.'

Rats. Sneaky, hairy, dirty rats. Rats with sharp, yellow teeth and evil, blood-red eyes.

I shivered. Thought about the cut on my wrist. The blood was congealed now. Did that mean the rats would not be interested or would they be drawn by the scent of quite fresh blood?

She must have felt my reaction because she said, 'Don't worry, Polly. Honestly, you're a lot bigger and scarier to them than they are to you.'

Something soothing about the way she spoke made me wonder if she had children. I opened my mouth to ask, then stopped. If she did have children, what had happened to them? They might have been left alone in their home with no one to care for them. They could have starved to death by now – or maybe Mother had done something to them too. Bringing up the subject didn't seem a sensible thing to do. Not yet anyway.

'Tell me if you don't want to talk about it, OK,' she said, 'but I can't help wanting to know why *you're* down here?'

She asked the question as if she knew why she was down here. Curiosity got the better of me and I blurted, 'Why are *you* down here?'

She laughed – this time a bitter, hard sound. 'Because she's mad. She's always been mad.'

'*Always* been mad? What do you mean? Have you known her for a long time?'

She didn't reply.

Icy fingers of dread unfurled across the back of my neck. 'Your name's Olivia, isn't it? You're her sister. Her twin sister.'

She was the girl in the photographs. The girl on the bed. The girl surrounded by dolls. The girl Mother said was rotten to her core.

The woman inhaled sharply, said, 'How on earth do you know that?'

I took a deep breath, unable to believe it.

'Polly? How do you know my name?' Her voice rushed out of her, urgent and panicky. She let go of my hand and moved closer to me on the bed.

'It's a long story,' I said.

'Tell me,' she urged, finding my shoulders in the dark, her fingers a little too tight. 'Tell me everything.'

Chapter 42

I told her everything, just as she'd asked. As I talked, I was surprised to hear hollowness in my voice, but Olivia made interested noises. Occasionally she gasped or groaned or rubbed my shoulders, while I twisted my hands together in the darkness, glad to be invisible as I tried to slow the storming of my heart. Talking about the past ten years was like inflicting lashes on my own back.

Why did she have to choose me, choose anyone?

Because she's insane.

There was, I told myself, a reason for her madness. There had to be. People weren't born evil – were they?

I sighed. 'I think her brain's all muddled up. I think, sometimes, she believes she really did save me,' I said quietly. 'She wasn't horrible all of the time. Sometimes, when I was little, she played with me, baked cakes with me, read to me at bedtime . . .'

'You're being too generous,' Olivia said.

'What do you mean?'

'You're trying to make excuses for her. Trying to understand her. She told you that you were allergic to light, for Christ's sakes. She stopped you going outside. And now she's locked you in a hole in the ground.'

'I know . . .'

'She's stone-cold crazy, believe me. *I* know – she's always been crazy.'

I said nothing. I didn't want to force Olivia to tell me anything.

Silence flooded the space between us, and my eyes grew heavier and heavier. The darkness pressed down and an irresistible sleepiness teased my mind. It was silent for a long time. I began to drift away.

Olivia sighed heavily. 'Four. We were four when I started noticing something strange about Catherine.'

I jerked upright, eyes wide, suddenly alert. I wanted to know everything. I wanted to understand *her*. Mother. Understand how she could bring herself to do the terrible things she had done.

'Strange?' *Catherine. So that's her name.*

'Yes. Strange. Disturbing. My earliest memory is her twisting the head off a doll then stamping on its face. I think she was angry because she'd been told off. I don't remember the details. She always had a terrible temper.

'Anyway. We didn't get on like twins are supposed to. Catherine hated me. I started to feel it when we were probably around six or seven years old. I'd sense her glaring at me from across the room as I sat on the old bastard's lap. Part of it, I think, was jealousy. I was prettier than Catherine and people commented on it all the time. And the old bastard – almost every day he'd admire me – in front of her. He'd dress us in these ridiculous dresses that looked like something out of a fairy tale, then stand back and say how I looked like an angel. *His* angel. I suppose I should have picked up the warning signs then, but I was too innocent to believe that adults could be so evil.'

'Did you and Catherine go to school?' I said, prompting her to continue.

'We did, for a while.'

'What was she like – at school, I mean?'

Olivia laughed humourlessly. 'Worse than at home.'

'How?'

She paused, took a ragged breath. 'It probably sounds petty but she stole every friend I ever made. And spread nasty rumours about me. Got me in trouble with the teachers. Like I said, it doesn't sound that bad now, but at the time it made my life hell. She bullied other children too. Eventually so many parents complained that the school expelled her.'

'What did he do?'

'Shut her down here for a few days. At the time I thought she deserved worse than that.'

'What was she like when he let her out?'

Olivia fell silent for a moment.

She sighed. 'She was quieter. A lot quieter, come to think of it. And she tried her hardest to please him any way she could. I'd still catch her staring daggers at me, but she spent most of her time – when I was around anyway – with her head in a book.'

'Do you think that's why she's like . . .'

'Like this?' She snorted. She sounded exactly like Mother. A chill crawled across my shoulder blades.

'Yes,' I said, 'I mean, being down here for so long. It must be hard to feel OK after that.'

She snorted again. 'I've no sympathy for her. She didn't have to do what he asked her to.'

'Didn't have to do what?'

She fell silent.

I swallowed and said, 'Did he home-school her?'

'Yes.'

'Like me,' I said.

Olivia seemed not to notice I'd spoken. In a flat voice she said, 'When I was twelve he started to abuse me. It went on for three years until I got pregnant and ran away.'

She was quiet for a long time. I waited. At last, she squeezed my hand so hard it hurt.

'He never, *ever* touched Catherine,' she said, her voice turning hard. 'But she knew – yet she never said anything to anyone.'

I gasped, unable to hide my shock. 'What? She—'

'Yes. Like I said. There's no sense trying to wrap your head round what she's done. What she's done is unforgivable. She's a monster and if I get the chance, I'll kill her.'

Chapter 43

We sat in silence, holding hands.

I groped for words but could not find ones that would do. I longed to know what had happened to the baby, but didn't dare ask. If Olivia felt like telling me, she would.

My tummy churned with hunger and emotion. Part of me wanted to close my eyes, go to sleep and forget everything she had just told me. Another part felt like tearing something to pieces, bashing my fists into the wall. Olivia had suffered so much cruelty and Mother had done nothing to help her. There was no question in my mind that Mother was crazy, but there was also no question in my mind that she was evil too.

'Shit,' Olivia said, 'I shouldn't have told you all that. You'll have nightmares for a month.'

'No, I won't. Don't worry about me. I want to know everything. I need to know.'

'Thanks, Polly.'

'For what?'

'For listening. I've never told anyone about my childhood. Even when I had the abortion and the nurses treated me like shit, I never told them what he'd done.'

'You had an abortion?'

'Yes. I don't feel guilty about it. Not when it was his.'

I didn't know what to say, so I said nothing. Blackness yawned in front of me.

'I'm married now to a wonderful man called Robert and we have twin boys, Andrew and David. They're three.'

'What are they like? Your sons?'

'Lovely. A handful but lovely,' her voice cracked. 'Every time I think about them, my heart breaks.'

I squeezed her hand and gave her a while to compose herself. Finally, questions pushed themselves off my tongue.

'How – er – how did she find you? What happened?' I said, desperate to know but equally desperate to take her mind off her sons. She sounded like she was about to break.

Her voice trembled. She cleared her throat and sniffed. 'I was stupid enough to come back here. I don't know why I did it. I think it was because I finally felt almost normal again. No one told me to do it. I just came. I'd been thinking about doing it for a long time and it was a nice day for April. The boys were at their grandparents' and Robert was at work. Work finished early, so I drove here. I only live an hour's drive away.

'I thought she was gone. All these years I'd created this fantasy that she'd moved to France, like she used to say she would when he was out of earshot. And I wasn't worried about him. I knew he was dead because a friend of his managed to track down my address and send me a letter telling me about the funeral, which of course I didn't go to. I was glad he was dead. Glad that he didn't leave me the house or any money. Ecstatic. It felt like a huge weight had been lifted from my shoulders. Like I was finally free. I think knowing he was dead was what allowed me to open myself up to the idea of falling in love.

'Anyway, where was I? Oh yes. It's my bloody fault I'm here. My stupid idea to come back, face my fears.'

'So you drove right up to the cottage?' I prompted, tasting blood from a torn cuticle.

'Yes. I noticed boards on the windows and thought some homeless person might have holed up inside. I didn't want to go in. I needed to see it; I don't know why – it's hard to explain.

'I got out of my car and wandered up to the front door. The same smells – smells of trees and grass and swamp and pollen – began to overwhelm me, and I started to cry. I couldn't be there. I knew I'd made a mistake – I wasn't ready. Would never be ready. So I turned to go and her car was pulling up behind mine, blocking me in. I froze. She got out of her car and we stared at each other. I was so surprised that I didn't speak. She looked so much older. Thinner, haggard, but those hateful eyes were the same.

'I found my voice and told her I was going. Could she move her car? She didn't reply; just walked towards me with her head tilted to the side in a really odd way and a strange smile on her face.

'I asked her again to move her car, but she ignored me and kept walking over. I asked her to move her car one more time. She didn't say anything, just smirked. I didn't know what to do. She slid her hand into her pocket then raised her hand. She was holding a knife.

'She said something like, "I'm so happy you came back, Sis. It's so great to see you." But I remember thinking that her voice was flat, strange. Disconnected somehow.

'I asked her what the knife was for, but she said nothing. She stopped a yard from me and said, "Your choice: shelter or knife."

'I tried to run past her, but she grabbed my arm and pulled me in front of her, pressing the knife against my throat, cutting into my skin. She pushed me into the back garden and locked me down here.'

I clutched her hands in the dark. 'I'm sorry.'

'You've nothing to be sorry for. I'm only sorry I ever came back. And I told no one where I was going. I've hoped and prayed someone would find my car and track me here, but surely they would have found something by now.'

I let myself imagine being rescued by a kind-eyed, gentle man, someone like Captain Crewe. Imagined the in-pouring of light as he opened the little door and let us out. Imagined the smell of the clean air, and the bright green of the trees. And Mother's face. Mother's angry, red face as she attacked Captain Crewe with her knife. I exhaled shakily and stroked the back of Olivia's hand.

'How's your neck now?' I said.

'It's fine. She only grazed me. It's the hunger that's killing me – and the dark – so much dark. It makes my mind do crazy things.'

'I know,' I said. 'When you were asleep, I began feeling really weird. I was *so* relieved when you woke up. I can't imagine how you've coped being alone down here all this time.'

'My boys. And Robert. They're all that's kept me going. But I'm ashamed to admit I'd started thinking of ways to end it, then you came along. You've saved me, Polly. You really have. Just talking about everything is helping a little.'

'We're getting out of here,' I said.

She said nothing. I could hear her stomach rumbling. The snip, snip, snip as she bit her nails too.

She was silent for a long time. We sat holding hands, both shaking with too many emotions to name.

Finally, she cleared her throat. 'How? How are we getting out of here?'

I didn't reply. I didn't know what to say.

Chapter 44

After braving the disgusting brick toilet I groped my way back to the bed and lay in the dark with my eyes open. Hunger and fear kept me awake, but Olivia slept again. I listened to her long, slow breaths and brought my hand to my lips. My fingers trembled, my mouth felt like it had been dried out with toilet paper and my head banged. Each bang was the fist of someone trapped inside my skull, desperate to get out. Each bang echoed the anger and fear that throbbed in my veins.

I was still running on adrenaline. I knew that and it terrified me. When that adrenaline melted away, fear would beat anger back down into the dirt, and I needed the anger that thrummed in my chest like a bird's wings. Anger gave me courage. Anger was good.

Before my anger could fade, I had to work out what was going to happen, but Mother was so unpredictable that there were too many ways this could go. I closed my eyes and pictured her face, trying to put myself in her position, think how she thought, see the world and Olivia and me through Mother's crazed eyes. Olivia said that their grandfather had never abused Mother, but he had locked her down here, which was a cruel punishment that she had gone on to use on Olivia and then me. That was behaviour she had learned and copied. From what Olivia had told me, I knew their grandfather had been cold, unloving, violent – traits that Mother shared, but Mother could also be caring.

She liked to turn little girls into her vision of the perfect doll; pretty, perfectly put-together, flawless. She liked her dolls to be obedient, quiet and calm. And young. Dolls were only perfect when they were young. That was why I was out. I was growing up and Mother couldn't handle that – but why? If I could solve that puzzle, maybe I could work out how to convince her to let us out. That was if she ever came back with the food and water she'd promised . . . she might decide to let us both starve to death.

I shivered, and shivered again. The dank, moist air was deep in my bones. Though the space was warm, so warm and muggy that I felt like I was inhaling steam, a nasty dampness had tunnelled into my flesh.

My stomach was already beginning to eat itself and I had not been down here for very long at all. It seemed impossible that Olivia had survived this long. She'd said nothing about Mother increasing or decreasing the portions she delivered, so that meant Mother was consistent – but now that I was down here too, would that stay the same or would she make us split one sandwich? Share one cup of water? She was punishing us both, but how far she'd go, I couldn't guess. A tidal wave of uselessness washed over me. It was simply impossible to work out what she would do.

My hand tickled. I flinched violently and squealed, swiping at the place where traces of spider legs lingered. My skin crawled. I shivered again and hugged my knees, rocking back and forth on the bed and telling myself to calm down. Tears leaked down my cheeks and I tasted salt. The taste brought back a sudden memory of crying over the loss of my imaginary friend, Polly. I remembered curling up in bed, hugging myself, weeping quietly for fear *she* would hear me. Even then I had been fearful. At the age of six, just one year older than Emma, I had been frightened and uncertain of her reaction. She had always been unpredictable to me and always would be, but there was a difference now.

I swiped my tears away and sniffed at my runny nose. When I was six, seven, eight, nine, ten, eleven, twelve, I had believed her to be some kind of perfect, all-knowing figure. Up until two weeks ago I had thought her invincible. But now I knew better. She was human and she made mistakes. It was a simple truth I had long known about myself, but I had never known it about her. Humans made mistakes and she was human. She was flesh and blood and bone. She could bleed too.

My lips formed a trembly smile. Shakily, I pushed myself up from the bed. The mattress wheezed and I heard Olivia move. I listened to see if she was awake but her breathing dropped back into its steady rhythm, and I was struck by the calmness of her breaths. In sleep and darkness, the emotions of the sleeping were hidden. I imagined what Olivia's face looked like now, so many years on from the horrific photographs of her on a bed. I pictured the same widely spaced eyes and elfin nose grown larger, wrinkles at the corners of her eyes. The vision was strangely strong and clear, given it was built from memory and imagination.

I thought about poor little Emma and wanted to scream. Was she still out there, lost and alone? And Patrick. What had happened to him? And Dot. What had happened to her? Mother had hit her so hard. Was she OK? Maybe Harold had found her and taken her to a hospital. Maybe not. Maybe that poor old lady was dead. Dead because of *her*.

Anger clenched my jaw and fists, and I strode forward

blindly, snagging my tights on the scraggy brick wall. The material on my left leg tore. I winced at the faint screak of tearing elastic and wondered how far the ladder ran, hoping it had not run all the way to my foot. My tights were another barrier between my bandaged feet and the grimy floor – not to mention the hundreds of spiders that haunted the place. Tights were my protection. My shield. My—

Tights. Tights? Tights . . .

Tights were strong, stretchy . . . tights could be useful . . . somehow.

The hint of an idea scratched at the back of my mind. Something to do with tights. Tights, tights, tights. I stretched and reached desperately for the idea, trying to pull the wafer-thin wisp into the centre of my mind and form it into something whole. I almost had it when Olivia gasped and the sound of metal scraping metal came from the door in the ceiling.

Chapter 45

'She's here,' Olivia whispered.

'I'm going to try to reason with her,' I whispered back, groping my way towards the stairs.

Olivia stayed silent.

My hands found brick and I sidestepped as quickly as I could, heading in the direction of the stairs. Above our heads the door opened a snatch and light winked and glimmered in the opening; one blinding ribbon of brilliant, shocking light that drew me like a bee to honey. Tripping over my feet, I stumbled, righted myself, sidestepped again. My foot found a step and I scrambled upward on my hands and feet.

The door opened several more inches, flooding the first three steps with light.

I glanced back into the gloom, which remained ink-black. 'Come up with me,' I whispered urgently, 'maybe she'll listen to you this time, if she won't listen to me.'

'Fat chance,' came her voice, which now sounded as hard as stone. But her voice sounded closer and I wondered if she'd moved off the bed.

'Please,' I begged.

A hand holding a sandwich lowered itself through the

opening. Food. My mouth began to salivate. I recognized those knuckles, that skin, those nails. It was her. Mother. Who else?

She placed the sandwich on the step, withdrew her hand then lowered another sandwich onto the step beside it. I was overcome with relief: she was evil but not so evil that she would starve two helpless people to death. Hope spiked in my heart. She was not a lost cause. She would listen to one of us, let us reason with her, let us persuade her – and I had one glittering diamond with which to bargain. Something priceless she craved. The diamond was fake, but she didn't know that.

'Mother?' I said.

The hand was lowering a large bowl of water through the gap now, quivering from its weight. The hand stilled an inch from the step, responding to my voice.

She was human. She was only human.

'Mother?' I repeated. I reached out my hand and touched hers. Her skin was papery and hot. Her hand flinched at my touch and water splashed onto the step. I kept my hand on hers, my touch light.

'Mother? Please let me out. I miss you.'

She placed the bowl on the step then withdrew her hand. I almost cried out for fear that she was going to lock us in again, but the door remained open. I raised my head and peered through. I could see her knees. She was kneeling on the ground on the roof of our prison. Behind her I could see lush green grass. I could smell fresh air and grass and pollen and hear a bird tweeting merrily, unaware of the fear and misery happening at its feet.

'Mother?' I said, my heart a throbbing lump in my throat.

'I can't let you out.' Her voice was flat and hard.

'Yes, you can. You can let me out and we can be a family again. I will help with all of the chores around the house and we can keep each other company and dance to the Eagles and—'

'No. That's simply not possible. Not now. Not now that . . .'

'That what?'

'That you know about *her*.'

I knew she was talking about Olivia. I felt a hand on my back and nearly gasped. Olivia was on the step below me. Now that she was there I could feel her heat and smell her sweat. My own sweat was cold and ran down my back. I looked at the sandwich, desperate to eat it.

'I won't tell anyone,' I said, intentionally not saying Olivia's name. Last time I had said her name, Mother had gone mad.

'I know that,' she said. 'But you'll *know*, and I know you, Mirabelle. I know you won't be able to stop yourself from trying to let her out – and that can never happen. She's evil personified. I've already told you that.'

A saying I'd read in a book popped into my head. *Pot. Kettle. Black*. I'd not understood what it meant at the time, but sudden understanding flicked on like a light.

'OK. I understand that, but you *can* let me out. I will be better, better-behaved, and I can help you find Clarabelle.'

The diamond was out there now. It was my only bargaining tool. If she didn't take it, I had no other options.

I held my breath, and her breath hitched. Olivia's hand found my shoulder. It trembled. I could picture Mother frowning, thinking it through, her mouth a grim line, her small, dark eyes narrowed to slits.

'How?' she said slowly, drawing out the word.

This was it. The big lie. 'She told me she was going to hide in the woods, near the cottage, next to this fallen tree we saw.' I nearly added, *when we were running away from you*.

'Which fallen tree? There are hundreds of fallen trees in the woods.'

'There was this huge one that I fell over. I can remember

exactly where it is. It's next to a deep hole in the ground. I can take you there and we can bring Clarabelle home and start afresh and be a happy family, and I can learn how to make dresses and we can make dresses for Clarabelle and—'

'That's enough. Be quiet now. I need to think.'

She let the door fall shut, making me jump.

'Bloody psycho,' Olivia whispered, 'she might actually be buying it.'

'Here,' I said, feeling for a sandwich then turning round to hand it to her.

'Thanks.'

I found the second sandwich and ate it like a wild beast, tearing chunks and chomping on them briefly before swallowing them down into my empty tummy. It was spam, but it was the best thing I'd ever tasted. When I finished the sandwich, I reached for the bowl and tipped water into my mouth, delighting, despite everything, in the deliciousness of the cold, crisp liquid. I was careful not to spill any. If Mother didn't let me out, we would need to make this water last a long time.

Carefully, I passed the bowl to Olivia and heard her drinking hungrily. She moaned with relief and burped. It would have been funny if not for the queasy uncertainty that plagued us. For a time that seemed impossibly long, we sat in silence listening, waiting and hoping she would open the door again, and that her answer would be the one we needed. I bit my nails and prayed to a god I didn't believe in. It was a simple yes or no answer. *Please say yes. Please say yes, please say yes. Please say—*

The door creaked open a few inches. Light shone in, golden and glorious. Birds sang.

'I've given it a long hard thought and I miss you too, Mirabelle. You'll never know just how much. Things have been hard, so hard. I've thought about letting you out hundreds of times. I nearly did once. I came out here and I stared at the shelter. I even pulled the key out of my pocket. I was so close to opening the door and letting you come back inside, but right at the last second I remembered how very badly you behaved, and I realized, as I've come to realize again, just now, that you are not the little girl you used to be. You used to be so pretty and kind and good. Such a good, beautiful little doll, but you've changed. You've developed these strange, wild ideas about me and about yourself. You seem convinced I'm not your mother and it's hurt me very deeply. Too deeply. You've given me a wound that will never ever heal, but worse than that – if that's possible – is that I know you can no longer be trusted. I know you're lying to me about Clarabelle. I know—'

'No, Mother, please. Listen. I'm not lying about her! I promise you I'm not. I know where she is and I'll take you there. I'll—'

'Stop. You're embarrassing yourself now. My goodness, Mirabelle, I've never heard you sound so pathetic. You're a nasty little liar. You're just as bad as her. You're both evil and evil deserves to be punished. Evil, evil, evil, evil!'

A scream-like roar tore itself from Olivia's throat, 'YOU'RE THE EVIL ONE, YOU MONSTER!'

She launched herself at the door like a bull on full charge. I slammed into the wall as she shoved past and watched in horror as she got her head and arms through the gap and reached out for Mother. Mother screamed and shoved Olivia's head back down into the shelter with a force that sent Olivia flying backwards, arms outstretched and flailing for the door opening. With a scream of rage, Mother slammed the door shut, trapping Olivia's right hand.

Olivia gave a blood-curdling scream, 'My fingers! My fingers!'

'Oh no, oh no – what can I do?' I gasped.

We were engulfed by darkness. I groped for her arm and trailed my fingers up towards her trapped hand. Mother was laughing manically on the other side of the door. She was trying to lock it, twisting the key in the lock and laughing but Olivia's fingers were stopping the door from locking.

Olivia screamed.

Still laughing, Mother opened the door an inch and Olivia whipped her hand out with a wretched groan. The door shut and metal scraped metal.

'Evil deserves punishment,' Mother shouted through the door. She banged twice on the wood and crumbs of dirt fell in my eyes.

Olivia moaned, 'My finger . . . is . . . hanging off,' then she slumped onto my lap.

I stared at the place where the light had come in, heart pounding at what felt like two hundred beats per minute. I ought to have been terrified but I wasn't. I was angry, yes. Frightened, a little. But my strongest feeling was excitement.

When the light had shone in it had revealed things inside the shelter that I did not know were here. Things I could use. A plan began to unravel in my mind like thread from a torn dress – or the ladder in a pair of ripped tights. The plan depended on a couple of things going my way, but if they did go my way, it might just work. It might save us.

Chapter 46

The air was full of the sickly-sweet scent of Olivia's blood and her body was like a dead weight. I heaved her off my lap and moved her down the steps as gently as I could, one step at a time. I was glad she was unconscious but worried about how much pain she'd be in when she woke up. I didn't have a clue what we were going to do about her hand. The only way to tell what kind of damage had been done would be to touch her hand, which would be agony for her. Her words rang in my mind, *hanging off*. Could shutting your hand in a door make that happen? Had Olivia imagined that or was her finger really hanging off? There was nothing down here to clean and bandage her hand with. Nothing to kill the pain. She was going to be in a lot of pain when she woke up.

Olivia was light so I was able to haul her onto the bed. I covered her with the bedcovers then perched on the edge of the mattress and took off my tights. My letter to my parents dropped onto the floor and I hoped my parents would never need to read it.

I was unable to rid my head of the hideous sound of

Mother's laugh. I still couldn't believe she'd laughed. It was like she'd enjoyed her sister's pain.

My jaw clenched. I tried to focus on that laughter and how only an evil person could laugh like that. Only an evil person could do all of the things she had done. She had hurt other people but she had also hurt me very badly and I would stop her from doing anyone any more harm.

I slipped my right hand into the sock part of my tights, then wrapped the tights round my four fingers as many times and as tightly as I could. Easing myself off the bed so as not to rock the mattress and disturb Olivia, I shuffled my way back to the steps. Beneath my bandaged feet the ground was gritty with dirt and who knows what else, but I didn't focus on that. I found the steps quickly now that I was getting to know my way around.

In my mind's eye I pictured the place I'd seen the nail. It had been in the wall on the left of the door in the ceiling. Buried deep in the brick, but not in completely. I needed that nail. It had been a big, long one – the longest, thickest nail I'd ever seen – and covered in rust, but it would do the job. If I could get it out of the wall.

I climbed to the third from top step and felt the wall with my left hand. Rough brick, rough brick, rough brick . . . metal! Scooting my bottom close to the wall, I grabbed the rusted nail with my tight-bandaged hand and begin to twist with all my might. Tears ripped through the outer layer of the tights quickly but despite my efforts, the nail did not turn. The layering was too thick. It was protecting my fingers but it was also preventing me from working out the nail. I unwrapped three of the layers and tried again. No luck. Unwrapped another three. Tried again. Yes, I could get a grip on the nail now, but after ten twists my fingertips were beginning to burn. I kept twisting and tried wobbling the nail from side to side. I twisted and twisted, wobbled and wobbled. It didn't budge. I kept going, gritting my teeth against the pain, knowing I had to keep trying. I felt wetness between my fingertips and the nail and knew my fingers were bleeding, but I couldn't stop. I kept at it until my fingertips throbbed and I felt like I was going to throw up. I was about to stop when I felt it turn. Only once, half the way round – a tiny amount, but enough to make me carry on.

I was sipping water from the bowl when Olivia moaned. I didn't know whether to be happy or scared that she was conscious.

'Polly! Help me – my finger – oh God, my finger.'

'Hold on. I'm coming.'

I carried the bowl down the steps and made my way back to the bed.

'You have to find something. Something to tie it on,' she said.

'Tie it on?'

Her breaths were fast and ragged. 'My finger. It's hanging off.'

'Which finger?' I said as calmly as I could.

'My index finger.'

I couldn't use my tights. I needed them, plus they were covered in muck, sweat and blood which wouldn't be good if she was right and her finger was actually hanging off. I racked my brain. I was wearing knickers and a dress. Nothing else. Both were dirty now.

'What can I use?' I said.

'I don't know. Oh God. It hurts so much. I'm losing a lot of blood. We need to stop the bleeding.'

'What are you wearing?' I said.

She moaned. 'Oh no – I'm going to be sick!' And she was. I felt something wet splatter my leg.

'Have you got a T-shirt on that I can tear up to make some kind of a bandage? I can use a little of our water to clean it.'

'Yeah. But I can't move my hand. I can't. You'll have to use my jeans. Pull them off.'

'No – what are we talking about – I can use some of the sheet, can't I?'

She moaned her agreement. The pain seemed to be getting harder to bear.

Quickly, I knelt on the ground by the foot-end of the bed, picked up the bed sheet and tried to tear it. It wouldn't work. I put it between my teeth and tore a strip off. Then another.

Olivia was muttering words I couldn't make sense of, moaning all the while. I dipped the first strip in the water and gently felt for her arm. She groaned.

'I'm going to clean it now,' I said.

'No, no, no, don't touch it! It's too painful,' she was crying.

'I have to. Like you said. We have to at least bandage it.'

She screamed when I took hold of her palm, which was caked with blood. I felt her thumb, which was fine. My fingertips drifted to the right and then I felt it: a wet, fleshy stump. There was no finger attached any more, and I wondered uneasily where it was. I dabbed the stump with the sheet and she screamed again. Vomit rose in my throat. I tasted sick.

'OK, OK. I won't clean it. I'm going to bandage it as quickly as I can. Squeeze the mattress with your other hand and scream as much as you need to.'

I didn't know how tightly to wrap it round her hand so I veered on the side of caution and didn't wrap it too tightly. She moaned and moaned and writhed around on the bed. I touched the bandage and felt blood soaking through.

'It needs more,' I said. I tore several strips off the sheet, trying not to think about how filthy they were, then wrapped and tied, wrapped and tied until I couldn't feel any moisture soaking through.

'It's done,' I said, close to tears and suddenly shattered.

She continued to moan. I helped her drink water from the bowl then told her to try to get some sleep.

I fell asleep on the floor not long after and had a nightmare about Mother painting my face with blood.

Olivia drifted in and out of consciousness as I worked on extracting the nail from the wall. I couldn't tell how much time had passed since Mother had left, but it felt like a very long time. I was plagued by hunger again, there was only an inch of water left in the bowl and the fingertips on my left hand were raw bloody nubs. But I kept at it with few breaks, changing hands when one felt too sore to twist the rusted nail. Wobbling the nail seemed to help; little by little I felt the thin metal rod edge out from its brick prison. That was one thing that kept me going. Another was the fact that Olivia's hand felt strangely hot. When I hovered my hand above hers, heat radiated off it. And it was beginning to smell. It was a putrid smell. Did that mean it was infected? Did it mean she was dying? I thought about her twin boys and her husband and how devastated they would be if she died, and I twisted the nail harder. I thought about Derek. He shouldn't have died. He wasn't a nice man, but he didn't deserve to die. I thought about Emma and hoped she had found her parents – or at least someone kind who could help her find them. I pictured Harold finding Dot and taking her to the hospital. I prayed she was alive. Prayed she made a full recovery. Lastly, I thought about Patrick and hoped he was still alive. I had barely known him, but he had been a good man and he'd tried to help us. Did he have people out in the world who were worried about him? Did he have a wife or children or a mother and father? If he did, they would be going through hell right now. They would not know what had happened to him, what Mother had done to him. They wouldn't know he was a hero. Mine and Emma's hero. If I ever did get out of here I would make it my mission to find Patrick's family and tell them how brave he'd been.

Olivia groaned so I rushed back to the bed.

'Water,' she croaked.

I lifted the bowl to her mouth and helped her sip.

'Careful. There's not much left now,' I murmured, but she seemed not to hear me. I tried to move the bowl away but she grabbed it with her unharmed hand and held it fast. I was surprised by her strength.

'I have to tell you something,' she rasped, 'before I die.'

'You're not going to die. She'll come back soon and—'

'She's not coming back,' Olivia said.

'Yes, she is. She always comes back. You told me she comes back with food and water. She came back before, she'll come back again.'

'It's too late. And I need to confess something. Something I've been holding in for a long time. Something I'll never forgive myself for.'

'Don't be silly. You need to rest. You need to sleep. Sleep now, OK?'

'No. Polly, you need to know . . . what I did.'

I shushed her and took the empty bowl away, placing it on the floor beside the bed. I didn't want her getting worked up. I patted her leg gently then went back to work on the nail, checking that my tights were still in position. When Mother came back, I would be close enough to grab the tights and carry out my plan. I only hoped I could get the nail out first.

Chapter 47

My fingers screamed. I took a breath, bit down on my lip and wrenched the nail out.

It was in my fingers now. I'd got it out. I'd done it.

Relief soared through me, making me feel like I was flying. Grinning, I tore off a strip of sheet and wrapped up my fingertips, glad for once that I couldn't see anything down here. If I could see what my fingers looked like, I might not have continued working on the nail, because now that I had it clutched in my sweaty palm, pain slashed at my fingers.

Fear rose and stamped on my relief. I began to wonder if it had been worth all the pain and effort. If Olivia was right and Mother never came back, my fingers would probably get infected and I'd die too.

Olivia was convinced she was going to die. If I didn't get her out of here soon, I knew she'd die. The stink of rot emanated off her hand in putrid waves and her body pulsed with unnatural heat. She'd tried again to tell me something but I'd silenced her. She needed to save her energy. I did too.

I got in position on the fifth from top step and pulled the

tights taut. I had tied the tights around the inner handle of the door – the handle I had seen when Mother had come. The handle I had known would be our saviour, if things went to plan.

My muscles cramped so I shifted position for the tenth time. I couldn't afford to move from the step. If Mother came back, I had to be here, ready. This was my only plan. There was no plan B. Plan A had to work or Olivia would die and I would be next. I could already feel the cuts on my bloodied fingertips and bitten wrist beginning to itch, burn and swell. Soon there would be pus and the rats would come.

I waited. Shifted position again. *She has to come soon. She has to.* Blackness tugged on my eyelids. I could not remember the last time I'd slept. I battled and battled against the urge to drift into delicious sleep and I won, for a time . . .

'She's here!' Olivia's voice hit my brain like a hammer.

My eyes flew open.

Metal scraped metal. I pulled the tights taut just as Mother began to tug on the door in the ceiling. She was strong but I was in a better position and prepared. My arm muscles clenched and I held fast to the tights as she tried and tried to open the door. I waited one more second. She had to be using maximum effort for this to work. I bit my lip and prayed again to a god I did not believe in, then I let go of the tights.

The door flew open and light burst into the blackness. Olivia gasped. I raced up the steps and out, out into the outside. Blinded, I raised the nail. Mother had fallen onto her back – just as I'd hoped. Sandwiches littered the ground. She was stunned and spluttering furiously, but she was already trying to stand. I threw myself onto her and straddled her ribs. Without hesitating, I stabbed the nail deep into her upper arm. She screamed and her eyes went wide with shock and pain. I pulled out the nail and tried to stab again but she roared and rolled over, sending me sprawling onto my side in the long grass.

She crawled away from me. I scrambled to my feet and chased her, nail raised. I jumped onto her back and wrapped my left arm around her throat. She seemed possessed by inhuman rage and tossed me off her back. I hit the ground like a rag doll and she turned and grabbed my wrists and straddled me.

'Stop,' she panted.

I struggled against her, writhing and thrusting and kicking out my legs, but she had me pinned. Still I thrashed and thrashed. I was possessed and I wasn't giving in. Her hands squeezed my wrists so painfully that I nearly dropped the nail. Somehow I clung on to it. Sweat from her stringy hair dripped into my face when she shook her head. I tried not to focus on her glaring eyes, instead shifting my gaze to the blue sky and sparkling sun – so much beauty. My lungs burned. I could not go back in the shelter.

I stopped struggling and turned my face to the side, forcing my body to go limp. I made tears come and fake-cried, made my chest heave with desperate sobs. She loosened her grip on my wrists and I brought up my knees and smashed them into her stomach. She made an 'oomph' sound and rolled onto her side. I sprang to my feet and ran. My plan was to lead her away from the cottage into the woods to the spot I remembered from before.

She chased me, screaming, sounding like a demonic beast. She was a beast. A dangerous, crazy beast.

I glanced back and saw her holding something that glinted in the sunlight. A knife. She always carried a knife. I still clutched my nail, now bloody with her blood, but a nail was nothing compared to a knife.

I was shaking, legs wobbling like jelly, heart rattling about in my chest like shattered glass, but I made my arms pump, made my legs move. I had never run so fast. I was a wild bird flying through the trees. The thought gave me strength. I ran on, jumping and dodging, thorns tearing at my bare legs, the torn bandages on my feet trailing behind me like intestines ripped from a fresh kill.

The canopy above blinked light and birds cried out in horror, branches rustling as they scattered in fear.

'MIRABELLE! STOP!'

I looked back. She was gaining on me. Catching up. Hair wild, eyes crazed.

I ran on, looking for the place that would save me, hoping I had remembered it properly, and then I saw something up ahead. A body. A body on the ground. I slowed down. Stared.

It was Patrick. Slumped up against a tree, his chin on his chest, eyes closed. Blood pooled around him. Caked him. Was he dead? I stopped. Maggots swarmed around his injured side. Flies buzzed in and out of the wound. His face was grey, his body was still. Dead. Patrick was dead.

A sob caught in my throat, but I was nearly there. Mother was still coming after me. I could hear her thrashing through the wood. I was too scared to look around, too scared to see how close she was to me.

I gritted my teeth. Gulped in air. I had to keep going. I had to find the place I'd seen before.

I ran.

Everything was a blur. Everything was strange yet familiar. There was no air. Fear strangled my lungs and panic pushed out every thought but somehow, through all the madness, I remembered where it was. I saw trees I recognized, clumps of moss, a clump of white fungi. And I knew. I knew I was close.

'Mirabelle.'

I whirled around. She stood a few yards away, chest rising and falling, eyes dark.

'Get back!' I screamed, waving my nail wildly.

I stumbled, nearly fell, regained my balance. She stepped forward and raised the knife. Her shoulder dripped blood. Her white blouse turned redder with every passing second. We stared at each other.

'I don't want to hurt you but you've left me no choice,' she said. Her eyes remained on mine. Her chest heaved.

I inched backwards. My heart began to slow. I smiled and said nothing, just carried on edging backwards. She followed and tilted her head to the side. Her eyes narrowed and she glared murder.

'Stop now. Listen to Mother.'

I continued to shuffle away from her, then I stopped, anger rushing through me. 'You deserved what your grandfather did to you. You deserved to be shut in there for a bit after what you did to Olivia.'

She barked out a laugh. 'I thought I raised you to be brighter than this.'

I frowned, confused. 'What do you mean?'

Her eyes clouded and glazed over. She spoke slowly, as if recalling a long-buried memory, 'He didn't just shut me in that one time. He did it many, many times.

'And she . . . she took *everything* from me. And he gave her everything and she loved it. Lorded all of her dolls over me. Bragged about how many she had. So beautiful, so perfect in Grandfather's eyes, but evil, and so, so, so spoiled.

'Did you know she got me expelled? Told the teachers I was bullying other children. But it was lies. All of it. And Grandfather was worried I wouldn't learn my lessons, that I was bad because of what she made him think I'd done, so he shut me down there every day to teach me a lesson. Oh yes, every day from the moment I turned thirteen. Every day for three years. And I learned all right. And you'll learn too.'

I shook my head, trying to process her words, knowing from the dreadful flatness in her voice that she was telling the truth about her grandfather. What that man had done to both of them was monstrous. Too horrible to imagine. Impossible to imagine. Who, I wondered, was telling the truth about Mother getting expelled? Mother or Olivia?

But it didn't matter. Not now. Only one thing mattered now.

Mother was eyeing the nail in my hand. She took a small step forward.

'Just let me leave,' I said, inching back. 'I'm not your daughter. Let me go home to my real parents. Let me go home.'

She rolled her eyes. Took another step.

'Don't,' I said.

She stayed where she was and jabbed the knife at me, each jab punctuating a syllable. 'I'm not perfect. What mother is? But you, Mirabelle – *you* were supposed to be perfect. You were supposed to be mine. My perfect little doll. Someone for me and only me. A perfect little doll I could raise as my own, a darling little creature who didn't need anyone else except for me. I wanted to give you everything I never had and I couldn't let the outside world spoil you like it spoiled her. I wanted to keep you safe. You understand that, don't you, Mirabelle? I've been doing all of this to protect you. I saved you from those evil people in the outside world. I saved you from a life of cruelty and lies. I saved you, Mirabelle.'

'I'm not Mirabelle. My name's Polly.'

She seemed not to hear me. She stabbed again. Only two yards away now. 'But you ruined that. All my efforts to make you the perfect little doll, and what do you do? Betray me.

Sneak around behind my back. Make up foul, hurtful lies about me. Try to leave me. Convince Clarabelle of your lies, make her turn on me too.'

'It's not lies,' I said through gritted teeth. 'It's the truth. You kidnapped me ten years ago, then two weeks ago you took Emma. You know that's the truth.'

'No! You lie. You're evil, just like Olivia. As soon as age claimed you, you changed, just like she did. First, you hid things from me, then you snuck behind my back, and then you tried to manipulate Clarabelle into liking you more than me and having vile thoughts about me, exactly like Olivia did with Grandfather.'

She laughed nastily. 'Well, it came back to haunt her, didn't it? When he finally succumbed to his darkest urges and acted on them, she came running to me – begged me to help her, but I didn't. I couldn't. She didn't deserve my help. She did it to herself. She ruined my life.

'And then,' her breath hitched and her eyes shone with madness, 'then, she got pregnant and instead of having the baby and giving it to someone like me who would love and care for it and give it everything it needed, she got an abortion. She *killed* her own baby.'

She clutched her stomach as if in pain. Misery dragged down her features.

I shook my head. 'She needed your help. She was only twelve when he started hurting her. You could have helped her. Even though she was mean to you, you *should* have helped her. You knew what was happening and you did nothing. You could have told someone. Anyone. She was too scared to speak up. She told you because she needed your help.'

She acted like she hadn't heard me. 'Rotten. That's what she is. That's what you all are.' Her eyes became glittering jewels of black hatred and she advanced quickly.

‘Get back!’ I screamed, but she kept coming, moving faster, holding the knife high so that it caught the light.

‘You have to be punished. You were never going to learn your lesson; I see that now.’

She lunged forward with an unearthly scream that echoed round us. The knife came. Long and lethal. The knife she used to slice through raw meat.

I threw myself to the side, hit ground, saw momentum carry her forward then down, down, down into the place I remembered.

Her body thwacked hard earth and I thought I heard bones crack. She gave a bitter, twisted screech.

I rolled onto my hands and knees and crawled to the edge of the hole. It was deeper than Mother was tall. Cube-like in shape, its steep walls were formed out of dark soil. She lay on her side on a bed of green and yellow leaves, her greasy hair snaking out around her head like Medusa’s serpents in the myth. Both of her legs were bent at awkward angles. The knife was planted in her thigh. Blood bloomed and spread around her like lava on snow, puddled in the leaves and seeped into the soil. She looked like a bleeding scarecrow. She stared up at me, eyes glistening, and raised one arm.

‘Mirabelle, please help me. Please help Mother. Mother needs you. Mother loves you.’

Tears filled my eyes.

I turned to go.

‘Mirabelle! Don’t you dare! Come back! Help me! Help Mother!’

I turned back and looked down at her crumpled body and dark, crazed eyes. More blood oozed from her leg onto the fallen leaves, turning them black.

I sighed. In a low, steady voice I said, ‘My name’s not Mirabelle and you’re not my mother.’

Chapter 48

I edged away from the hole and collapsed.

For a long time – too long – I knelt on the damp soil and stared at a tree, my body racked with shivers. Mother continued to cry for my help. I put my hands over my ears and rocked back and forth and attempted to block out her voice, but it was useless.

When I thought I could stand without passing out, I pushed myself to my feet and turned my back on her. I tried to ignore her screams, but they chased me like thunder, rolling closer and closer as I stumbled further and further away.

With screams ringing in my ears, I moved on, running, knowing I had to be quick. Olivia was bleeding. She was also starving. If I didn't help her reach a hospital soon, she was going to die.

My body shook all over. My knees wobbled and my heart throbbed, but I kept moving. I didn't look back even though she still called to me, her voice echoing through the wood like a howling spirit, tempting me to return.

But I wouldn't go back and help her out of the hole. I needed to move on. I needed to get back to the garden and help Olivia.

I paused to catch my breath and leaned against an upturned tree. Mother's voice stopped abruptly. I exhaled with relief then sucked in a breath; was she dead? Visions flitted through my mind. Had an animal jumped into the hole? Was it tearing her to pieces? Was it eating her alive? Patrick had said there weren't wolves in England any more, but there were bound to be other creatures stalking the woods. Creatures turned mad by hunger. Creatures starving enough to feast on a helpless human being.

I tried to swallow and saliva stuck on my tongue. It was like I'd forgotten how to swallow. Panic bit and I tried to relax my mouth. I tried again and this time it worked and saliva slithered down my throat.

I looked back and strained my ears for her voice, but the trees were thick with silence. Dusk melted them into each other, creating a ghostly army dressed in grey. I swallowed with difficulty. Imagined a badger tearing a chunk of flesh out of Mother's hand – a hand that had stroked my head when I was poorly. A hand that had kept me clean and fed for years.

I bowed my head as memory after memory of me and Mother swept through my mind. She was crazy, yes, but for years she had taken care of me. For years she had been my mother.

I didn't want to face her again, but I couldn't let her die down there. Not like that. I knew I'd never forgive myself.

I pushed myself off the tree and looked back the way I'd come. Though pale grey, there was still enough light to see the way. I scanned the ground and spotted a large branch. Whether it was big enough to fend off an animal, I didn't know, but it was better than a nail.

Knowing speed was important, I ran back through the trees, eyes darting up and down, heart frantic. I couldn't believe I was going back to help her, but I knew I had to.

I'd never forgive myself if I didn't. And I couldn't let myself become like her. She hadn't helped Olivia because Olivia had been horrible to her, but she should have helped her when she was at her weakest. If she'd helped her, everything might have turned out differently.

Besides, she didn't pose any threat any more, so the least I could do was help her out of the hole then give her something to protect herself with while I went to help Olivia.

It didn't take long to reach the hole. I crept up to the edge and peered down.

She was gone.

Chapter 49

Spiders' legs crawled across my neck. I scanned the silvery trees. Listened. The wood lay silent and still. Shivers criss-crossed my spine. I looked back down at the hole. Blood darkened the leaves and soil, turning the ground purple-black. One side of the cube-shaped well had caved in a little, its wall crumbling and full of stab marks.

She must have pulled the knife out of her leg then used it to help drag herself up and out of the hole.

A trail of blood led away from the hole, further into the woods. I followed the path as far as I could with my eyes, but it was soon swallowed by shadows.

I wondered how she had the strength to haul herself out of the ground like that. Her legs had been bent at strange angles; I'd thought they were broken, but they obviously weren't. I bit my lip, annoyed that I'd wasted time going back to help her.

I looked down. I'd dropped the branch. I picked it up. If Mother came after me, I could use the branch to defend myself, but I doubted that she would have the energy to do more than sit and wait for help. I told myself to relax; it was good she was out of the hole – she could defend herself from wild animals much better now, but she was too weak to come after me, too injured to do anything but crawl. She was harmless.

For a moment, I hesitated, stunned by the calmness of my thoughts. Despite everything, I was using logic to survive. I thought about my trick with the tights and smiled; how clever of me to come up with something like that.

Hope lifted my shoulders and I ran away from the hole, back towards the cottage. I had made it this far – I could make it to the end. I could help Olivia reach a hospital and I could make it to the police. I wouldn't give up. I would keep going until I found my parents. My real parents. Jane and Peter Dalton. My MUMMY and DADDY. The words sounded so special. So magical – like they ought to be written in capital letters.

Fear nibbled and gnawed when I thought about how they might react to me, but an explosion of happiness came when I imagined seeing them. At the same time, my need to see them was so strong I worried my heart would pop out of my chest and fly into the sky like the kites in *Mary Poppins*.

As I weaved in and out of the trees, I entertained myself with exciting questions. Did I look like them? Did I have my mummy's nose and my daddy's eyes? I'd always thought how unlike Mother I looked. In books, sons and daughters usually resembled their parents in some way or other . . . it had been another clue that I had missed. Another clue that she had not been my real mother.

What would have happened if I had realized earlier, when I was nine or ten? Would I have known what to do?

No. You'd have done or said something stupid and she'd have punished you. Badly.

It was a horrible thought. One that made me feel sorry for my younger self. I had been so trusting, so willing to believe her lies. It also made me think that it was just as well I hadn't realized the truth until now. Though I had never stepped foot outside the cottage until recently, I had read and learned enough of the outside world to survive. If I had escaped sooner, I probably wouldn't have known how to cope in the real world. And now I was free, and I was going to see my real parents for the first time in ten years.

Excitement bubbled up inside me. I ran on and jerked to a stop as a black board slid down over every happy thought. It was Patrick. Patrick's body.

I glanced around and saw a large leaf. I picked it up and placed it gently over his face, shivering as I did, unable to look at him. A sweet-sick smell filled the air around his body. Flies buzzed. I stumbled away and headed for the back garden.

'Olivia? Olivia? It's me.'

The garden was empty. Nothing but wild, tangled grass filled the space. I hurried over to the door in the ground, knelt down and called her name again. The idea of going back down there was chilling, but if Olivia was still in the hole, I had to get her out.

'Olivia? Are you in there?'

I heard a groan and looked around. There, sitting on the ground, leaning against the back wall of the cottage, sat Olivia.

I rushed through the high grass and sank to my haunches beside her. She cradled her wounded hand in her lap. Her eyes were pink from crying. This was the first time I'd seen her. She looked like a prettier, skinnier version of Mother. Although I knew it wasn't her, the similarity of their appearance brought bile to my throat.

'Can you walk?' I said.

'You're alive,' she said, 'I thought you were dead. I thought she was coming back to kill me.'

Her chin trembled and fresh tears trickled down her cheeks.

She was milk-white and smelled worse than before, sort of un-human.

'Come on. I'll help you walk. We need to get going. She's injured and I think she's harmless, but I don't know where she is.'

I slipped my arm under Olivia's shoulder blades and almost gasped. Her bones stuck out like shards of glass.

'Where're we going?' she croaked.

'To the closest house.'

She shook her head. 'It's too far. I'll never make it.'

'No, it's not. There's this farmhouse I found before, Knackers Yard. There's a telephone inside. We can use that and call the police.'

'I don't think I can walk.'

'You can. Lean on me.' I helped her stand.

Despite her thinness, I struggled to hold her up. We tottered to the side and almost fell.

'See?' she said.

'You can't let her win,' I said, trying to think. 'There must be a way . . .'

Her head snapped up. She looked at me, eyes alert. 'Her car! If we can find her keys, I can drive us to the hospital.'

I frowned. 'She kept all of her keys on her belt.'

'But she must have a spare somewhere. Everyone has a spare car key.'

'OK,' I said, trying to hide the doubt in my voice. I'd looked for keys before and only found the one that opened Mother's bedroom door. I thought hard and realized that when Patrick had tried to help us get out of the cottage and I'd searched her bedroom for the front and back door keys, I'd been in a frantic rush and had searched quickly – so quickly that I could have missed a small key. Besides, a lot had happened since then. She could have moved everything around. Maybe there was a spare car key in her bedroom. I concentrated, racked my brain. Other places that seemed likely hiding spots that I'd never searched properly were the attic and Emma's bedroom.

Thinking about Emma sucked the air out of my lungs. An image of her drowning in mud scuttled around my mind like a black beetle.

'Polly? We need to move.'

'Sorry,' I said, helping her towards the back door.

Dread at going back inside the cottage made me stop. Nausea raced up my throat and saliva pooled on my tongue. I turned away and threw up all over the wall.

Chapter 50

I stared at the back door. It was wide open as if beckoning me back inside. I shook my head at Olivia.

'It's going to be OK,' she said, 'I'm with you. We'll be in and out in a matter of minutes.' She sucked in a sharp breath. Her face trembled.

'I can't,' I said.

'Polly, look at me. You *can*. You *must*. I can't wait much longer and you can't leave me in case—'

'I'll run. I'll run as fast as I can to Knackers Yard and call the hospital. I know the way. I know the numbers to press. I'll be really quick and—'

Tears filled her eyes. She looked up at the sky. I followed her gaze; dark clouds that looked like bruises crowded the very top. Below them sat an orangey-pink colour; a shade so delicate and unusual I couldn't tear my eyes away. The sun was hidden behind the dark clouds as if scared to come out.

'What if she comes back and you're not here to help me?' Olivia said. 'I'm too weak to run. I can't fight her, not in this state. Please. We have to go inside and find her keys. We have to do it now.'

I thought about Mother hurting Olivia, maybe even killing her like she'd killed Patrick and Derek, and my gut churned. A cold sweat broke out over every inch of my skin, but I nodded and helped Olivia up the small step into the kitchen.

As soon as my foot touched the floor, gloom seeped into my mouth, down my throat and deep inside my heart, making it race so fast I thought I was going to pass out.

Sensing my fear, Olivia held my arm and I clung onto her fragile frame. She murmured reassuring things and my feet moved, and then I was guiding her through the room as quickly as possible, somehow managing to stay upright, my gaze locked on the ground, my breathing shallow and fast.

Focusing on my feet, I hurried her down the hallway. We reached the foot of the stairs and Olivia used the banister and my support to drag herself up each step, her grunts of pain and the creaking floorboards creating an unsettling melody that made me shiver.

On the landing, I flicked on the light and led her to Mother's bedroom. Out of the three rooms where she might be keeping a spare car key, I thought her bedroom was the most likely. She nearly always kept it locked. It might have been to stop me from seeing her crazy doll display, but it also might have been to stop me from finding any other keys. Or something else too horrible to name.

To my surprise, her bedroom was unlocked. I realized she'd probably stopped bothering to lock it when she moved me into the hole in the back garden.

I tried Emma's old room and that too was unlocked.

'I can kneel on the floor and search through drawers and behind things,' Olivia said. 'As long as I'm not standing, I think I'll be able to help look for the key.'

'OK. You look in here. I'll look in Mother's room. If we don't find it in either of those, I'll have to look in the attic. And if I don't find it up there, we'll have to look downstairs.'

It was a struggle to speak without crying. My body seemed to have frozen, making my movements stiff and jerky. I knew it was because I was back inside the cottage. Back in the dark. Back outside Mother's bedroom.

She nodded and I left her kneeling in Emma's room rummaging through the drawers of the little white desk, looking as though she might faint at any moment.

I paused, took a breath and wiped sweat from my forehead. I didn't want to be in the cottage again. I definitely didn't want to go back inside Mother's most private place. A place that could contain more horrific displays of craziness that would stay in my head for the rest of my life.

'Hurry!' Olivia's voice was quiet but urgent.

I jumped, exhaled a shivery breath and entered the room.

Chapter 51

I tried not to breathe in the scent of her, but the smell found a way in. Orange-blossom soaked into my skin, drifted into my eyes and oozed up my nose. It was like a toxic mist with a mind of its own. I could taste her, feel her presence in the room even though she wasn't there.

I dry-heaved then dropped to my knees, lay on my front and edged as close to the bed as possible. With trembling fingers I lifted the valance and peered underneath. Unlike before, I took my time and scanned every part of the space. When darkness prevented me from seeing further, I crawled around to the side of the bed and checked under there. I moved to the back of the bed and there, tucked right at the back against the wall, was a small box. I couldn't believe my luck. I lay on my front again and stretched my arm under. My fingers hit the edge of the box, but I was too far away to pull it towards me. I turned my face and pressed my cheek to the carpet. Like that, I could wriggle under and get hold of the box.

Dust matted the carpet. I sneezed and wriggled my upper body underneath. My hand connected with the box and I managed to pull it closer. I wriggled back out and pulled the box with me.

Hot from the effort, I swiped my brow, sat cross-legged and tried to open the box, which was made of bronze and very simple with no markings or decoration at all. At first, the lid seemed glued on, but after a few moments, I managed to use my nails to prise it open.

Inside the box was one photograph and a very small piece of fine, black hair. Nothing else. I picked up the picture and brought it close to my face. The photograph was of a baby with its eyes closed. There was no colour in the baby's face. It was wrapped up in a pale pink blanket.

I turned the photograph over. On the back in Mother's writing it said *Annabelle. 3.3lbs. Born 1/3/63. Died 1/3/63.*

Gently, I replaced the photograph in its box. I looked at the tiny curl of hair. It must have belonged to the baby. *Mother's dead baby.* I shook my head. Mother had given birth to a baby girl? Was that why she'd done all of this – because her little girl had died? I touched the black curl. The hair was so soft, so silky. My heart hurt for the baby, for me and Emma and Olivia, but also a very tiny bit for her. For Mother. A sick feeling swirled in my tummy as I wondered about the baby's father. Had Mother been attacked too? I closed my eyes, unable to look at the little curl of hair. I didn't want to feel sorry for her. I wanted to hate her.

I shut the lid. She had suffered, but she had made me and Olivia suffer. It was all so complicated that my brain hurt trying to understand it. Maybe I would never be able to understand it. But at least she wasn't trying to hurt me any more. She was alone in the woods, bleeding and hurt.

Focus on finding the key. Stop thinking about her.

'Any luck?' Olivia's voice was just loud enough for me to hear.

'No. Not yet,' I shouted.

'Me neither,' she said, 'I've looked everywhere.'

'I still need to check the rest of her room. I'll come get you and you can help me look in here.'

I left the box on the carpet beside the bed and pushed myself to my feet. Swaying with exhaustion, I left the room and helped Olivia out of Emma's bedroom. As we crossed the landing, I stopped mid-step.

'Did you hear something then?' I said.

Olivia frowned. She was so pale she could have been a ghost. 'No. I don't think so.'

We hovered on the landing and listened for another minute. There wasn't any sound. I looked at her and shrugged.

She shrugged back and said, 'We're paranoid.'

I helped her into the room and onto the floor in front of the small bookcase beside the bed. She began pulling off books with difficulty, using only her uninjured hand, her pace slow, every movement a struggle. Her other hand rested limply on her thigh.

'Are you sure you can do this?' I said, forcing myself to approach the wardrobe.

She nodded, her mouth a grim line.

I took a deep breath and stared at the wardrobe. The doors were closed, but I'd seen what hung behind. I didn't want to see them again. I didn't want Olivia to see Mother's twisted dolls either. I hoped she would be too focused on searching the bookcase to look around.

My hands found the doorknobs and began to pull. A thud made me turn around. Olivia was lying on the floor. I dashed across the room. I couldn't see her chest moving. I put my ear to her chest and waited.

After what seemed like for ever, I heard her heart beat. With a huge sigh, I laid her down on the floor so she was in a less awkward position then stared down at her unconscious body, not sure what to do next. I wondered how long it would take for her to wake up. If I found the car key, I needed her to be awake.

I pulled a pillow off the bed and slid it under Olivia's head. Her skin was cold and clammy so I covered her with the duvet then hesitated, lost and confused, not sure whether to keep looking for the key or try to wake her up. I knelt back down and gave her a gentle shake but she didn't stir.

Thinking a little water splashed on her face might help to wake her, I left the bedroom and stepped onto the landing, pausing at a creak.

Dread seized my neck. I froze. Listened as another creak and then another cut the quiet in half like a blade.

Unable to stop myself, I went to the banister and peered over the top.

Chapter 52

It was her. She was almost at the top of the stairs, dragging herself up on her hands and knees, her face veiled by hair and blood.

'Mirabelle,' she rasped.

Her arm flashed out and shot between the banister poles; fingers latched onto my ankle and wrapped around the bone. I cried out and tried to yank my leg out of her grasp but she clung on, holding with inhuman strength, nails scouring my skin like claws. She thrust herself up, releasing my ankle and swiping out with her free hand. I darted back, but she seized a handful of my dress and pulled me over the banister on top of her.

I screamed and fell, and our foreheads collided. My head rang with pain as I rolled down the stairs and smashed into the wall. She shrieked and scrabbled down the stairs on her bottom, using her hands to push herself down, movements jerky but fast as a spider. I stared up at her distorted face, unable to move as pain shuddered through my back – and then she was on top of me holding the knife above my chest, her eyes wild and split with streaks of blood.

I looked at the knife and a crazy idea popped into my

head. She was not the woman I'd thought she was, but I knew what drove her.

Looking into her eyes, I said, 'Who's Annabelle?'

A puzzled look washed away some of the wildness. She blinked a few times, but didn't move the knife. In a soft voice, she said, 'Annabelle. Poor, sweet, little Annabelle.'

'Who is she?'

'My baby. My first little doll.'

'Where is she now?'

Her eyes grew wet. She frowned. Her chin trembled. One of her tears hit the blade of the knife.

'Why have I never met her?' I said.

Mother tipped back her head and blinked rapidly. Her chest rose and fell with abnormal speed. 'I can't. I can't talk about Annabelle.'

'Why? Did something happen to her?'

Her chin snapped down and she stared into me, her eyes intense and dark. Suddenly, she was present, more present than before. More present than ever. I held my breath. Glanced at the knife.

In the gentlest voice I'd ever heard she said, 'Annabelle was my little doll. My real little doll. But she's dead now. She's dead and buried and gone for ever.'

I swallowed. 'I'm sorry.'

She narrowed her eyes and tilted her head to the side. 'You're not my little doll. You're not my Annabelle. She's all I want. She's all I ever wanted. Don't you see?'

I didn't say anything. I didn't know what to say.

Tears dribbled down her cheeks and mixed with her blood.

In the not-too-far distance, sirens sang, their song the most beautiful sound I had ever heard, but it was going to be too late.

'I've done terrible things,' she said flatly.

Tears poured down her cheeks. I stayed silent.

'All I ever wanted was someone to love me back,' she said. She was distant again, frozen in a faraway time, looking beyond me into the past, maybe far back into her terrible childhood.

I tensed as she jerked down and brought her face an inch from mine. She smelled awful, her breath like rotten fruit.

'Please, don't—' I said.

But she had already made up her mind. I saw the decision painted there in tears and blood. Her blood, my blood, Olivia's and Derek's and Dot's and Patrick's blood. She'd hurt so many people, and now she wasn't just going to hurt me. She was going to kill me. I was never going to see my mummy. I was never going to see my daddy. I was going to die here, inside this wretched, never-ending gloom never having experienced a proper life. A life lived in colour with people who loved me.

I closed my eyes, held my breath and tried to imagine my parents. They were all I wanted to see, but no matter how hard I tried all I could conjure up was the face of the grandfather clock or the deep darkness of the hole in the back garden. And that was my final vision: blackness – a long black tunnel with no light at the end.

A tear hit my eyelid and I opened my eyes and flinched as she brought the knife down whip-fast and placed it on the ground beside my face. I frowned, confused and frightened, as she pushed herself off me. She didn't look at me or say anything, just drifted away with limping steps towards the kitchen.

I raised my head off the floor, terrified to move in case she came back, but she walked into the room and closed the door.

I listened and listened and heard a drawer scrape open, heard a chair scrape across smooth, hard tiles. A moment of silence followed and then I heard her gasp. She gasped once more and then all was silent again. Nothing broke the quiet apart from the grandfather clock striking the hour.

Unable to believe it, I scrabbled to my feet, reached for the front door and stepped outside.

Chapter 53

It was the first sunset I'd ever seen. I sat in a police car and watched the sky through the open window. The sky was layered. At the top ran a light, brilliant blue layer. Beneath the blue ran a delicate lavender, followed by the most magical shade of light pink. It looked like someone had taken three brush strokes to the canvas above and painted the sky in three separate sweeps of colour. It didn't look real. Sitting in the police car on the dirt road outside the cottage looking up at the sky didn't feel real.

Olivia waved at me. She was being rolled past in an ambulance bed. I wondered if Mother had been telling the truth about Olivia getting her expelled. Knowing I would never know, I waved back.

The ambulance drove away. Policemen rushed around the cottage like giant ants. A policewoman stood in front of the car window, trying to hide the next bed that rolled past, but I could see the black body bag anyway. I knew it was Patrick. I had told a policeman where to look for him. I remembered my promise to find Patrick's family and tell them what he'd done for me and Emma. Another ambulance approached and Patrick was put into the back of the huge vehicle and driven away.

'You OK?' the policewoman asked. 'Can I get you anything?'

'I'm kind of starving, to be honest, so yes, please.'

She smiled. 'I think I've got some crisps in the glove compartment. Hang on a second.'

While she rifled inside the front of the police car, I turned my attention back to the sunset. It was beautiful and if a thing could be perfect, this sunset was. There was magic in those colours.

'Here you are,' the policewoman said, handing me a packet of crisps.

'Thank you.'

'I've just been told we need to leave the scene now. Make sure you strap in.'

A memory of Mother strapping me in when she'd driven me back to the cottage made me flinch. I focused on my crisps, on the strong, salt and vinegar crunch of every bite.

As the policewoman started the engine, I swivelled in my seat to look out of the back window. Mother's body was being wheeled into view. One of her hands was visible. It hung down the side of the bed. Blood covered her wrist.

I spun round to face the front and my eyes met the policewoman's in the small mirror.

'I'm sorry you saw that,' she said.

'It's OK. I've seen worse,' I said. And I had. I hesitated, then said, 'There was a woman called Dot and a man called Harold who—'

'They're fine. They're both fine. Mrs Bancroft sustained a minor head injury, but she'll make a full recovery. Mr Bancroft had a flat tyre, which was why he didn't return to Greenfield House for so long, but once he returned he was able to get his wife to a hospital and report the fact that you'd been taken.'

I exhaled, pleased beyond words that Dot was OK. I was scared to ask about Emma but I needed to know. I couldn't bear the not-knowing any longer. I exhaled, took a deep breath. 'She took another girl too but she got away. Emma—'

'Emma's fine too. She's an extremely brave little girl, just like you. She saw someone going for a run and asked him to take her to the police station. She told us about the knacker's yard and described the woods and the general direction the two of you had come from. It didn't take us long to find this place.'

'Was she hurt?'

'Other than a few scrapes, no. She's at home with her family, safe and sound, all because of you.'

I smiled. Emma was OK. She was safe. She was with her family.

I wanted to ask more questions but was too choked up to speak.

'Would you like the radio on?'

I caught the woman's eyes in the mirror and nodded.

She turned it on and for a moment I was seized by the terrifying idea that the Eagles' music would come on, but it wasn't them. The radio man introduced a song called 'Somebody to Love' by Queen. I liked it.

My mind tried to return to when Mother and I had danced, so I stuck my head out of the window and looked at the fields and the sky and the wide, open space of the outside. Cool air rushed at my face, soothing my aching head. The policewoman passed me back a can of something called Coca-Cola that I had never tasted before. I liked that too even though it made my teeth feel sticky.

We drove through countryside, past sheep and cows and

beautiful sleek brown horses. I saw a few rabbits and more fields and more trees and bushes and a stream and then I saw houses, and more houses and I realized we were in an actual village or town. The policewoman said something but I didn't hear her. I looked down at my cleaned, bandaged hands and watched them shake. I was beginning to feel nervous and cold, so I wound up the window and let my head lean back against the padded headrest. Tiredness dragged me down and I fell into a heavy, dead sleep.

'We're here,' the police officer said.

I opened my eyes and looked out of the car window at a big building called Bristol Royal Hospital for Sick Children. I didn't like the name of the hospital. A shiver ran across my neck and I snuggled down into the blankets that the policewoman had piled around me. I stared at the huge, ugly, brown building and tears swam in my eyes. I didn't want to go in there. I didn't want to be inside. I wanted to be in the outside. I wanted to be free.

The car engine cut out and the radio went dead, cutting a slow, sad-sounding song in half. The policewoman told me to stay where I was and got out of the car. I closed my eyes and pulled the blankets up over my head. I wanted to stay where I was. Good luck to whoever was going to try to get me to go into that horrid building.

I heard the door next to me click open.

'Polly? Polly, it's OK. There're some people here you need to meet,' said the policewoman, her voice thick as if she was trying not to cry.

I stayed hidden, safe in my blankets, taking strange comfort in my self-inflicted darkness. The blankets were warm and soft and they smelled like soap. I squeezed my eyes shut. There was a moment of silence then I heard a woman's voice. A different voice.

'Polly? Baby? Is that really you?'

My heart somersaulted. I recognized something in that voice. My brain seemed to click awake at its sound. Slowly, I unpeeled the blankets from around my face and stared at the fair-haired woman standing next to the police officer. She inhaled sharply. Silent tears spilled down her cheeks.

'Polly? Oh my goodness. My little girl. My baby.'

She held her hands out to me. Her arms were shaking. Her whole body was shaking. She smiled, chin trembling, her eyes exactly like mine.

Behind her stood a man with light brown hair. He was crying too. He sank to his knees and stared at me, his eyes wide and shiny with tears.

'Polly? My sweet Poll?' he said. He could barely control the tremors in his voice.

The policewoman smiled and stepped back.

I looked from the lady to the man. A memory stirred – a memory of the three of us playing in a carpet of sand somewhere warm and bright.

I stared at them. My MUMMY and DADDY.

Tears made me blind, but they were happy tears. The happiest tears in the world.

'Mummy? Daddy?'

Without a second thought I tore off the blankets and threw myself into my mummy's chest. Her arms wrapped around me and she held me and rocked me. She whispered my name over and over again. Her voice was so soft, so full of love. She kissed my cheek and stroked my hair and told me she loved me more than anything in the whole world and she would never let me go again. She felt and smelled so familiar it was like I'd known her all my life. I buried my nose in her shoulder and breathed her in.

Another pair of arms wrapped around me. These were firmer and stronger, and I knew they belonged to my daddy.

A light tapping sensation on my head made me look up

and I found myself staring into the eyes of a little boy with blond hair.

Without letting go of me, my mummy said, 'Polly, this is your little brother, Jake. Say hello to your big sister, please, Jake.'

The little boy patted my head again. He grinned at me revealing two missing teeth.

I smiled back. I couldn't believe another dream had come true. I had a little brother. I was never going to feel alone again.

'Hello,' he said. 'I'm Jake. I like birds. Do you like birds?'

I looked down and grinned. In one hand he held a small, cuddly robin.